WORLDBURNER

Also by J. Warren

Published by Rebel Satori Press

The Consort

Tygers

Unbalanced Mercy

Remains

The Jacob Connor Trilogy
Stealing Ganymede
Silencing Orpheus
Drowning Narcissus

WORLDBURNER

BY J. WARREN

QUEER SPACE
New Orleans & New York

Published in the United States of America by
Queer Space
A Rebel Satori Imprint
www.rebelsatoripress.com

Paperback ISBN: 978-1-60864-361-5

Part 1: A Knock At The Door

1.1.1

"Are you awake?" the voice asks.

I'm trying to answer, but I'm too far down.

"Are you awake?" the voice repeats.

I don't recognize the voice.

I've never heard it before.

I open an eye, but the light is so bright, I close it immediately. I raise my hand in front of my face.

"I know the light is very bright, but you'll adjust quickly," the voice says.

"Where..." I start to ask, but sandpaper in my throat won't allow me to get anything else out.

"Here," the voice says, and there's something plastic in my mouth. "Drink."

I sip and it's cold, wonderful water. I start to sip faster.

"Whoa, there; slow down. Too much too fast and you'll just get sick." What I'm assuming was a straw is pulled away from me.

There's something I'm trying to remember, but it won't come to me.

I open one eye, then the other one. They tear up as they try to adjust from huge, bright blur to a solid image. First, I see my hand, then the ceiling.

I look over at the man standing near me. He's enormous; six and a half feet easy. Dark hair pulled up into a topknot. Sharp pointed goatee. Green eyes. He's got his sleeves rolled to his elbows, so I see that his arms are covered in tattoos.

"Hey, Baldi; he's up," the man says to no one in particular.

"Oh? On my way," a scratchy voice says from somewhere behind me.

There's something terribly important I'm trying to remember but can't.

"Hold still," the huge man says. "We'll get you checked out real fast and then you can sit up."

I hear footsteps clanging on metal coming closer. A shorter, thin man comes into view. He's looks half starved, and his pointy hair sticks out all over. He lowers his glasses from the top of his head and as soon as they are over his eyes, I can see the telltale sparkle that means he's getting information on the lenses.

"Mmmmhm. Okay. Sure," the thin man says.

"This is Baldi. He's what passes for a doctor on this tub," the big man says to me.

The thin man touches his hand to the rim of his glasses, then goes back to staring at me. "Ah, ok. Well, sure," he continues mumbling. After looking me all over, he steps back from the bed I can now see I'm on.

"And?" the big man asks.

"Looks like he's okay," Baldi says. "Careful, though; there's likely to be delayed responses. Maybe some memory loss."

"Alright, kid; you can sit up, now. Nice and slow."

I try to sit up but stop. I ache all over. The big man steps over and puts his hand behind my back. He helps me to sit up.

"Where am I?" I ask.

"We'll get to that."

"Who are you?" I ask. There's something right on the tip of my tongue that I can't get out.

"I'm Eli. The Captain told me to make sure to go slow, so for right now, just know that you're safe."

"Wait," I say. Flames. I can remember flames, and the loudest sound I've ever heard. "Explosion?" I ask.

"Nice and slow," Eli says. "And remember, you're safe."

An explosion. A huge explosion. Flames. Heat.

"Where am I?!" I can feel myself sliding into panic.

No one says anything.

"Where am I?!" I demand. I can feel my heart pounding against my chest.

"We may have to put him out again," Baldi says.

"Nah. It's a shock but let him go through it."

"Where am I?!" I yell again. And again. And again.

The one called Baldi presses a button and there's a pinch in my left arm.

It takes a while to stop yelling. The crying takes longer than that. After a while, though, I can think again. My voice isn't steady, but it's mine once again.

"He's back down out of the red zone, at least."

Somewhere in the back of a memory, warbly, as if through some sort of sound effect, I hear someone say the words "...red zone..."

And then an explosion...a giant fireball that consumes everything it touches.

I blink, waiting for my heart to race, my breathing to speed up again, but it doesn't happen.

"Akari, right?" Eli asks. "Your name is Akari?"

I recognize that name. There's something I'm supposed to remember, I can tell, but it doesn't come to me. I can feel it way down in the darkness, whatever it is, moving around, huge and menacing. Whatever it is, though, I don't remember.

I nod.

"Okay, good," Eli says.

"He's steady. You can probably take the restraints off."

I hadn't even noticed they were on, but Eli removes the cuffs that had held down my wrists and ankles.

"Where am I?" I croak, my voice having gone horse from the yelling. Just then, my stomach growls.

"We're going to get you a whole bunch of answers in just a bit," Eli says. "First, though, I think we should feed you. You were out for a while, and I'm not at all convinced that liquid fed through a tube into someone's arm is 'everything they need.'" Eli says. I can tell that last part was aimed at Baldi.

"C'mon," he says, helping me off of the bed.

"How do you know who I am?" I ask as we walk down a long metal corridor. It's cold, and I pull my hands into my sleeves.

"It was on your badge," Eli says. He steers us through a hatchway into a room about the same size as the first. There are tables with benches. Along the wall are lots of metal cabinets and a couple of counter tops.

"Badge?" I ask. The thing way down in the dark of my memory moves again, but still doesn't come up anywhere close enough to see.

He makes a motion for me to sit at one of the tables while he busies himself pulling things from a few cabinets and sliding them through a slot in the wall.

"We found it right next to you. Force of the blast must have blown it right off. There wasn't much information on it, and all the communication functions were trashed," Eli says. There is a small chime and a tray with a bowl comes out of the wall. Steam comes up off the bowl as he brings it over and puts it in front of me. He presses on the center of the table and there's a click. A container rises up from the middle with napkins and silverware. He hands me a fork.

"Here," he says. While I'm looking at the meat in some kind of sauce over rice he goes to another cupboard and comes back with a cup with a lid on it. When he pulls on a tab at the top, steam comes up from inside. He pulls the top off and I see the cup is filled with tea.

"I hope you're not a vegetarian. Nobody else on the ship is, so we don't have a lot of vegetables around," Eli says and his sits.

"Ship?" I ask.

"I promise—answers coming very soon. First, though, eat."

It turns out to be a kind of okay chicken curry over pretty good rice. The tea is lousy but it's hot. After the first forkful, I realize I'm starving. While I'm scarfing down food, a woman walks in. The second she does, Eli sits up straighter.

4

She's shorter than me, with brown hair that comes down to her shoulders and big green eyes.

"Captain," Eli says as she sits across from me.

"How is he?" she asks him while looking at me.

"Baldi says he's stable. Looks to be hungry as a horse, so that's a good sign, I think," Eli says and the Captain nods.

"Akari, this is the Captain. Captain, Akari Tatsuro."

Is that my full name? It feels strange to have someone else know it when I am not certain.

I finish the last of the food and down the last bit of tea and burp loudly before I can stop myself. The Captain grins and Eli laughs. "Sorry," I say.

"Well," The Captain says. "I'd say that's a good enough way to start."

1.1.2

"Where am I?" I ask.

The Captain nods. "You are aboard The Hokhmah, my ship."

"Why?" I ask.

The Captain looks at Eli for a second, then back at me. "There was an accident. Your outpost was...destroyed," The Captain says. "I'm sorry, but you were the only person we found alive down there, after."

They both just look at me for a few moments.

"It was your badge, actually," Eli says. "It somehow had enough juice to send a signal through all the rubble. You're lucky you had it on...or, at least, that it didn't fly too far from you when it fell off."

"And...uhm...you're sure that..." I don't look at either of them.

"We looked for a long time," The Captain says. "I'm sorry."

I tear up.

There's a beep and The Captain looks down at her wristband. "Go ahead."

"Looks like the coast is clear, skipper," a voice says through the static.

The Captain gives another look at Eli, then at me. "Give us just a second, okay?" She stands and Eli stands, too. He follows her back out into the hall.

Even as I do it, I know somehow that I shouldn't. I *know* it.

It's like a reflex.

I close my eyes and steady myself with a quick deep breath.

A quick, deep breath and an image comes into my mind.

The bud of a flower opening up to the sun.

As soon as I do, I feel myself stepping outside myself.

I'm hit with a wave of dizziness...

…and immediately I am inside Eli's head. Luckily enough, he seems to be a very calm person. As he's talking to The Captain, he is paying close attention, and not having a lot of stray thoughts.

"I have a bad feeling about this," The Captin says.

"Well, yeah, okay, but what were we going to do? Just leave him in the rubble? We had to do something."

Eli feels care for me, which is good, but also danger.

"This whole thing went south so fast…" Eli says.

The Captain stares for a minute.

"Like it or not, he's here now. We can decide what to do with him soon. For now, though, he's going to freeze to death if we just let him run around the ship in regular civvies," The Captain says. "Break into the stores and at least try to keep him from dying of hypothermia before we figure out what to do. He's your responsibility."

I hear her boots clang on the metal floor as she walks away. Eli sighs, then walks back in.

I let go of his mind, the flower in my head closing, wrapping itself back up like a little cocoon.

"C'mon, kid; I think there's some spare body suits and jackets down in one of the lockers. Maybe we can make one fit."

I'm numb and I don't know what else to do.

He turns away and starts walking and I follow.

"That looks like about the best we're going to be able to do," Eli says as he steps back from me. The suit is about two sizes too big, but we roll the cuffs on the pants and the sleeves. "Not going to win any fashion contests, but it'll keep you warm. Old ship like this, the heaters can only do so much, y'know?" Eli finds a tech vest small enough to fit, too. I zip it up and feel not just warmer, but safer.

"Here," Eli says, handing me a small black rectangle. "Zip this in one of the pockets. It's a locator so that we can find you if, y'know, something happens." He nods at me and I nod back.

"Yes, please," I say.

He leans forward, "Huh? You gotta speak up over the generators on almost all the decks. You're kinda a soft-spoken little guy, I can tell, but you if you don't, no one can hear ya."

"Yes, please," I repeat, louder.

Eli laughs. "What?" I ask.

"Please. That's about the first time I've heard anyone use that word on this ship." He laughs, turns, and I follow. "Let's get you in a bunk for the night and we'll figure out what to do in the morning."

"Morning?" I ask. Before the explosion, it had been early. I can't remember what time exactly, but I remember that the sun was just coming up.

"Ship's time. You'll get used to it if, y'know, you're here long. For us, this is the end of a very, very long day." I follow him around a few corners and down a ladder. Eventually we stop in front of a door. He presses the green button beside it. The door opens and The Captain comes out.

She pauses for a second at the door and I can tell that she and Eli are having a conversation without talking like adults do sometimes. She shakes her head and sighs, then leaves. I follow Eli into the room.

There are two bunk beds set up along the walls. There is a woman with brown hair, a long tan cape, and expensive looking clothes standing near one. On the top bunk, there is a lump of blankets that moves a bit but then settles.

"Hello," Eli says to her, then gestures to the other bunk across the room. I sit down on it. "Settle in and try to get some rest. I'll come get you in a bit when it's morning." He nods to the woman as he walks out.

I lie down and turn my back to the room.

I close my eyes, do the breaths nice and slow, then picture the flower open and I jump over into the woman's head.

...poor thing. I hope they treat him well, but I can't get involved. I have to

make sure that Cassandra makes it to safety. That has to be my only...

She's thinking about me and she's not dangerous, so I let her mind go.

It's then that the enormity of all of it hits me.

It's all gone.

Whatever happened, it destroyed my whole life.

Even if I can't quite remember what that life was, I still feel its loss.

I don't want to cry, but I end up doing it, anyway.

At some point I fall asleep.

1.1.3

I wake up shivering.

The cold seeps under through the body suit and past my clothes.

"Having trouble sleeping?" The woman with the cape is sitting next to me on the bed.

Something in me doesn't want to admit that I am. That I'm weak.

"It's okay," she says. "Sleeping on a ship for the first time is always... difficult." She takes off her cape and drapes it over me. I want to refuse it, but it's so instantly warm that I can't.

I stop shivering almost immediately.

She crosses her legs and nods. I want to say something to show that I'm strong, that I don't need his help, but I can't.

She leans forward and flips a switch over my head that I hadn't seen. A small box on the wall just above me glows deep red. The room starts to warm.

"I saw that the big one hadn't shown you where the heater was or even where to find a decent blanket," she says as she flips another switch right next to the first. The room dims. "Turns out I was right to worry."

I want to fight it, but it's so nice to have someone thinking about my comfort in this moment that my eyes start to drift closed again. I struggle, trying to stay awake enough to say thank you, but I don't make it. My eyes close.

"Who is he?" a young girl's voice whispers.

"I didn't catch a name. At any rate, he is none of our business. Again, if you would please." I recognize the voice of the woman whose cape I am currently sleeping under.

There is a loud sigh. "amō, amās, amat, amāmus, amātis, amant," the young girl's voice says.

"Good. Again, please."

I think about reaching out to the woman's mind again, but I'm also thinking about trying to dive back down into sleep.

"But we specifically asked for a private room, didn't we?" the young girl's voice asks.

"As you know, things changed when they found us and started chasing us. I'm sure the crew is doing the best that they can," the woman's voice says. "Now, again, please."

"amō, amās, amat, amāmus, amātis, amant. I don't see why I have to learn a language that was already dead and ancient before anyone even landed on the first moon."

"Because it is what properly educated young people do," the woman says. "Again, please."

The girl growls but starts the sequence again.

I suddenly feel how badly I need the toilet. I roll over and sit up and stretch. The young girl I have been hearing is on the top bunk. She must have been the lump of covers I saw before I went to sleep. She has long blonde hair tied in many intricate braids and rings, and her eyes are the most striking green I've ever seen.

They are both staring at me.

"Good morning," the woman says.

When the silence continues too long, the woman taps the young girl on the shoulder. "Good morning," the young girl says, but I can tell she doesn't mean it.

"Good morning," I say. I stand up and walk toward the door.

"Make a right turn and then it's the third door on your right, you'll find," the woman says.

I want to ask her how she knows exactly what I am looking for, but the matter grows fairly urgent.

I go to the room she described. As I'm using the toilet, I can see that the room is set up to be communal toilets and showers.

Luckily enough, no one else is in there yet.

I wash my hands and step back out into the hall. While I was in there, the lights have come up. I can hear footsteps on metal, but I don't see anyone.

I'm alone.

"There you are," Eli says.

For a big guy, he moves very quietly.

"Good morning," I say.

"You alright?" he asks, stopping in front of me.

I nod, but don't mean it. "Can...can I ask questions now?"

"In a bit. Let's swing by the caf again so I can introduce you to the crew. That way they won't try to kill you if they see you in the halls." From his tone, I can tell this is only kind of a joke.

He puts his hand on my shoulder and we walk back through the same twists as last night and back into the room he called the caf, which I'm guessing means the cafeteria.

The Captain is leaning against a wall with a mug in her hand. She looks at me and nods when we come in, but she doesn't say anything. "You already know The Captain," Eli says.

At the far table in the corner, sitting in the seat in the exact corner of the room is a lean black man with a shaved head. Even though we're all inside, he has sunglasses on. He's smoking what I'm told used to be called a cigarette. "That's Salvadore," Eli says.

Right near the door is a woman with brown hair cut very short. She's wearing one of the flight suits like the one Eli gave me. She has a portable terminal pad in front of her and she's flipping through screens very quickly. "This is Sweet Caroline." She waves without looking up.

Sitting across from her is a man who, even though he's sitting down, I can tell isn't very tall with brown hair and green eyes. He's the only one who smiles and raises his mug to say hello. "That's Max, our pilot." Max snaps a sloppy salute.

Still getting things from the cupboards along the wall is the wiry man I already met named Geribaldi. "You remember Baldi from yesterday. He's our doc."

"Folks," Eli says. "This is Akari, the kid we…picked up…yesterday after the…thing."

"You're lucky to be alive, kid," Max says with a laugh. "If you could have seen the damage that…"

Eli gives him a stern look and he shuts up and takes a swig of his coffee.

"Right after breakfast, come on down and we'll take one more look at you," Baldi says as he puts a sandwich into a heater.

"Okay," Sweet Caroline says. Her voice sounds strange for some reason. "Got it."

"Maybe we should wait," Eli says.

"No," The Captain says. "Let's have it."

Eli puts a hand on my shoulder and leads me over to the cupboards. He shows me the foods that they have. I'm not particularly hungry, but I don't know when I'll get to eat again, so I put a few of the pre-packaged sandwiches on the tray and a couple of the fried potato patties.

I walk over to the same heater that Baldi used and Eli shows me how to program time and heat level. Then he shows me where the dehydrated juice is and how to get water.

Behind us, all of the crew except Salvadore have gathered around Sweet Caroline. They're talking just a bit above a whisper, but I can't hear them over the heater and the air exchangers.

The heater dings and I take out my breakfast. Eli leads me over near Salvadore. I can tell it's on purpose.

"Morning," Eli says.

"Eli," Salvadore says. His voice is like gravel, but it's also comforting in a way.

"Hi," I say.

Salvadore nods. Now that we're close, I can see that he's cleaning something. It's in a million pieces on the table in front of him, and he's wiping and inspecting each part.

"Did you sleep okay?" Eli asks.

"Yeah," I say. The second the first bite of one of the sandwiches hits my mouth, I realize I'm actually starving. I'm trying not to gobble, but it's hard.

Across the room, the rest of the crew are talking animatedly. I'm too busy with food to jump over there and listen in.

The woman and the young girl come in. The Captain makes a gesture at them, and the crew all waves hello. The woman takes the girl over to one of the other tables. Once the girl is seated, the woman goes and begins to gather food and puts it in the heater. She fixes juice and then a mug of coffee.

Something about it seems odd, because of how fine their clothes are, but at the same time I can tell they've done this a million times.

"Who are they?" I ask.

Salvadore clears his throat.

"Our passengers," Eli says. Something in his voice sounds funny.

Just then, The Captain leans back from the conversation and looks at me. I look down at the tray. I don't need any special ability to know her thought right at that moment is worry.

She's worried about me.

1.1.4

"Okay," The Captain says as she stands up. "Let's finish up and get on station, folks. We've got work to do."

As I open my eyes, I see Salvadore putting the pieces and parts he's been working on back together at astonishing speed. I know it's rude to stare, but I can't look away.

Faster than I can count to twenty, there is what looks like an old style long-barrel revolver pistol in front of him. It looks like it came straight out of photos from ancient Earth. He slides it home in the holster on his hip as he stands, everything one smooth motion. He stubs out his cigarette and walks out.

The rest of the crew finish up their meals and swig the last of the coffee, then leave.

Eli clears his throat and swigs the last of his coffee.

"You finish eating," he says, "then go back to the room you slept in, okay?"

"Until when?" I ask.

"Until I come get you later," he says. "Likely at some point, The Captain is going to want to have a sit down with you. Sooner rather than later if I know her. I'll be there, too."

I nod. He follows Salvadore out.

I finish eating. It's then I realize that the little girl is staring at me from the table across the room. When I look back at her, she ducks so that the older woman is between me and her.

"You can come over here and sit with us if you like," the woman says without turning around. I'm not comfortable sitting by myself, so I take my

15

tray and glass over to sit with them.

"My name is Nyssa," the woman says, "and this is Ardra."

"Hello," I say. The quiet stretches out between us.

"It's customary on most worlds to give your name once others have introduced themselves to you, I believe," the woman says. She's smiling, but I hear a bit of authority in her voice.

"I'm sorry," I say. "Akari."

"As passengers, we're not being told much, which is, I suppose, customary, but I take it that you were brought on board after the chase?" Nyssa asks.

"Chase?" I ask in return.

"That big man came to us and told us to buckle into the emergency chairs in the room we paid for," Ardra says. I don't know if she means it, but I hear the accusation in those last few words. "Then there was a crazy time of maneuvers and loud sounds. It was like the amusement ride we went to that one time," Ardra says while smiling and looking at Nyssa.

"Yes. Very unsettling," Nyssa says.

"Then he came back and said that we were going to have to set down for a bit to do repairs. After a while, something woke me up and it was you," Ardra says. Again, it's hard not to hear the accusation.

"Eli brought you in to our room and you went to sleep," Nyssa says. "And now here we all are."

"Nyssa sang a lullabye for you," Ardra says.

"A lullabye?" I ask.

"Don't you know what a lullabye is?" Ardra asks.

"That will be enough, young lady," Nyssa says.

"It's a song you sing to help people sleep," Ardra says, then asks, "Can I have some more juice?"

"Of course," Nyssa says and starts to get up.

"I want to get it myself!" Ardra says and is on her feet moving to the far wall before Nyssa can say anything.

"Alright. Remember where the fill line is, though." Nyssa waits a moment to watch Ardra, then says, "You'll have to pardon us. You see, we paid quite a bit to have both a private room and...well, not to be indelicate, but for a private trip. There weren't supposed to be any other passengers."

"It's not like I want to be here," I say. I'm getting a bit tired of people being jerks for something that is out of my control.

"This was not meant to be an accusation," Nyssa says. "I am merely curious. For them to have brought you aboard after...some very delicate conversations...that means that you weren't a scheduled passenger."

"Yeah, so?" I ask.

"So, if they didn't mean to pick you up, and you aren't happy about being here, I am left to wonder under what circumstances do you find yourself aboard?"

Just then Ardra plops back down into her seat. Predictably, her glass is almost overflowing. Nyssa sets about getting a napkin placed under it and gently scolding her.

I'm left thinking about what she just said.

Several times now, Eli has made mention of an accident. I don't know much about how things on spaceships work, but it sounds like before whatever accident Eli has been talking about, there were high speed maneuvers. Trying to avoid hitting something? Trying to get away from someone?

"How old are you?" Ardra asks.

I think for a minute, but I don't know. "I'm...I don't know."

"How can you not know how old you are?" Ardra asks.

"Ardra, it's impolite to take that tone when someone answers a questions you've asked," Nyssa says.

"But how can he not *know* how old he is?"

"As we discussed earlier this morning, our new friend Akari has been through a trauma quite recently, it seems. What can sometimes happen when someone experiences a trauma?"

"They can lose their memory," Ardra recites without looking up. It's the same tone of voice from when she was going through that language exercise from earlier.

"That's correct," Nyssa says.

Another thing I'm getting very tired of is being discussed as though I'm not in the room.

"Ardra has more work to do on her Latin this morning. I imagine you might enjoy reading for a bit before The Captain calls for you. Would you like to borrow one of my books?" Nyssa asks.

"Oh! You should borrow the one where the young knight falls in love with the king's wife. It's very good!" Ardra says.

"I suspect that Akari might not find stories of romance quite as interesting as you or I," Nyssa says. She gets up and takes all of our trays to the counter and feeds them through one of the large slots. "Come along and we'll all go back to our room," she says as she comes back and takes our silverware and glasses to the same slot and feeds them in, as well.

She walks to the doorway and holds out her hand. Ardra, who has already gotten up, walks over and takes it. To say they seem completely out of place in the grime and rust around them would be a huge understatement.

I get up and follow them back to the room.

When we get there, Ardra pulls out a few actual paper books. I'm shocked.

One that she has them, and two that she will actually allow me to touch them.

I can't stop myself from saying "Wow" when I see them.

"Please be careful with how far you open the one you pick, though," Ardra says. "Too far can damage the glue and then pages can come loose."

"That's the one I like," Ardra says of one that has a picture of a man in full armor riding up to a castle. Next to it is one that has a picture of a boy on beach standing near an old style wooden chest that he appears to have just dug up. The last one has a picture on the front of a large boat on the ocean with a huge whale underneath it.

"I believe that one is the one you might like the most," Nyssa says, pointing to the one with the boy and the chest.

"Thank you," I say. I lay back on the bunk and open to the first page.

I can hear them start up their lesson again, but instead of reading, I close my eyes and breathe through the relaxation. Then I picture the flower opening.

Finding Eli is fairly easy now that I have been in there a few times.

They're all sitting in a control room of some sort. I guess that it must be the flight deck. Sweet Caroline is sitting at a console, her fingers flying, the screen shifting almost too fast to see. The rest of the crew are sitting around her.

"So," Sweet Caroline says, "I dumped the badge and the core that was attached to the pod he was in. Or, I should say, I did my best to."

"We know you tried," Max says.

"Go on," The Captain says.

"There already wasn't going to be a lot, considering," Sweet Caroline says. "Still, I have a few things. First thing is this: cross referencing the settlement with nav records results in a goose egg." She looks up from her screen. "There was no permit for a settlement or anything else on that planet."

"Claim jumpers?" Max asks.

"That, or something worse," Baldi says.

"What could be worse?" Eli asks.

"Some kind of Black Site. Something off the books. Invisible budget stuff," Baldi says.

"We don't need conspiracy theories right now," Eli says. He tries not to look at me, but he does.

"So when they came in so hot after us, it was because they didn't think they had to be careful. According to their records, there was no one on that planet," Sweet Caroline says.

We all lean back in our seats looking at each other.

19

"What else?" The Captain asks.

"This is stranger. The badge identifies the kid as Akari Tatsuro, age fifteen. Thing is, though, none of the data goes back that far. Now that could be a result of the damage..." Sweet Caroline says.

"Or?" Salvadore asks.

"That's what I don't know. The data is throwing codes all over the place. Something about it is hinky but I can't put my finger on it. Just...the files aren't what I'd expect to see from a kid who has been in the system for fifteen years. In some places it's too organized. In others..."

"What?" Eli asks.

"In others it's scattered. Things you'd expect to find, like the name of a grandmother, or a date for when his family moved to the colony, something... none of that stuff is there. But then there are meticulous charts on his height, his weight, his endorphine saturation at precisely eleven oh-one a.m. on the fifth of whatever."

"That almost sounds like..." Max trails off.

"Like a lab rat," Salvadore says. The Captain nods.

"What if," Sweet Caroline starts but then stops.

"Go on," The Captain says.

"What if that container we found him in wasn't some kind of survival pod? What if that was a vat?"

We all stare at one another again.

"The memory loss?" The Captain asks.

"Touchy stuff," Baldi says. "Always has been. His memory could come back all of a sudden in five minutes, or he may never get it all back. Depends on how hard the knock to his noggin was as well as how safe he feels. One thing is for sure, though—there's nothing I can do to help it along. It either comes back on its own or doesn't."

"Okay," The Captain nods, then says. "Sweet, keep working on it. Eli, let's you and me wander down and ask our young friend some questions. Max, steady as she goes—let's get our friends offloaded as close to when we promised as possible."

20

"Aye, aye, skipper," Max says.

I let go and come back to myself. The flower closes.
I feel like I want to run.

1.1.5

"Comfy?" Eli asks.

The Captain and Eli came to get me and they took me to the medical bay again. Baldi put on his special goggles and looked me over. Once he was done, The Captain looked at him and he took off. I'm left sitting on the exam table.

"Akari, I have some questions I want to ask you and I need you to tell me the truth," The Captain says.

I nod. To my left I can see that the bed is still scanning my vitals. The Captain keeps looking over at them.

"Can I ask some back?"

"Sure," The Captain says. Something in her voice says I shouldn't, though.

"How old are you?"

"Fifteen," I say.

"And you're sure about that?" The Captain asks.

I shrug. "It's how old I am."

"Do you remember your fifteenth birthday? What did you do to celebrate?"

I feel like I know the answer, but when I think about it, nothing comes.

Do I tell her that, or do I make something up? If I make something up, will the scanners be able to tell?

"I don't remember. Maybe I hit my head?" It's something I heard Baldi say.

"Maybe you did, but the doc says you don't have a concussion."

"Oh," I say. "Will you tell me what happened?" I ask.

22

"As soon as we're done. I promise," The Captain says.

"Do you know the names of your parents, your mom and dad?" Eli asks. I can tell from his tone of voice that was the easiest question and so he wanted to be the one who asked it.

Again, I feel like I do, but when I try to remember it, nothing comes.

"I…I think…no," I say. Something down in the deep parts of my mind stirs, but nothing comes to the surface.

The Captain nods, then crosses her arms over her chest.

"Nyssa and Ardra are our passengers. They paid us quite a lot of money to get them from where they were to someplace safer. That's why we're so far out here on the rim. We thought there wouldn't be any patrols out this far, so we weren't thinking too much about hiding ourselves," The Captain says.

"That's an understatement," Eli mumbles.

She gives him a look, then to me she continues, "We were running at top speed to get our passengers where they wanted to go, so when a patrol popped out of nowhere and demanded we stop our engines, it took us by surprise. We…didn't react as coolly and professionally as I would have liked. It turned into a nasty battle and in one of our maneuvers, we damaged the patrol ship very badly. Before we could stop it, it slipped into the atmosphere of an uninhabited planet that was nearby, and it crashed on the surface."

"The problem was," Eli says, "the planet *wasn't* uninhabited."

"I'm very sorry," The Captain says. I can tell it's not something she says often.

"But, wait…" I start to say but then stop. It hits me then. The fire, the huge wave of pressure…

"If we had known…" Eli starts to say.

"If we had known anyone was down there, we wouldn't have tried a maneuver that desperate. Though, chances are, it was the sheer desperation of the move that made it work. I love this ship," she says looking around, "but head to head with a police interceptor, there's no way we win."

She stares off into the distance for a moment, then comes back.

When her eyes focus in on me, I shiver.

"It was only after, when we were in orbit scanning to make sure they weren't coming back up to finish the fight that we saw there was a settlement on the surface," The Captain says.

"And in that scan, we found you," Eli says.

"Take a minute if you need it," The Captain says, "but then I need to ask you some questions."

I know they're waiting for me to cry. I feel like I should cry. Nothing happens, though. I feel that there is a loss, but I don't *feel* that loss at all.

"Okay?" Eli asks.

I nod.

"Do you have any idea why your parents and the others had a settlement on a planet that wasn't listed anywhere in the directory?" The Captain asks.

I don't have any idea, so I shrug.

"Do you have any idea what they were researching or making or…?" The Captain asks.

Again, I don't have any idea. I shrug.

I can see she's already annoyed.

"Do you know if they were working for someone? A government or a company or…" The Captain asks.

"I don't know," I say. She glances at the screen that is showing my vitals, then back at me.

"When we found you," Eli says, "you were in a kind of plexisteel canister. The heat of the impact had cracked it open and you were half in and half out, covered in some bioelectric reactive jelly. Do you have any idea what that was all about?"

I shrug.

"Were you maybe recovering from an injury or something? Had you recently been sick and maybe you were isolated?" Eli asks.

"I'm sorry; I don't know."

"Maybe we should take a different route," The Captain says. "Do you remember an explosion?"

"Yes," I say.

"What happened just after it?"

"I remember a lot of…pressure and…then…" I shrug as my thoughts trail off.

"What about just before the explosion?" Eli asks.

An image of a large fish tank but inside is a person. I can see their arms and legs, but not their face.

An image of a computer screen reading information. The information makes me happy.

"Hello?" Eli asks, a small grin on his lips. "Where'd you disappear to?"

"I remember looking at a screen. The readouts made me happy."

"You don't know what they were telling you?" The Captain asks.

I shake my head. She doesn't move for a second, then asks "Anything else?"

Someone's eyes staring straight into mine as the flames rolled around me. Then nothing.

The Captain is looking at the screen with my vitals.

"No," I lie. I expect alarms to scream from that screen.

Nothing happens.

The Captain sighs. "Okay." She turns to Eli, "I think you're right—he's got his bell rung and we're not going to get anywhere. Not for a while at least." She turns back to me. "Do you remember the names of any family that might have been somewhere other than that outpost?"

"No," I say. "I'm really sorry."

She purses her lips. "Not your fault." I can tell she feels it is, somehow, though. "So, look; we're going to knock around the databases and see what we can find. This ship is many things, but an orphanage it ain't," she says.

Eli gives her a look.

"I'm very sorry about your parents," The Captain says, then walks out.

"Hold still," Baldi says from behind me, then I feel a sting on my arm.

25

"Hey!" I flinch.

Baldi steps away with a syringe filled with blood. "This will help us find you in the databases."

Eli laughs a bit. "We can't exactly just call someone," he says. "We're not exactly...law abiding citizens in good standing."

Baldi laughs too.

It's hard to feel like I'm not the one being laughed at.

1.1.6

"So," I start to say as we get closer to the door to the room I've been sharing with Nyssa and Ardra.

"Don't," Eli says.

"What?" I ask. We both stop.

"You're about to ask me if you can follow me around the ship instead of being stuck back in the room. You're going to promise me that you'll be quiet and not get in the way, but then you'll accidentally bump into someone and then it's my butt in front of The Captain getting chewed out and then you have to go back and stay with them anyway."

I wonder for a second if he isn't able to read minds.

"I already got in enough trouble when I bought Milo on board," Eli says.

"Milo?"

"The cat," Eli says. "He's...somewhere around here. Unlike the rest of us, he knows enough to hide so he doesn't get assigned work to do."

"A cat? Aren't you worried he'll...I don't know...fall down a vent shaft or something?" I ask.

"Nah. He's smarter than the rest of us. If you're going to worry about someone falling down a shaft like that, worry that it'll be Max," Eli says and presses the button to open the door.

Ardra is asleep on the top bunk, her book open on her chest.

Nyssa is sewing something.

On the bed I've been sleeping on there is a large black and white cat. He has a large white spot on his chin exactly where a beard would be.

"Ah," Eli says. "There's Milo."

Nyssa shushes us. Eli waves to say he's sorry, then gestures for me to go in.

For a second, I think about maybe trying to run, but then think about how there is nowhere to go. I go through the doorway and it shuts behind me.

Nyssa nods at me.

I go over to the bed and sit down. The cat stares at me. I try to remember if I've ever had a pet, but I can't. The cat walks over and stands with its front legs on my leg and stares right into my eyes.

"Hi," I say. His whiskers are really long. He blinks at me a few times, then walks across my lap, his tail hitting me in the face.

"That usually means they like you," Nyssa whispers.

The book she lent me is still sitting on the bed. Again, it's such a valuable object I can't believe she's trusting me with it. She's gone back to her sewing.

"You might consider using this down time to get yourself cleaned up," Nyssa says without looking up. I don't need to read her mind to feel that this is more than just a suggestion. I don't know how long it's been since I have had a shower.

There are lockers across from the showers back down the hall.

For a moment, I look around, feeling very unsure.

I close my eyes for a moment and feel the flower open to the sun.

All around the ship, everyone is going about their business. Now is the perfect time to do this if I'm going to.

Pulling off the clothes that Eli gave me, I can actually smell myself. It isn't nice.

On the far wall, I can see a door marked "Autowash." I open the autowash door and leave the clothes inside. I have no idea what's going to happen. When I close the door, a green light comes on and I hear it rumbling.

Standing naked on an unfamiliar spaceship who knows how many hundreds of thousands of miles from where I called home yesterday feels very strange. Figuring out the shower controls doesn't take long and after a blast of cold water that makes me yelp and dance, I find myself under a flow of hot water, which feels nice.

In that moment, though, I panic.

I start coughing, and I can't get my breath.

There is a flash across my mind of watching someone through water, their face distorted. I can hear them saying something, but I can't hear what. It's just a jumble of sounds.

I sputter and slip, finding myself on my knees under the shower.

I turn off the water and sit there for a moment.

My breath returns, but ragged, halting.

I notice I've got scars on my arms and chest. I don't think they have been there long. One looks like it's been sewn up, probably by Baldi.

Once I feel steady again, I stand up, but it's very cold in this room.

I turn the water back on and the panic happens again. I get control of my breathing, though, and it subsides with each lungfull.

More scars. circular cuts near my wrists where it looks like maybe some kind of hose was plugged in. A place on the top of my right hand where several smaller hoses were, maybe.

In that moment, surrounded by strangers, on a ship that I don't know, going someplace I have no idea about, I feel exactly how small I am. How little footing I have.

While I'm standing there, I decide to listen in. Maybe I can find out more about who they are and what they want for me…from me…

I close my eyes and do the calming breath, then open myself and find Eli fairly quickly.

"…we don't have. Instead, let's list what we do have," The Captain finishes her sentence. Seated at a table with her are Sweet Caroline, Salvadore, and Eli.

"So far, it doesn't look like our little mishap has sparked too much interest back at the core," Salvadore says. Even his voice feels cold. Eli is very thankful for

that, wondering what would have happened to the passengers if things had gone differently. The pictures in his head are very dark.

"Good," The Captain says. "Sweet?"

"Same," Sweet Caroline says. "Nothing on the nets about it, either."

"Maybe we got lucky just this once," Eli says. He's trying to be funny to lighten the mood, but it doesn't work.

"And our guests?" Salvadore asks.

"That has already hit the webs, I'm afraid. They are missing and presumed kidnapped," Sweet Caroline says. "The good news there is that it's still early in the news cycle, so they're likely only just getting the search together. It won't be long, though."

"How long until we reach the coordinates they gave us?" The Captain asks.

"Max says a little over 24 hours at this speed," Salvadore says. "Says he can't go any faster without people taking notice."

"Okay," The Captain says. "What about our information search?"

"DNA markers are still processing, but so far I can tell you that all the regular channels are coming up zip," Sweet Caroline says.

"Meaning?" The Captain asks.

"Whoever he is, no one is looking for him. He's not listed as missing anywhere. That checks out with the story of him living there on that outpost, and the outpost being off the books," Sweet Caroline says. "It also means that no one is aware that the outpost was destroyed. At least, not yet."

"Something?" The Captain says looking right at Eli.

"Maybe nothing. I don't know."

"Out with it," The Captain says.

"Well, it's just this…have you noticed how he doesn't seem all that sad?" Eli crosses his arms. "I mean, his parents and everyone he's ever known are gone and…well…he doesn't seem to feel anything about it."

The Captain nods. "Could be shock. Keep an eye on him. Salvadore?"

Salvadore inhales, exhales, says, "once people start picking through what's down there, it's going to be very obvious pretty fast that the ship that crashed was *a Police interceptor. Those don't tend to crash on their own."*

The Captain nods. "And if somehow any of the recording data survived…"

Salvadore nods.

"Buddhist or something else?" a woman's voice says, and I snap back to my body.

Nyssa is standing over near the lockers.

I immediately move to cover myself and nearly fall over turning sideways and raising my leg up.

"What?!" I say too loudly.

"Relax, young man. I may not look it, but I have already served two full generations of children for House Rhinestadt, and helped with more than my fair share of others before getting this posting. You don't have anything that I haven't seen before." She laughs and opens a second autowash on the wall. She dumps and armload of clothes in and then says, "finish up; you don't want to use up all of your hosts' hot water on your first day aboard." With that, still grinning, she walks out.

I stand in front of the door to the room not wanting to go in. Nyssa is in there and I'm embarrassed. I look down the long hallway one way, then the other.

She comes out of one of the doors up the hall and walks toward me.

What was she doing in one of the other rooms?

"So…Buddhist or Val Edra Gorah or…?" she asks as she stops next to me. I can feel the heat in my neck and ears.

"Huh?"

"The meditation you were doing. I've seen you do it a few times. You close your eyes and change your breathing. Is it from a particular religion or was it something you were taught?" she asks.

"Oh," I say. Do I tell her? Is she someone I can tell?

"I'll ask you to forget what I said about serving the House of Rhinestadt.

31

I misspoke…" she says. I can tell she's lying. I can see her giving me the same look I feel like I'm giving her. We're both wondering if we can trust the other with something.

"It's not," I say.

"Pardon?" she asks.

"Meditation," I say. "It's not. It's…something else." I want her to like me. I can't explain why, but I do. "Something…different."

I watch her think for a moment. "What is it?"

"Why don't you want anyone to know that you worked for the House of whoever? Why was it so important that you be the only passengers on this ship?" I ask.

I can see on her face I've surprised her. She thought she was lying better than this.

She looks at the door to the room then back at me. "Have you been lying to the crew of this ship? Do you remember more than you're saying?"

"Are you and Ardra criminals?" I ask.

She sighs. "I have to keep Ardra safe," she says.

"And you feel like people knowing information about you will make you less safe," I say. "I think I understand that. And I feel the same about…me. About what I am."

Just then there is a terrible loud sound, the whole ship lurches, and all the lights in the hallway shift from white to red.

1.1.7

There is another lurch back the other way and I fall against Nyssa as we both smack against the wall.

Before I can say anything, Baldi comes running from down the hallway. He doesn't say anything as he sprints past us. There is another horrible loud sound and the lights dim for a moment, then another lurch.

Nyssa and I look at one another. She slaps the button on the door and leans in to the room. "Stay here!" she yells, then turns and runs after Baldi.

"What's going on?" I ask as I catch up to her.

"Go back to the room!" Nyssa commands. Baldi looks back at us but keeps running.

I don't say anything. In a moment, we're all on what I recognize as the flight deck of the ship. Everyone is sitting in the same chairs I saw earlier. On the screen at the front of the room is a picture of another ship.

"Careful of that turret!" The Captain says. "He's coming around again."

"I got it," Max says. The ship lurches again.

"What's happening?" Nyssa demands.

"Get back to your room!" The Captain demands without looking back at us.

"Tell me what's happening!" Nyssa demands.

"Another patrol cruiser," Eli says over his shoulder. "This just really isn't our day."

"How?" Nyssa asks.

"That's a great question," Eli says again.

"Increase to maximum," The Captain says. "No sense in trying to hide now."

"Recommend evade pattern delta," Salvadore says.

"Max?" The Captain says.

"Got it!" Max says. The ship lurches under us again.

There is another terrible sound and the ship jumps. Baldi has strapped himself into one of the seats. I see Nyssa see that there are open seats along the far wall at the same time I do. We both run for them and strap in.

"That was very close!" Eli yells.

"Update on the orders on us," Sweet Caroline says. "Looks like we got upgraded to Code 3."

"Shit!" Baldi says.

"Code 3?" Nyssa asks.

"I told you to get back..." Before The Captain can finish what she's saying, the ship groans and we're all slammed around.

"Captain, I am not going to be about to outmaneuver them. We're too big and too heavy," Max says.

"Guns?" Nyssa asks.

"This ain't that kind of bus, sweetheart," Baldi says.

"We don't have anything heavy enough to get through the armor on an interceptor like that," Eli explains. "Five minutes to overheat," he says.

An idea occurs to me. "How close are they?" I ask.

"Huh?" Eli asks.

"How close are they to us?" I ask again.

"Far too close," Salvadore says.

I breathe and drop my shoulders. I breathe in and out again. I picture myself opening up.

From a long way away I hear Nyssa ask, "What are you doing?" but I'm already searching.

Over on the other ship, the pilot is laughing.

"That old tub won't be able to keep this up much longer. Five minutes to

overheat, tops," he says.

Behind him, the other man presses a button and says, "Tommy, get ready for boarding. If this is who I think it is, they're going to be filled with contraband."

"Roger that," a voice comes back over the communicator.

I think about what I need to do.

I concentrate on the pilot.

He's thinking about how his own ship is getting a little overheated. He's hoping that we'll surrender soon because he doesn't want to have to admit to the man behind him that our own pilot, Max, is better than he is.

What can I do to confuse him? I know that I've done something like this before. I can feel it.

He's thinking about the things he'll need to do once we surrender. That'll come after we overheat. In his mind, he sees it all like a checklist.

He keeps watching his own temperature gauges.

That's it, I think.

I concentrate very hard and slow my breathing even more. I feel myself sink further down.

Back on the surface, I can hear someone asking, "Why is he bleeding?"

I concentrate on the pilot and on the heat gauge.

I make him pay close attention to it.

I make him see it going up faster than he feels it ought to.

I feel his surprise when he sees it.

I make him see it going up even faster than before.

What? he thinks. Why is the ship overheating?

What do I do what do I do what do I do he starts thinking.

I make him see the heat gauge go into the red. I hear him think about how that means there's a chance they'll blow up. I feel him start to panic.

I make him see the heat gauge go further into the red. I feel his panic set in.

I put one word in to his mind: STOP.

I keep repeating this word, making him see the heat gauge tell him his ship is about to blow up.

He snatches the speed control all the way back to zero, yelling out in panic.
I let go of him.

"They stopped!" Max yells. "They just went engines off!"

"Then go!" The Captain yells.

"Akari?!" Nyssa is yelling.

I'm shaking and I can't stop. I can feel something wet on my upper lip.

I feel gravity pull against my chest as Max slams the speed control on his own panel forward.

"Go go go go go," I hear Max mumbling.

"What's going on?! Is he bleeding?" Eli asks, unstrapping himself. He flings himself out of the chair and over to me.

"Did it work?" I ask.

Before anyone can answer, I pass out.

1.1.8

I'm very far down in the dark.

From somewhere above me, I hear bits and pieces.

"....that it was him?" someone says.

"I think so..." someone responds.

"...still don't know how they managed to sneak up..."

"....damage that I can see, but I better keep an..."

"....changes things quite a...."

Then I drift back down into the deep darkness.

I come back up near the surface and open my eyes, but then immediately close them because it's too bright.

"Scan says he's awake," Baldi says. "Akari? Akari, can you hear me?"

I nod.

"Good. Here, let me lower the lights a bit," he says. "Okay. Try now."

I open my eyes and it's much easier to keep them open.

Baldi is sitting near the bed with his goggles on. He takes them off, rolls to the wall and punches a button.

"Skipper?" he says.

"Go ahead," The Captain's voice comes back.

"He's awake."

"On my way," she says.

"You gave us quite a scare," he says. His face softens up a bit from its usual pinched expression.

"I didn't mean to," I say.

He laughs. "Yeah, I figure you didn't. Fair warning, you have some explaining to do once the skipper gets down here. First, though, I have a question. Any idea what 451 is?"

I shake my head.

"Hmmm," he says, leaning back in the chair.

"Why?" I ask.

"It's tattooed on your left shoulder blade. You've never seen it?"

I shake my head.

"No idea how it got there?" Baldi asks.

I shake my head again.

The door opens and The Captain walks in with Salvadore and Eli.

"Akari," The Captain says as she stops near the bed I'm in.

"What happened?" I ask.

"Well, it looks like the police cruiser broke off pursuit just as they were about to have us. We were pretty confused about it ourselves, but I'm not one to ask questions when we get a break." Eli smiles at this. "So, we kept monitoring them even as Max went a hundred and ten percent on the reactors and we found ourselves someplace to hole up for a bit."

I nod.

"Later, though, Sweet monitored something interesting. The people in the interceptor sent a report that they had experienced massive engine overload. That's why they stopped following us. They were afraid they were about to blow up," The Captain says.

"Sweet went back over the data we got from our own sensors and during the time they were chasing us, their engines were fine. They never went beyond eighty-five percent on their own reactor," The Captain says.

"So we took a look at some more data only to find just about the time they cut off pursuit, you blacked out..." Eli says.

"Bleeding all over my flight deck," The Captain says.

"...and Sweet Caroline says there was a spike in this particular electromagnetic band. One she says is usually associated with weird phenomenon," Eli finishes.

"Weird phenomenon?" I ask.

"It's a band that tends to spike when people are doing things like reading minds, moving things without touching them, that kind of thing," Eli says.

"So," The Captain says, "we put some things together. It seems," The Captain goes on, "that we just keep asking you questions. I'm hoping this time you have more answers than last."

"I'm sorry," I mutter because I don't know what else to say.

She nods. "First off, the big question. Back there, with the interceptor... what did you do?"

I don't know if I should say anything.

"Look, we know you did *something*. You started bleeding from your nose and tear ducts like someone had stabbed you in the brain and then you went unconscious. Garibaldi says your readings were like someone who'd just run a marathon on a desert planet. So, time for some truth. What did you do?"

I close my eyes and sigh. "It might be easier to show you."

"Under no circumstances," Salvadore says. I notice his hand on the butt of his gun.

"If he was going to hurt one of us, don't you think he'd have already done it?" Eli says.

"Maybe this is what he was waiting for, a first step to a takeover," Salvadore says.

"Come on," Eli says. "He's a kid."

"I've seen kids used as living bombs before," Salvadore says.

"Whatever it was he was doing," Baldi says, "I have that reading in the EM spectrum at this point and this one." He points to two spikes in a series of peaks and valleys on a display. "It was electric, or at least, used a helluva lot of electricity."

"We didn't see anything," Eli says.

The whole time I notice that The Captain is watching me.

"Okay," she says.

"Captain," Salvadore says. He almost whispers it, but it has the same effect as a yell.

"My choice," she says. "Go ahead."

I close my eyes and breathe. I can already feel the edges of the flower frazzled and burnt as I open them. I open my eyes.

"Hello," I say to The Captain in her head.

She steps back from the bed

"This is what I can do," I say to her in her head.

"What is it?" she asks out loud.

"What is what?" Eli asks.

"Stop. Now," Salvadore says stepping back from the bed and wrapping his fingers around the handle of his gun.

I look from him back to The Captain. Her eyes are wide.

"Telepathy?" she asks.

I nod.

"But I thought only females..." Baldi says.

"He's a telepath?" Eli asks.

Salvadore's hand does not leave his gun.

"That would explain it, then," Baldi says. "Telepathic waves moving along the electromagnetic spectrum. Still, though; you are a male, right?"

I nod again.

"Then that's...that's odd."

"Explain," The Captain says to him.

"Well, people are born with ESPer potential all the time. We all have bits of it. A sudden flash of insight, or knowing when someone is behind you, that kind of thing. Some people, one in a couple of million, have more than that. One in a couple of billion of those has something truly spectacular. One in a billion of those has enough juice to be really powerful. Thing is, when we find someone who is on that level, they are almost always female."

"So you, what, you read the minds of the people flying the other ship?"

Eli asks.

"I…confused them." That's the closest I can come in a way they would understand to tell them what happened. "Tricked them."

"At that kind of distance?!" Baldi slides his chair back from the bed and whistles.

I nod.

"What does the number 451 stand for?" The Captain asks.

"I'm sorry," I say. "I don't know."

"He says he didn't even know he had the tattoo," Baldi says.

"Sweet has looked all through the networks. No one knows anything about you, no one is looking for you…whatever was happening on that outpost where you were living, it was…secret," The Captain says.

I don't say anything because I don't know what to say.

"She says that all of this is starting to add up to a pattern she says she's seen before."

I don't say anything.

"She says it looks like they were doing something that was illegal if they were civilian scientists, or off-the-books top level secret if they were military. Which one sounds right to you?" The Captain asks.

"I don't know," I say.

"Captain, this could just be…" Eli starts to say.

The Captain raises her hand and holds up one finger in his direction. He stops talking.

"Give me one good reason why I should trust that you won't…confuse… us?" The Captain asks.

"I helped you get away from those people," I say.

"That could be a trick to make us feel comfortable," Salvadore says.

"You saved me," I say. "I wouldn't hurt you."

The Captain nods. "We're going to have to trust you," she says.

"You can," I say.

"Oh?" she asks, raising an eyebrow. "You don't know anything about

41

yourself from what you've said, so how do you know that I can trust you?"

"I just…know," I say.

She looks into my eyes for a moment, then nods slowly. With that, she turns on her heel and walks out, Salvadore trailing behind her.

I get the feeling I just dodged a bullet.

Baldi pulls the nutrient line out of my arm and puts a patch over it to stop the bleeding.

"Ow," I mumble.

"Oh, stop," Baldi says.

"So," Eli says, sitting down in the chair next to the exam bed. "A telepath?"

I nod.

He shakes his head and whistles.

"Let him get some more rest," Baldi says without looking away from the screen where what I assume are my vitals are being displayed.

"Okay," Eli says. "I'll come back later."

"Bring his dinner so I don't have to, alright?" Baldi says.

Eli nods, smiles at me, and walks out. Baldi lowers the lights around the bed even more. I close my eyes and breathe. Again, it feels frazzled, worn thin and damaged. I open myself up, anyway, and look for The Captain.

1.1.9

The Captain and Salvadore are standing in a hallway that dead ends in an escape pod.

"We seem to keep having the same conversation with the kid," The Captain says. "What does he know, he doesn't know anything, what does he know, he doesn't know anything..." She's thinking about a circle.

Salvadore holds up his hand with his index finger up. The Captain squints.

"How do we know he's not listening in to us right now?"

The Captain nods. Nothing we can do about that she thinks to herself

"Thoughts?" she says.

"We might have an even bigger problem than we think."

"Go on."

"I've read the same stuff Garibaldi was talking about. What he didn't say is that those that have been studied that have the ability to actually truly read minds? They tend to have another ability that comes along with it," Salvadore says.

"Which is?"

"The ability to move objects without having to touch them."

"Telekinesis," The Captain says. Salvadore nods.

"We need to offload our little friend as soon as we possibly can and high tail it. Go to ground someplace for a bit," Salvadore says. "If he can do that to the pilot of another ship that is...how far away were they?..."

"Agreed," The Captain says. "But Eli? He's gotten attached to the kid. The last time I saw him like this, the ship gained a cat."

Salvadore smiles. Somehow it makes him even more menacing.

"Still," she says. She's thinking about a kind of headband, only she calls it a crown and some part of her smiles at the irony, she once saw years ago. The person wearing it smiled and told her that the person who owned him could press a button and explode the crown whenever they wanted to.

Salvadore cocks his head to the side in way that I think means he already doesn't like what she's about to say.

"Hear me out here," The Captain says. "What if...what if we could use him?"

"I bet every person who ever wound up dead because of a telepath had that same thought at some point," Salvadore says.

"That's what I mean, though. What if there was some way to...I don't know...control when he could turn it on and turn it off? Somewhere there has to be technology like that, right?"

Salvadore purses his lips.

"Don't give me any talk of moral high ground," The Captain says.

"I didn't say anything," he says.

"Yeah," The Captain responds, "but you say nothing so loudly."

Again, Salvadore smiles. Again, it makes me feel cold.

"You don't like the idea," she says.

"What I would like is to offload our little friend as soon as we possibly can and high tail it, as I said. I would like for us to find someplace to burrow in for a while and let the heat die down," Salvadore says.

"Noted," she says, turns on her heel and walks away from him. She's thinking about that crown again. And about something else, something deeper, darker. It glitters so far down in her mind that he can't see anything more than its vague outline. Something even she only calls "it."

I let go of her and shiver, and, exhausted, I fall asleep again.

When I wake up, Nyssa is sitting next to the bed. She looks up from her sewing, sets it on her lap, and watches me for a moment.

"You're awake. Good. How are you feeling?" she asks.

"I'm okay," I say.

She glances over at the screen, checking my vital signs, then looks back at me.

"Were you dreaming?"

"I don't dream."

"Everyone dreams. The human mind goes insane if it doesn't. Likely you were just too far down to remember them," Nyssa says.

Not far away in what looks like an office, Baldi is talking with Sweet Caroline on a screen. I want to listen in, but Nyssa is here. She sees me looking.

"They're having a rather interesting discussion regarding how the police cruiser was able to find us," Nyssa says. "Of course, it could simply have been an accident, but I get the feeling that on this ship, nothing is ever regarded as merely a coincidence."

She leans forward a bit.

"I understand you had something to do with our escape," she says. "For that, I and Ardra thank you."

"Water?" I ask.

She takes a small container from the table nearby and hands it to me. I lean up on one elbow and sip water from it. I have to stop myself from gulping because it is so refreshing and cold. As if she knows what I'm thinking, Nyssa nods.

"Is it true?" she asks. "Can you…read minds?"

I want to deny it, but I know that I can't. I nod.

She shakes her head and mumbles, "Forbidden…"

"What?" I ask.

"How long have you known you could?" she asks.

"I don't know," I say. "I don't remember when the first time I did it was."

"All your life?"

"Maybe," I say.

45

She shakes her head again.

"That must be horrible and wonderful all at the same time," Nyssa says.

I nod.

"Do you know, then?" she asks quietly.

"Know what?" I ask.

"About…us?" she asks. I know she means Ardra and herself. "About who we really are and why we're running?"

"I haven't read your mind," I say.

"Is that the truth?"

I nod.

In the office, Baldi switches off the screen and looks over at us. Nyssa waves to him. He goes back to what he was doing on a data pad.

"Or hers?"

"Or hers," I say.

Nyssa looks at the floor for a moment. "They were going to marry her off," she says. "A girl that young. Marry her. To a man far older. I…" she trails off. I don't know what to say. "Politics are often beyond me. I just try to raise children to have as many possible paths as I can and I stay out of it. But this…this was too far."

"Are the cruisers that keep attacking after you?" I ask.

"We don't know," she says. "Maybe. It seems to me like it's too early for them to already know we're gone and to know that this specific ship out of all of the ones it could possible be is the one we're on."

"What will they do if they find you?" I ask.

"Ardra will be taken back to be married off just as if nothing had ever happened. I…I will almost certainly be disappeared," Nyssa says. She sighs and claps her hands on her thighs. "I'm afraid I also owe you an apology."

"For what?" I ask.

"I saw the number tattooed on your shoulder. I was the one who reported it to Salvadore."

"Why?"

"I need their help to get Ardra where she will be safe. I need them to not only help us because of the money, but to *want* to help us. I thought..." she shakes her head. "I thought that maybe you were...I don't know...a spy sent onboard from some group of...I thought that anything that could go wrong needed to be dealt with. So I told them that something was out of place with you. I'm sorry," Nyssa says.

"I don't know what it is," I say.

"No idea?"

I shake my head.

"I should let you sleep. I simply wanted to be one of the ones to say thank you for what you did to help us."

I don't know what else to do, so I nod. She stands up and puts her hand on my shoulder, which feels nice.

Once she's gone, I breathe deep once, then again. I close my eyes and open myself up. I find The Captain. She's sitting at a console on the flight deck with Sweet Caroline.

"...and so he thinks that we might be in danger. What do you think?"

Sweet Caroline doesn't say anything for a moment.

"Go on," The Captain says. Again, she thinks about the crown.

"Well, remember that while you and Salvadore went to go see if there was anything left of the interceptor, you sent Eli and Baldi and me over to have a look at the rubble nearby. That's when the guys found Akari," Sweet Caroline says. The Captain nods. "Okay, well, while they were dealing with getting Akari hoisted and back to the ship, I found something," Sweet Caroline says.

"What did you find?"

"A memory drive," Sweet Caroline says. "So I picked it up, brought it back, and I've been nursing it back to health the same time you guys have been focused on Akari."

"And?" The Captain asks.

"I got it. Well, some of it, to be more precise. It's corrupted, as you'd expect,

but it's got some files…and some video," Sweet Caroline says. She turns to the console and presses a few keys. On the screen, an image of room appears.

In the room there are three consoles. A mess of wires runs from each one to a metal pedestal in he center of the room. On that pedestal is a large cylindrical fish tank.

In that cloudy tank floats a person.

People are talking, but none of them can be heard all that well.

One steps from one of the consoles to directly in front of the camera.

He's speaking, but the language isn't standard. He adjusts his glasses as he speaks, and refers to his data pad a few times. At the end he nods, and then the man and the camera move closer to the tank.

When they get up close, the man says a few more things. He smiles, looking very proud of himself. The voice behind the camera says something, and the man in front smiles even larger, says something, and bows a bit.

He looks down and checks his wrist communications device. He says something into it. His badge lights up, processing the information.

"Do you see it?" Sweet Caroline asks.

"See what?" The Captain says.

"That's the same device we found near Akari."

On the screen, the man turns to the tank, and wipes away some of the condensation.

As soon as he does, the face of the person inside becomes clear.

The person in the tank is me.

Sweet Caroline hits a button and the image pauses. "What if," Sweet Caroline says, "…what if he wasn't the kid of one of these researchers who was out here doing go knows what kind of cloning or genetic manipulation or…I dunno." She presses another button and the camera zooms in. There is no doubt that it's my face. "What if Akari is the experiment they were out here doing?"

1.1.10

I let go and come flying back to the room. I can't catch my breath.

I wake up to find the medical bay mostly dark. The dim light above me is the only one on except in the office, but Baldi isn't in there. I sit up and then slide off the bed. The metal deck is cold on my feet.

The flight suit is on the bed nearby. I slide into it, zip it closed, and put my shoes on. Being covered up and warm already makes me feel better.

I walk to the door and lean out when it opens. No one anywhere nearby.

I walk a few feet down the corridor and realize that I don't know how to get anywhere from where I am. Rather than wander aimlessly, I lean back against the wall and breathe deeply. I inhale again, open myself up, and look for Eli.

"...has to be some solution," Eli is saying.

"Like what? This isn't a stray cat to adopt. This kid could be a killer." Salvadore leans back in his chair.

"Could be," Eli says. "That's not the same thing as is."

"You want to wait until he destroys us, too?" Salvadore says.

Eli is so mad he wants to take a swing at Salvadore. It makes me feel strange to know someone wants to defend me so much.

The Captain sees that things are about to escalate, though, and she makes a quick motion with her hand. "We need to make a decision sooner rather than later," she says.

Salvadore nods.

"There's a picture that's starting to form around this kid," The Captain says. "It isn't good, Eli. Salvadore isn't wrong. This may look like some lost kid, but the truth is that we may have brought something very dangerous on board."

"Some thing? Is that where we're at now?" Eli says. "If we were just going to make his life even worse, why did we even bother to bring him on board? Revive him? Why didn't we just leave him there in the rubble to die?"

"If you'll recall, you didn't exactly give any of us a chance to make a decision on that. You and Sweet already had him back aboard and Baldi was working on him before either of us made it back," The Captain says gesturing toward Salvadore.

"So that's just it? We don't even ask him about any of it?" Eli asks.

"To what end? We've asked him and asked him and all we keep getting is that he doesn't remember."

"Well, he doesn't."

"Or maybe he's just saying he doesn't," Salvadore says.

The Captain makes another gesture with her hand, cutting off Eli before he can say anything. It's pretty clear who she's listening to.

"He trusts you," she says. "Maybe he'll say something to you he won't say to me. Go back down there, turn on a recorder as discreetly as you can, and see if you can get some answers. But," The Captain says, "This is it. He either starts giving us information, or our choices get very limited. Understand?"

Eli nods. *I'll make sure he understands*, he thinks.

"Hey," Baldi says and startles me out of it.

"Hi," I say.

"Feeling better?" he asks. Again, it feels strange to have such a caring tone come from someone who looks so frazzled and scarred. Before I can even answer, he has a small tool out of his pocket and he puts it into my ear. I try to move, but he puts his hand on my shoulder. "Hold still."

He pulls the instrument back out and looks at the tiny display on it.

"Okay, hotshot. Looks all good. I'm going to want to check back in on you before bedtime, got it?"

I nod.

"Do you know how to get back to the passenger room from here?"

I shake my head no.

He gives me quick directions. "Do not go wandering. This ship is old and some of it is only held together with tape and a few whispered prayers."

I pass by all sorts of doors both open and shut on the way.

Through the window of one of the doors I see flickering blue light. When I get up on tiptoe to look, I see Max welding something.

Through an open door I pass by I see Sweet Caroline sitting in a chair with a long cable running from just behind her ear to a set of cobbled together computers and consoles. Her eyes are glazed over.

Eventually I reach the passenger room.

When the door opens, Eli is sitting on the bed I'd slept in. Neither Nyssa or Ardra are there. I step in and the door shuts behind me.

"Hey," Eli says. "Baldi says you check out."

I sit down beside him.

"So, Sweet Caroline has put together some information from a recorder she found at the site of...where we found you. It's...it's not super clear, but, as The Captain would say, there's a picture emerging."

I try not to laugh at how dead-on his impersonation of her in that moment is. I think for a moment about telling him I already know, but something tells me that if I say I've been listening in, things go downhill fast.

"First off, I want to say that, nobody has said how sorry we all are about what happened yet. So, look, I know we're all really sorry. In that moment, it was a choice between us and them, sure, but I can't tell you how much I wish things would have happened differently," Eli says. Without even listening in I can tell how much he means it.

"After the...the crash...we realized what had happened and we set down to see if there were...you know...survivors. The only person alive we found was you. When we found you, you were sort of half in, half out of this… tank. Like a large glassteel cylinder. From the video we've recovered, we now know that…well, that you were in that cylinder at the time of the…accident," Eli says.

My brain flips through a few quick flashes. Coldness. Darkness. But at the same time, seeing numbers on a tablet and being happy. For just a second I can both see someone else's face and also see my own through glass.

"So, we scooped you up and got you back here as fast as we could. Luckily enough for you, this old crate used to be a long-range medical ship. Kind of a big ambulance made to go long distances without any help. We have a lot of what Baldi calls toys on board that many ships that…do what we do… wouldn't have," Eli says.

I remember feeling warm. I remember hearing voices. I remember waking up to Baldi's face, and Eli standing over me.

"Sweet Caroline has gone digging in all kinds of places, from the shallow information system we all use to the scary corners of places I would rather not know existed, she says, and she can't find anything about that outpost. The place we found you didn't exist as far as anyone else is concerned. Sweet says that means whatever was happening there, it was scary stuff. Now, for this next part, I need you to kind of try to stay strong," Eli says. He puts his hand on my shoulder.

He doesn't know that I already know.

"Sweet says that all of this combined with what she's been able to piece together of the video files we found when we found you…it looks like maybe…maybe *you* were the thing they were working on."

Just like the first time I heard it, it is both shocking and not shocking at all. It feels like the truth.

I nod.

"We don't know what that might mean, yet, because the files she's recovered so far are mostly video from that lab…the lab where you were… where we found you. But Salvadore says that, for that lab to have been able

52

to withstand the hit and explosion that it did and you to come out alive, it was heavily shielded, and the...the tank...doubly so," Eli says. "He says that means they really, really didn't want anyone to be able to scan what was going on inside."

He squeezes my shoulder.

"The Captain says this all starts to look like maybe you weren't the kid of someone who was working at that outpost. She says that it looks like maybe they were...that they were growing you. That maybe they were trying to create a telepath on purpose," Eli says.

I can tell he keeps pausing so that I can have time to process and maybe to say something, but I don't have anything to say. The second I heard all of this I knew it was true, and oddly enough, I'm fine with it.

"I don't remember anything," I say. "That's why I'm not feeling sad. I don't remember anyone on that station. If I was someone's kid, I should remember them, right? A mom, a dad, something. But I don't."

Eli nods.

"The last part came through just before Baldi let you go. As soon as Sweet decoded it, we asked Baldi to run one more scan, and he confirmed it," Eli says.

Here it comes, I think.

"To us, you look like you're maybe fourteen or fifteen. But the logs, at least what Sweet has been able to recover and decode of them...the logs say that it's only been about two years since you were conceived."

"Oh," is all I can think to say.

Again, none of this is shocking. Even if I hadn't already overheard it, I don't know that it would be.

Some part of me...knows this.

And there's something deeper. I don't know what it is, but I can tell that there is something else that part of me knows, but that I can't seem to get at.

"I guess I was thinking some of this might be shocking to you," Eli says and looks at the floor. When he finally looks back at me, he says, "Can you see why The Captain thinks there's more you're not telling us? No matter what we find out, you don't seem to be shocked by any of it."

I shrug. When he leans back and sighs, I say, "I promise I'm not hiding anything on purpose."

"Okay," Eli says. "Then...then what is it?"

"I can't...it's like I keep telling you—I can't remember. It isn't that I don't want to, it's that...it feels like there's nothing there, sometimes. Other times it feels like there is something, but I can't...grab it. Like...something buried in dirt that's also slippery."

"But you still know how to talk," Eli says.

"I don't know. I know how to talk, I know how to turn on a faucet or whatever. I just...I can't really remember things like what my house looked like."

"Okay," Eli says again and leans back in his chair. "I guess that makes sense given the...the tube thing." I can tell he hesitated because he doesn't know if him saying something like that hurts my feelings. It doesn't, but I don't know how to say that to him. "You're a telepath. You can read people's thoughts. You know that."

I nod. "But, it's like...I don't *think* about it, it's just something I do."

Eli looks confused.

"You fix stuff," I say and Eli nods. "How often do you walk around thinking to yourself, 'I am a fixer; I fix stuff'?"

"Okay," Eli says. "I guess that makes sense. Are you doing it now? Reading my thoughts?"

I shake my head no.

"Is it what you're doing when you start breathing deep? Or is that just some kind of meditation?"

I look at him for a second, then nod.

"Is...is it just what that person is thinking right then or do you...can you go deeper?"

"Just what they're thinking now. I think...I think to try to go backward or deeper down would take...more."

"More?" Eli asks.

I shrug. "I don't know how to explain. One thing is kind of easy, the other would be hard. It would take...more," I say.

"You can see why even that first one would make people uneasy, though, right? I mean, especially on a ship like this. We're all...none of us are exactly... good."

I don't know what to say to that.

"That's what they're all worried about. I have to be honest with you, The Captain and Salvadore...they want to just dump you off somewhere. They're that worried about what you...do."

I nod.

"Do you...do you want to go?" Eli asks.

"I don't know," I say. "Being here is making people nervous, and I don't want that. But I don't know where else I'd go. I don't have..." Anything, really, I think, but the second I go to put that into words, my eyes well up. I sniffle. "If I really am...if I'm an experiment, then I don't have any family to go to. I don't have anyone except you," I say.

I can see Eli's eyes well up, too. He looks away blinking.

"Yeah. That's...that's pretty much what I feel, too. I'm...I'm really sorry that these people did this to you," Eli says. He puts his huge hand on top of mine. It makes me feel uncomfortable to have contact with someone and also makes me feel better all at the same time.

"Why did you guys save me?" I ask.

"We saw a kid lying in the ruins of the outpost that we kind of accidentally destroyed. There wasn't a lot of choice," Eli says.

"But...if you had a choice?" I ask.

"What, like if you were a puppy at the pound or something?" Eli laughs.

I smile. "Yeah, I guess."

He thinks about it for a minute. "Me? Yes. The Captain, though...She's not great with people."

"But she's the leader?" I say.

"Ironic, isn't it. See, she..."

The speaker on the wall comes to life. "Everyone get up here," The Captain's voice says.

"Uh oh," Eli says. He stands and walks to the doorway, then stops. "You coming?" he asks.

I quirk an eyebrow at him.

"They better need to start getting used to you sooner rather than later," he says.

I toe into my boots and follow him to the flight deck.

1.1.11

More than a few eyebrows go up when I walk on to the flight deck after Eli. They look at him, then at me, then go back to what they were looking at the large screen at the front.

"Captain," Eli says. She nods at him.

On the screen is a scene of wreckage spread out in all directions from a center point.

"...still have no idea who these settlers were or what they were doing here. Again, news of the crash of this police cruiser is only just now coming in. We're receiving word that there are no survivors..." The Captain gestures to Sweet Caroline to turn the volume down.

"They have found the crash," The Captain says.

"And if they're releasing *this* information to the media, then the actual police have more," Salvadore says.

"I can tell you that if there was a flight recorder down there, we would almost certainly have found it," Sweet Caroline says.

"Can you give me more certainty than that? I mean, how thorough was your search after you found..." The Captain is about to say something about me, but then decides not to.

"We had already searched the area around what was left of the cruiser before we found the kid," Max says.

"I hope you're right," The Captain says. "Anything?" she asks, looking at Eli.

He looks at me then back at her. "He legit doesn't know anything."

I see Salvadore's face harden. Sweet Caroline looks away from me and back down at her console.

"But if you think about it," Eli says, "that makes sense. If…if he *was* some kind of…an…experiment…" even without reaching out to him, I can feel how much he hopes that doesn't hurt me. "…then he wouldn't have any memories of anything that was going on, would he?"

The Captain steps closer to me, her jaw set. Before she can say anything, though, Sweet Caroline says, "Got it."

Without looking over her shoulder at Sweet, The Captain says, "got what?"

"The code to get me in to the filed reports from the sector we just left." The Captain looks down at the floor then turns and walks over to Sweet Caroline. "And?" she asks.

"Just a second…" Sweet Caroline says. Eli puts his hand on my shoulder and guides me to an open chair. When I sit down he gives me a look that says to stay still and quiet.

"Okay, here it is. See, after a message gets sent across the network, there's a copy of it that floats around for a bit in the buffers. So back at headquarters, they can encrypt it and store it deep in a vault somewhere all they want to; for a little while, it's still bouncing around out there."

"Okay," The Captain says. "What did this last cruiser say about us?"

Sweet Caroline is quiet for a moment, then says, "You're not going to believe this."

"Try me," The Captain says.

"It looks like it was a fluke. They weren't looking for us, or, really, anyone specific. We just happened to stumble across their patrol route."

"But I thought you said we had a very accurate map of those," Max says.

"It looks like these guys changed their approved route manually. They mention something about deviation discretion. They don't mention why they…oh, I see…" Sweet Caroline says, then a picture pops up on her already crowded screen of a run down looking space station. "Their deviation from the regular patrol route would take them very close to this," Sweet Caroline says. "It's unlisted, but I bet if I dig around some I can find out what it is. I'll probably need a node, though."

"Why?" The Captain asks.

"Like I've said before, I'm doing the best with what I have, but this old tub was never going to have state of the art communications equipment even when it was brand new. I keep telling you that we should invest in…"

"Yeah, I get it," The Captain says.

"So, if you want me to really dig in and see what's going on and maybe do a little…" Sweet Caroline says, wiggling her fingers a bit.

"Or we could just count ourselves lucky and get our passengers to their destination. Move on with our lives," Salvadore says.

The Captain closes her eyes and sighs. Again, she walks over to me. Eli sits down next to me.

"What if the kid's bugged somehow? Chipped, like a puppy or something?" The Captain asks.

"We'd have found anything that was broadcasting, would we?" Eli asks.

She doesn't say anything. Her expression doesn't change.

"I promise that I'm not trying to hurt you," I say. "That I won't try to in the future, either." I'm surprised to hear myself talk this much. I think Eli is, too. "If what Sweet Caroline has found out is true, then…then they were doing something to me. Maybe they even *made* me just so they could do… whatever it was they were doing." It's only just now as I say it out loud that I truly understand what that might mean. "If those things are true," I say, "then you rescued me. You saved me from them. Why would I want to hurt the people who saved me?" I ask.

The Captain's face softens.

Salvadore says, "The thing you wanted me to look into? It's doable."

"Okay," she says over her shoulder. "Max, how long at present speed until we reach the coordinates?"

"Just a bit over twelve hours now," he says.

She nods, then sits down next to me. Somehow, even though her voice

59

gets quieter than it has been, she seems more in charge than ever.

"Eli wants us to keep you on. Says he can always use an extra pair of hands. He even goes so far as to suggest that because we were involved with the accident that destroyed the outpost, you're our responsibility. My gut is telling me to dump you off somewhere. Do you know why?" she asks.

"Because I'm a telepath," I say.

She nods. "Every story I know of that has someone like you in it always ends in disaster. Always." She stares at me for a moment. "Thing is this, though—between you, me, and the wall? A part of me keeps coming back to how it might be useful to have someone with your particular...talents... around. Problem is, while I want you to be able to tell me what cards someone else has in their hand, I'm not so keen on the idea of you rattling around in here," she taps her temple. "If what we've managed to piece together is true, then life hasn't been kind to you at all. I do see that. But these people here? They're my family. And I protect my family. So, feel for you or not, I have to do right by them." She looks over at Salvadore. "How long?" she asks him.

"Two hours, tops," he says. I can tell he's not happy about whatever it is they are discussing.

"Eli says he trusts you. And I've learned to trust Eli when it comes to people. So I'm going to give you a choice. Salvadore says he's got a way to create a device...a kind of...headband...that will detect the specific waves that come off you when you're...doing the thing," she says, gesturing toward her head. "Says it can alert us, maybe even stick a shocker in there so we can stop you from doing it until we want you to." I can feel the effort it took for her to not call it a "crown."

Eli stiffens up and is about to say something.

The Captain gestures at him. He doesn't relax, but he doesn't speak, either.

"You agree to put that on? *Then* I can trust you. You put it on, you can join my crew. You work like any one of us, get a share like any one of us, this ship becomes your home. You become family," she says. "If you say no, then we dump you on the next station or planet that comes along and you find your own way."

Somehow, this doesn't shock me. Since the moment she had the thought while I was listening in, I knew that this was where things were headed, even if I didn't realize it.

Eli is shaking he's so mad.

"Salvadore is going to go ahead and start making the...headband... because it seems to me that might be a handy thing to have around regardless. You've got until he's finished. Once it's done, you have to make the call and we go from there. Got it?" she asks.

I nod.

The Captain stands, turns, and she and Salvadore leave.

1.1.12

"This is unfair," Eli whispers through clenched teeth. I catch Sweet Caroline sneaking a glance at me. She looks away quickly.

I know that part of this was her idea.

"Come on," Eli says. When he gets up, I follow him.

Once we're far enough down the main corridor, he says, "this isn't fair."

I don't know what to say, so I don't say anything.

He stops us in front of the room I've been sharing with Nyssa and Ardra. When the door opens, Nyssa has a small stringed instrument out and she and Ardra are singing a song together. They jump when we come in.

"Sorry," Eli says.

"It's quite alright," Nyssa says, setting the instrument down. "Music lessons weren't going particularly well this afternoon." I hear the crack at Ardra in that. "What can we do for you?" Nyssa asks looking at Eli.

Eli sits down on the other bed. I sit down next to him.

"The Captain just did something pretty rotten," Eli says.

"Oh?" Nyssa asks, "and what was that?"

He looks at me. I get the impression he wants me to say something about it. In that moment I realize that I don't talk much, but that I also don't know what to say half the time.

"The Captain wants me to make a decision," I say.

"Regarding your...talents...I suspect," Nyssa says. I nod. "I would imagine she is being pressured to remove you from the ship, yes?"

I nod again.

Eli halfheartedly punches the mattress.

"I see," Nyssa says.

"Why?" Ardra asks.

"People are often afraid that if someone were to know their thoughts and true intentions in things, they would seem foolish…or villainous," Nyssa says, "or perhaps both."

Quiet settles in the room.

"Are you reading our thoughts right now?" Ardra asks.

"No," I say.

"Why can't they just ask him if he's doing it when they are afraid?" Ardra asks.

"That's a very good question," Nyssa says. "I think because many suspect that someone who could read thoughts might try to use it to gain advantage. What I've heard most often, though, is that those who have this…trait… often only use it when they feel threatened."

"Like an octopus changing its color?" Ardra asks.

"Yes, very much like that," Nyssa says, looking at me.

I hadn't thought of it, to be honest. I wondered if I had been using it to gain advantage or if I had only used it for self-defense.

"Still," Eli says. "It ain't right. Scared or not, it's who he is. You can't get mad at someone for who they are."

Nyssa folds her hands neatly in her lap. "I admit, I am somewhat concerned about this, myself. However, I do believe that Akari can be trusted. Most young people can, given simple guidance."

"The Captain doesn't see it that way," Eli says. "She wants him to wear a thing."

"A…thing?" Nyssa asks.

"A headband thingy that will alert people if he's…y'know…" Eli says.

"Ah," Nyssa says. "Accompanied by some sort of physical inducement to discontinue such behavior, I would imagine?"

"Yeah," Eli says, "it'll shock him."

"This is in return for staying on the ship?" Nyssa asks.

I nod.

Nyssa sighs. "Well, then, you'll simply have to be given another alternative." She looks at Ardra pointedly. Ardra nods. "Rather than be dropped off on some random planet that The Captain happens to decide on because you won't wear her device, would you like to come with us?"

I hadn't even considered it. I can see from Eli's face he hadn't either.

Nyssa had been so wonderful to me, and even though Ardra could be a brat, I still liked her very much. I felt as though the future I had resigned myself to almost instantly back when it was put before me, wearing that "crown," felt brighter.

"Would you like to?" Ardra asks.

Eli looks at me. In that moment, I see something cross his face that I haven't seen before. I feel myself start to change my breathing and almost reach out, but I stop myself. There, in that instant, I see it. How I had been behaving.

I couldn't remember any time before being on the ship, but since waking up here, I had been reading people's thoughts. Not only without them knowing I could, but without even being in the room. I could see how people might think it was unfair, how they might have things they didn't want me to know.

I swear that I hadn't thought of it until that very moment or couldn't remember having thought of it before then. At least, not in a fully realized way.

"When one wants to know what another is thinking," Nyssa says, seeming to read my mind, "one can simply ask, 'what are you thinking?'"

"What are you thinking?" I ask Eli.

"I don't want you to go. I...I would miss you," Eli says. "But, if it's between you having to wear a headband like some kind of choke chain...like a dog... or being free..." He doesn't finish his thought.

Nyssa nods. "I must warn you; Ardra and I, we will need to move around quite a lot, even when we make planetfall. She and I have been prepared for this for some time, and this is the first you're hearing of it, but that is the situation. However, if you believe you can bear such a life, you are welcome to come with us."

I know that there is something Eli and Nyssa and Ardra know that I don't. I don't like being the only person in the room who doesn't.

"It would also be fair to reveal to you, should you decide to join us, why we are on the run, so to speak," Nyssa says, and I notice she is looking at Ardra as she says it. Again, the little girl nods. Nyssa nods at her in return, then looks back at me.

That's the choice I'm given—between Eli, the only person who has stuck up for me and cared for me in the short time that I can remember, or Nyssa who is wonderful but who I barely know.

"Of course, we have given you a very difficult decision to make. One that should not be made quickly. There is no need to answer immediately," Nyssa says. I can tell she means it. I think for a second about how kind she is versus how cold The Captain feels.

"You…" I start to say but stop. She looks at me with eyes that are so kind, so patient. "You don't worry at all that I'll…" I gesture toward my head.

"Of course I have some concerns," she says. "I wouldn't be a normal person if I didn't. However, and I don't wish to speak ill of someone who has done so much to help us," she says, glancing at Eli and then back at me, "unlike our captain, though, I believe that you have the ability of self control. If I ask you to not read my thoughts, I believe you would respect that request."

I vowed that I would never read her thoughts without permission.

I could see Eli consider the idea for a moment.

"The Captain means well and all…" he starts but doesn't finish.

"I'll go with you," I say.

I see how it hurts Eli, but I also see that he knows this is the only thing I could have chosen.

"Excellent," Nyssa says. "Eli, perhaps you'd be so good as to find some things, clothes and such, that you might be able to secret away for Akari given that he has nothing."

"Yeah," Eli says, standing. "I can do that. Come on," he says. He stops at the door and turns. "Thank you," he says to Nyssa.

"I believe this decision is to all of our advantage," she says.

Eli and I walk out.

1.1.13

When Eli comes to get me to pack because we've made it to the planet, it seems as if it was too fast. That everything is happening too fast.

I'll soon have to leave this ship, and it is the only home I've ever known.

"Here, you'll need a jacket," he says, handing me a beat-up old leather jacket that is split in a few places. It's several sizes too large for me. "You'll have to roll the sleeves up some," he says, "but it should work." I put it in the old large duffel he's fished out of the storage lockers for me.

We've been down here a while.

For the first bit, nothing that he pulled out was anything enough. Not tall enough, not thick enough, not…it went on like that for a while.

"Here, give me those," he says, gesturing toward the boots I've been wearing. "Put these on," he hands me a pair of much nicer boots. I can feel the steel toe in them. "They're a bit big, but you'll grow into them. They used to belong to…" he pauses. "Well, that doesn't matter, really. That was a long time ago. For now, just lace them up real tight like this." He bends down and laces the boots up for me. "Watch me so you can do it later."

He keeps stuffing things into the duffel until I'm sure I won't be able to carry it, but I don't want to say anything because these things will become all I have in the entire world.

When he asks me to pick it up by the strap I fall over. "I guess that is a bit much," he says. We start to take things out, being more critical of each item. He tries to hide it, but I can tell that each thing we take out pains him. I don't have to read his mind to know he's thinking that I might need it.

"Why?" I finally ask.

"Why what?" he stops and looks up at me.

"You've cared for me since I...woke up. Why?"

He sits down on the floor near the bag. "When I was young...younger than you are now...something...terrible happened. I was left alone. A friend of my dad's took me in. It wasn't easy; he didn't have any kids and had never really wanted any. Still, he made sure I was fed, that I had clothes, all that stuff. He...he didn't have to do any of that. He could have just said 'that's a shame' like everyone else and turned away, but he didn't."

I don't know what to say, so I put my hand on his shoulder.

A smile touches his lips, but not the rest of his face.

He pats my hand.

"Look, are you sure?" he asks.

"Sure?" I ask in return.

He sighs. "They're...they're going to be on the run for the rest of their lives. No rest, no...no settling down. I mean, unless they can find some place truly off the grid somewhere, which I guess *could* happen, but...it's going to be a longshot." He looks away and we both go quiet. He looks back after a moment and says, "They're just going to be on the run. If you go with them, so will you."

"Aren't you, too?" I ask.

I see that stings him a bit. I want to apologize for it, but before I can he says, "That's...that's true. I guess. I mean, we spend a lot of time trying to get around the law, but we're not wanted, per se." I can see him trying to build to some sort of lesson, but I can also see that it isn't coming.

"I want to stay with you," I say. "But if it means that I have to..."

"I know," he says.

"You could maybe come with us?" I ask. Before I do I know it's a stupid question.

There's a beep overhead and then some feedback as the nearby speaker comes on.

"Planetfall. Repeat: planetfall," Max's voice announces.

I already know his answer.

"You don't understand; this old tub is flying true right now, but most times…most times it's all anyone can do just to keep it flying. Without me they'd…"

"Okay," I say.

He looks at me for a second. Then he nods, too. "Okay."

Eli grunts as he gets to his feet. He zips the bag closed and holds the strap out to me. This time I can pick the bag up.

Eli nods. Then he reaches into his pocket and pulls out a small wad of bills. "Here," he says. "Put this in your pocket."

"I can't take that from…" I start to say.

He grabs my hand and shoves them into it. Then he turns and gestures for me to follow him. I put the money in my pocket.

When we get back to the room that I've been sharing with Nyssa and Ardra, they are both folding seats down out of the wall.

"Hurry, now; get strapped in," Nyssa says to Ardra. She makes sure that the strap goes over the stuffed horse Ardra is clutching.

Eli folds another set of chairs out of the wall on the other side of the door. When they click into place he gestures for me to sit. I set the bag down but when I reach for the harness belt Eli is already pulling it across me. He clicks both into place and nods at me.

I look over and Nyssa is already fastened in as well.

Eli flips a switch on the wall. "Captain, Eli."

"Go," The Captain's voice comes back.

"Passengers strapped in."

"Roger that," she says.

Eli looks at me one more time then leaves. Around us the ship starts to shake just a bit. Then there are sounds like someone wailing. Then the ship starts to jump and buck, shaking. A few of the toys that Ardra had left out bounce around the room.

The sound as if someone is being tortured gets even louder.

The jumping of the ship gets worse. If not for the harnesses I know I would have been thrown from the chair.

Just when it seems like things are getting too violent, that something is about to break, the vibration dies down. The shaking stops. The shrieking quiets.

The feedback happens again.

"Caution: autogravity off," Max says over the speaker.

I do feel a tiny bit lighter.

A few minutes later Max says, "Caution: landing."

The ship jolts then noticeably settles.

"Welcome to Saberhagen 45c," Max says.

Nyssa unstraps herself and then unstraps Ardra. They begin to pick up the few toys and things that had bounced around the room. I unstrap myself and pick up the pony that had slid over near me. I take it to Nyssa. She takes it from me and smiles.

"I see that you've acquired some luggage yourself," she says.

I nod.

"I'll go over it in a few moments to make sure that it's light enough for us to take. We may have to remove some items. I hope that won't upset you... or Eli...too much."

Until that moment, it hadn't occurred to me that she might also be taking on guardianship of me when I decided to go with her. The thought didn't make me upset, though.

The door opens and The Captain comes in. He doesn't enter, but I can see Salvadore out in the hallway.

"Well," The Captain says to Nyssa, "this is goodbye."

"Are we at the station?"

"Yes," The Captain says, "safely tucked in to one of the outermost hangars, just as requested."

"Good," Nyssa says. She begins to move their things from the drawers she'd put them in to the bags she and Ardra had stowed under the bed.

"How long before your contact arrives?"

"Should be very soon," Nyssa says. "As soon as he does, you will receive payment in full."

The Captain turns to me. "I understand that you've decided to go with them."

I nod.

She nods back at me. "Very well. But here's something to remember," she says, leaning close to me. "There are those who will find out who and… what…you are. They won't be as nice as me about it. If you're going to be wandering around out here, you need to protect yourself." When she says that a shiver runs down my spine. "You do that by making sure people *don't* find out who and…what…you are. Do you understand?"

A part of me wants to protest. To remind her that I saved them. That she wouldn't know what I was unless I *had* saved them. To remind her that I wouldn't even be on her ship if they hadn't made a horrible mistake that had killed maybe a hundred people.

That should have killed me, too.

But for some reason hadn't.

It's there that the urge to argue back dies on my tongue.

I could see, too, that my arguing would do nothing. She'd already made up her mind.

I was a problem that she was relieved to find had solved itself.

"Good. It will be nice to get my engineer back," she says. "I'll be opening the hatch as soon as we're equalized with the planet," she says to Nyssa and then she leaves.

When the door closes, Nyssa says, "I find her somewhat unpleasant."

I can't stop myself—I laugh out loud. I look over at her and she winks at me and smiles, too.

Part 2: Past The Edge

1.2.1

As soon as Nyssa, Ardra, and I stepped on to the cargo deck, the door at the far end opened. Wind came in through the gap and I nearly gag.

"Don't worry," Eli says from over near the wall. "Every planet has a smell. Rotting vegetation, meat, etc. You'll go nose-blind to it fairly quick."

What had been the inside wall of the ship was now the ramp leading down into a huge, dirty, concrete hangar.

"Eli, Sweet, you're with the ship. The rest with me," The Captain says, already walking. We all follow her down the ramp and across to the far wall of the hangar where there was a door.

I pause for a second to look back at the ship. It's pitted and scarred hull was actually handsome in many ways. The lines bulky but beautiful in their own fashion.

Then I see Eli standing at the bottom of the ramp looking at me.

I wave to him one more time.

We had tried to say goodbye before everyone gathered in the cargo bay, but it was ugly and we both started crying. Then we pretended that we weren't crying, which only made me want to cry more.

After a few rounds of that, The Captain had called over the intercom for everyone to gather to disembark.

Eli waves back and I turn to follow the rest through the now open door and out onto the planet.

The smell gets worse. Ardra struggles to hold her nose closed while she carries one of her small bags. Nyssa has a few of theirs. I have the rest of theirs plus the one that Eli gave me.

"Let's keep up, people," The Captain says from the front. I move faster.

Salvadore is directly in front of me. He has his sunglasses on, his long leather jacket flowing behind him, and his huge pistol on his hip. I've never seen a more graceful or more dangerous looking person. He glances back at me just once, and I can't help but feel like I'd been fully assessed and catalogued.

I move closer to Nyssa. Again, she smiles encouragement at me.

"Thank you for carrying the rest of our things," she says. Just outside the door to the hangar there was a broad street. I see that there was another huge hangar directly across from us, and then two more sets just like this one all the way down the street. At the end of the street was a dome. People flowed in and out of that dome continuously.

"It's no problem," I say.

As we pass by the last hangar on the same side as the one we'd just left, a roar erupts from it as well as a strong wind. From out of the top, a small ship lifted off, pointed itself upward, then shot at the sky. I'd never heard anything more exhilarating and more frightening in my life.

The Captain looks back over her shoulder but keeps walking.

When we arrive at the dome, I can finally see how massively tall it is and how huge around. Just to the side of the three entrances I could see were small rectangle buildings. Above the door of each was the same thing in many languages. I couldn't read any of them.

"Come with me," The Captain says to Nyssa.

"Watch Ardra," Nyssa says and steps into the building, just barely big enough for three people, with The Captain.

I leaned against the outer wall of the dome near Ardra. She was taking her hand off her nose for longer and longer periods of time, then putting it back. I'd already stopped smelling the horrifying smell of this planet.

"We should go in there," Ardra says.

"No," I say. "Nyssa said to wait here."

"But she could be in trouble," Ardra says.

I look around and the rest of the crew have gone. Without even saying goodbye, they've all scattered to somewhere. Still, Nyssa said.

"We wait," I say.

Ardra stamps a foot but doesn't move any further.

The Captain walks out of the little building shoving a purse into the side pocket of her jacket. She glances at me once then turns away and walks into the dome entrance. Nyssa comes back out.

I want to ask if it went alright, but she motions for us to follow her. We walk in to the dome, as well.

We walk a long tunnel that leads to a riot.

The room is a chaos of people and colors and noise and movement.

Two seconds after we walk inside, I've lost sight of everyone I was following. People move past me without even looking at me. The ones that do look at me, I wish weren't.

Suddenly there is a woman pressing up against me. She pushes me back against the wall.

"Well, hello cutie pie," she says. "What's your name?"

"Akari," I say. She's at least a foot taller than me and has a larger framed body than I've seen before, and she's using it to make sure I can't move.

"Mmm," she says. "Sounds Old Earth. I love it." She runs a hand through my hair.

Her hands start to rove down my body. Again, I try to move but I can't.

"How much money you got, honey? You and me? We could have a real good time." She arches her eyebrows and I wonder if that's supposed to mean something.

Eli appears behind her and puts his hand on her shoulder.

"Mags! You old so and so. How are you?" he says to her.

She moves just enough to turn and face him. I slide out and away from her.

"Eli," she says.

"Look, this little one isn't worth your time or trouble. Howzabout you and me make some magic?" He does the same thing with his eyebrows she'd done to me. Again, I wonder what it's supposed to mean.

She shakes her head. I move behind Eli.

"I know better than to think you have any money," she says to Eli.

"Well, that's your loss," he says, laughing. Before she can say anything, Eli puts his arm around my shoulder and leads me away. He moves through the thick of the crowd as if they weren't even there.

He stops us both in front of the bar.

"You looked like you needed a little help," he said.

"I thought you were supposed to stay with the ship," I said.

"Yeah, well..." he says. "You seem to have gotten separated from your party. That's a bad thing. Try to make sure it doesn't happen in the future." He sounds stern, but I can see in his face he's happy to see me. I'm happy to see him, too.

"What is this place?" I ask.

His height allows him to see over everyone else's heads. "It's got a bunch of names, most of them not very nice. Mainly everyone just calls it The Dome. It's where you go when you need to get things done that you wouldn't want many people knowing about." He puts his arm around my shoulder again and we start moving through the crowd. "Lots of places like this all over, but this one is especially...difficult to find...unless you know what you're looking for."

I'm trying not to stare at all the people. Some are ordinary like me, but others are modified in all kinds of ways. One man has half of his face replaced with a chrome plate that shines like a mirror. A woman has four extra mechanical arms. One person in a long flowing robe has tentacles coming out from the arm holes.

"Biopunks," Eli says when he sees me staring at that person. "Modify the body at a DNA level. Kind of cool stuff, but I'd never try it, that's for sure."

Eventually we wind up in front of Nyssa and Ardra's table.

"There you are!" Ardra says.

"Looks like he got a little discombobulated," Eli says. "Your guy here yet?" he asks.

"I imagine so. It's just a matter of whether or not he feels safe enough to contact us." She looks around then back at Eli. "Thank you for returning Akari to us, but…"

"A guy like me standing next to you isn't exactly going to help your contact feel safe. I get you," Eli says. He turns to me, looks me square in the eye and says. "You be good, ok?" I can tell he means a lot in that one sentence. He hands me a rectangular piece of plastic. "When you guys get set up wherever you're going, and Nyssa tells you it's safe, you put this into any communications system, and it'll dial me on the ship. You call and you let me know how you are, ok?"

I take the card and put it in my pocket and I nod. "Thank you for…"

Before I can finish, he's tearing up, so he claps me on the shoulder and walks away.

"Sit down," Nyssa says. Her tone of voice isn't angry at all, but I can tell she means immediately. I squeeze in next to Ardra.

"He's a good man," Nyssa says, her head moving to scan the crowd.

"Who are we meeting?" I ask.

"A man that I contacted before Ardra and I left. Someone I trust. He will take us to a place where the Royal Family cannot reach us."

I nod and start looking through the crowd even though I have no idea what I'm looking for.

Far across the room, I can see The Captain and Salvadore settling into a booth with some other people I don't recognize. I could listen in if I wanted, but the coldness in The Captain's voice from before crept back to me and I shivered.

A man steps up to the table blocking my view. He's older than Nyssa, tall with long red hair, and he's carrying several weapons.

"It is a lovely night for dancing," he says, his face unmoving.

"The Tango is always the right choice," Nyssa says. "Sarnex Dessicant."

"Nyssa—that's the name we're using these days, right?"

"Yes," she says.

The man's face relaxes. He sits.

I immediately don't like him.

"I'm glad that you have made it," he says.

"I am, as well," Nyssa says to him.

"If I may ask, who is this?" he asks gesturing to me.

"It's a very long story. One that I would prefer to tell once we are out of orbit and accelerating away from this sector," Nyssa says.

"The money was for two, not three."

"He's small—he won't take up much space," Nyssa says.

"Space isn't the problem, hiding an extra heartbeat is."

"Do you want the money or not?" Nyssa says. I hear her doing an impression of The Captain, but he wouldn't know that.

He looks around the bar, then back at her. Neither says anything for a moment.

"Come with me," he says in return. He stands and we all follow him toward the door. I want to look back at the other crew one last time before we go, but we're moving too fast and the crowd is too thick.

We're heading back toward the hangars. Nyssa's head swivels back and forth, constantly finding Ardra, then me, then looking through every alley and doorway we pass.

Eventually, we reach a hangar farther back than the one Eli's crew had set down in. The man looks around, then punches a few buttons near the door and, when it opens, ushers us inside.

I feel his eyes on my back as I pass him.

The second he's inside, the energy around all of us changes.

I turn back to see what's happened and I see that he's got the three of us at gunpoint.

1.2.2

"Sarnex," Nyssa says as she raises her hands above her head. "What's going on?"

"What is going on, 'Nyssa,' is that I know who you are. And, more importantly, I know who *she* is," he says motioning toward Ardra with his head. "Him, I'm not sure about, but he's pretty enough, I'm sure he'll fetch me a coin or two on the open market for pleasure slaves."

"What's going on?" Ardra asks.

"Quiet, honey," Nyssa says softly.

I put my hands up, mimicking Nyssa.

"And us?" Nyssa asks.

"Well, the little one is going straight back to her parents. And, luckily enough for you, the reward specifically states that they want you returned alive, as well. To face whatever punishment they decide to dole out to you, I would imagine."

"How much?" Nyssa asks.

"Oh, my darling. Are you truly going to attempt to convince me that you have enough money to buy me off? To pay more than her parents will?"

It's then that I notice there is no ship in this hangar.

I also notice that he's left the hangar door open.

I have never tried it like this, but I start to slow my breathing down. It'll be hard to close my eyes on a person who has a gun aimed at me, but I think I can do it.

"How do you know what I have and what I don't? I had enough money to pay for a ship to get us to you, and to pay the original outrageous price you asked for transporting us, don't I? Don't you think it would make sense that there is more, somewhere?"

I close my eyes and reach out. I feel his mind. Though guarded, I slip inside and see the whole situation through his eyes.

Immediately, Nyssa pulls something from the inside of her jacket and throws it at Sarnex's face.

I can feel him wanting to move, the surge of energy that is his reflex wanting to come through, but I'm in the way. The signal doesn't reach its destination.

I let go of his mind just as the blade that Nyssa threw hits Sarnex in the neck.

I come back to my own body just in time to see Eli come charging through the door to the hangar. Eli hits Sarnex square on, and Sarnex hits the decking hard; I'm sure I hear something snap. Eli, having used the other man to cushion the fall, sits up and starts to punch Sarnex repeatedly until the man goes unconscious.

Nyssa crouches in front of Ardra, shielding the girl with her own body. I see she has another of the throwing knives in her hand ready to go.

"Go close the door," Eli says to me. It takes me a moment to snap out of it, but I do as he asks.

"Everyone okay?" Eli asks.

"Yes," Nyssa says as she walks over to pick up the gun.

"Good," he says, standing. He pulls the knife Nyssa threw out of Sarnex's neck and hands it back to her. "Good throw," he says.

She takes it, wipes it on Sarnex's pant leg and then puts it back inside her jacket.

I get to the controls near the door and press the button with the down arrow. The door slides closed. We're left looking at each other in the cold fluorescent light of the hangar bay.

"How did...?" Nyssa starts to ask.

"I just had this feeling. Something about him seemed...off," Eli says.

"Where's his ship?" Ardra asks.

"That's...odd..." Eli says. He bends down and starts to search through Sarnex's jacket and pockets. Nyssa keeps the gun trained on the body.

There are a handful of things that Eli piles up near Sarnex's body, but I can see on his face none of them is what he had hoped for.

"No disc, no remote, nothing," he says.

"If he doesn't have the key to his ship on him, then maybe it's tied to his bio readings," Nyssa says.

"Well, that won't do you much good, if so," Eli says, gesturing toward the body. "And, why didn't he close the door himself? He would have had to move you to wherever his ship is, but even on this planet, someone marching a group of people around at gunpoint would be...noticed."

"He must have an ally. Or more than one," Nyssa says.

Eli stands back up and looks at me. "At the last minute, there, he hesitated. Was that...?"

I nod.

Eli nods back at me.

"What do we do now?" Ardra asks.

Just then something in Eli's vest beeps. He pulls out a box, clicks the button on it and holds it close to his ear.

"Yeah," he says then pauses. "How long?" He nods, looks at me, then at Nyssa then back to the floor. "The guy she went with turned out to be a bounty hunter." He waits for a moment then says, "I don't know either, but we can't..." He listens for a moment, then says, "Shouldn't we worry about that later? I mean, we could just as easily..."

"What's happening?" Ardra whispers.

Nyssa looks at me for a moment, then looks away.

Eli shuts off the communicator and puts it away sighing. He looks at me and then nods. "Okay, new plan. Let's go." He starts moving for the door.

"What's happening?" Nyssa asks.

"We're all going back on the ship and we're getting out of here," he says, opening the door. He pokes his head out and looks both ways.

"I don't understand," Nyssa says.

"Come on," Eli says and steps out. Nyssa looks at Ardra, then at me, then follows him, pulling Ardra with one hand, holding the blaster with the other. I follow them.

There's a lot of activity out around the hangars. People are moving very fast to get from the dome to their ships. Others pile in to skimmers and flitters of all types to get away.

"Sweet Caroline says that a couple of police cruisers just showed up in orbit. Only they didn't settle in, they started entry. They're coming down here," Eli says. We're struggling to keep up with him as he leads us back to the hangar where we first arrived.

"It's us," Eli says into the communicator as we come around the hangar. The door is closed, but it opens, revealing Salvadore with his pistol drawn. I stop for a second as his eye falls on me.

Eli moves past him, but he stops the rest of us. Eli turns when he realizes we're not behind him. "What's going...?"

The Captain reaches the door just then. "What's going on is that there's just about to be real trouble here. How much do you want to bet that it has to do with them?" I see her hand is on the blaster at her hip.

"Captain—," Eli starts.

She holds up her hand. Salvadore hasn't moved. He's still watching me.

"I can pay. There's the money that I was going to give to..." Nyssa says.

"Whatever money you have isn't nearly enough to pay for the kind of trouble that's just about to show up," The Captain says.

"So, what are you going to do? Leave us?" Nyssa asks.

The Captain doesn't say anything. Just then there is a huge boom that sounds all around us. Everyone's hands go to their ears except Salvadore.

I look up and I can see three fiery trails overhead.

"Captain," Salvadore says.

"Captain, if we leave them here, then what was the whole point?" Eli asks.

"The point was a fare," The Captain says.

"She's got more money—are we saying we don't need it?" Eli asks.

There's a loud beep from The Captain's jacket and Max's muffled voice says, "whatever we're doing, we need to do it *now*."

The Captain looks at me, then back at Nyssa. All around us there is the sound of engines as other ships launch from their hangars.

I look up. What had been just fiery trails a moment ago are now clearly defined gleaming metal triangles.

"Shit," The Captain says and her jaw sets. "Get them on board," she says to Eli.

Salvadore says, "Captain."

"Later," she says and gestures toward the ship.

Eli waves us through, "Come on!"

Salvadore watches me as I move past him.

"Fire her up, spin up the guns," The Captain says into her jacket.

We're all running for the ship's ramp. Salvadore brings up the rear and as soon as we're all aboard, he closes it. We all run for the front of the ship.

"This one's gonna' be a squeaker," Max's voice says over the speakers.

"Sweet?" The Captain yells as we pour onto the flight deck.

From her console, Sweet Caroline says, "already on it, but remember they've got big boy toys. I'm doing what I can."

Salvadore slips into the console I've seen him at before but then slides a helmet over his head. "Weapons hot," he says.

The Captain finishes strapping herself in next to Max. I get my own belts buckled just as Nyssa finishes the last of Ardra's. She throws herself into the last free chair and starts to buckle herself down as the ship lurches upward.

"Blasting our way out of some dog's butt of a spaceport is not the way I thought today was going to go," Max says.

"Me neither," The Captain says. "Go full on the reactors."

85

The ship shudders and whines, the bones of it creaking as Max pushes it too hard too fast. On the screen at the front I can see the distinct shapes of the police cruisers that have entered orbit and are already firing on the other ships leaving the hangars.

"Any company topside?" The Captain asks.

"No," Salvadore says.

"Angle the deflectors as far port as we can get them," The Captain says. "Full reactors now!" she yells at Eli.

"One hundred percent available," he says.

"Hang on!" Max yells.

We're all shoved down into our seats as the full power of the engines roars to life somewhere behind us.

We're rocked sharply. The ship groans and shakes, trying to right itself.

"How bad?" The Captain asks.

"Armor soaked up most of it. Returning fire," Salvadore says.

We're rocked again and then again. I can see on Salvadore's screen that we're being hit. I can also see that he's firing back at them.

"Go one ten on the reactors!" The Captain says. "I want FTL the second we're out of the gravity well."

"One ten coming up," Eli says. I hear the edge in his voice when he says it. His fingers fly over the four different control pads at his console.

We're rocked again. The lights dim a lot. Some smoke and sparks fly up from Eli's panel.

"How bad?" The Captain asks.

"We're still flying," Eli says.

"Out of gun range in fifteen," Salvadore says.

"Sweet?" The Captain asks.

"Almost there," Sweet Caroline says.

"Hurry!" The Captain barks.

"We'll clear gravity in twenty-three," Max says.

"FTL is spotty. That last hit," Eli says.

"I need FTL now!" The Captain yells.

"I'm working on it," Eli says.

"Do you need me to get out and push?" Max says.

"Evasive," The Captain says, then we're being thrown in all directions. On the screen I can see Max corkscrew us through a series of blasts, then twist us up and through another series of blasts.

"Eli?!" The Captain yells.

"Almost there," Eli says.

I close my eyes and start to slow my breathing. I can't get myself under control, though, with the smoke, and the constant movement. Finally, I let go. Whatever is going to happen, I can't help.

We're rocked by a two more hits in quick succession. Sweet Caroline's console explodes, spewing glass and fire. The lights go out.

I can see that she got her arms up in front of her face in time, and so she's not injured, but her console is smashed. "Sweet?!" The Captain yells.

"I'm okay, but that's it. I'm out of it. Whatever you're going to do, you better do it," Sweet Caroline says.

"Eli!" The Captain yells.

"Now!" he yells back.

"Here goes nothin'!" Max yells and slams the throttle forward.

There is a slight bump as the ship gathers itself and leaps forward, then the world quiets.

1.2.3

We're all left looking at one another for a moment, wondering if something will go wrong. When nothing does, we all take a breath. The crew starts unbuckling themselves.

The Captain leans back in her chair and sighs. "Okay," she says, then stands. "Max, cut her back to ninety-five percent, and then back to eighty after an hour or so. Just long enough to make sure they aren't following. Eli, I'd like a damage report. Sweet, you, too." With that, she walks off the flight deck.

Eli, already unbuckled, stands and motions for us to follow him. Nyssa helps Ardra get loose and we all trail behind him.

"That's what we call 'a rough one,'" Eli says. We take a ladder down and then a long, curved hallway until we cross through a large door. In front of us is a room the same size as the cargo bay. Unlike the cargo bay, though, this room is filled with pipes and generators and other components.

"Over here," Eli says. He takes us to an area on the far side of the room. Here is a ragged couch and several display screens. Many of them are flashing red messages to him. Oddly, there are also a few potted plants hanging from hooks in the ceiling.

Eli sets about working with the controls and the alarm messages begin to disappear. Nyssa dusts off a section of the couch as best she can, and then motions Ardra to sit. I perch on one of the arms.

"So, what now?" I ask.

Eli finishes with last red message and then turns to us.

"That'll be up to The Captain." His tone isn't good.

"I assure you…" Nyssa starts.

"Yeah, I know," Eli says. "You thought you could trust the guy. Instead, it turns out he was working for whoever it is that you're trying to get away from. This isn't the first time this has happened to us, believe it or not," he says. He stands, takes a watering pitcher from a niche in the wall and begins to tend to the plants. "If we're honest, this isn't even the first time this has happened this year." He shrugs, "hazard of the trade, I guess."

Watering so many plants over his head causes him to have to stretch and his tattoos become more obvious. His entire left arm is a solid sleeve of pictures and words. The right one seems to be all the way to the elbow. They creep up his neck from his chest.

"It also means that my original escape plan is fully known. We can't go to the place I had thought we'd be safe," Nyssa says.

"I was just thinking that, too," Eli says. He finishes watering the plants and then sits back down.

"Do you think that she'll be…sympathetic…to our cause?" Nyssa asks.

"Money will help. I hate to ask, but…do you have much left?" Eli asks.

Nyssa shakes her head. "There was enough to pay him off, but after that I was counting on the kindness of the locals once we arrived. By now, they are all likely…" she doesn't finish her thought.

"Did something bad happen to cousin Ohvem?" Ardra asks.

"I'm sorry, sweetling. I think it may have," Nyssa says.

Ardra starts to cry and Nyssa pulls her close.

The speaker on the wall nearby comes to life. "Status?" The Captain's voice demands. "Are our…guests…with you?" she asks. He looks at us and I get a sinking feeling in my stomach.

"They are," he says.

"Could you all meet us in the galley, please," she says. Her words are polite, but I hear the command in them. Eli does, too, I can see.

"On our way," he says and flips the toggle closed.

In the galley, everyone except Max is gathered.

We arrive as Sweet Caroline is giving the tail end of her report on the status of the ship. From what I can understand, it could have been a lot worse. The Captain assigns each person something to fix, then her attention falls on us.

"What happened?" she asks.

Nyssa sighs. "Someone that I thought I could trust betrayed us."

"I gathered that. Why were there heavy cruisers involved?"

"When I first contacted you, you said that you preferred it if all the sticky details, as you said, remained hidden so that even if you were boarded you could say you didn't know. I thank you for helping us. We would not have survived without you. But if I answer your question, then you will know those…sticky details," Nyssa says.

I can almost feel The Captain's brain working.

"I don't suppose you have some secondary site that you didn't tell anyone about that you might now direct us to?" The Captain asks.

"I'm sorry, I don't. Finding him and getting to New Ivory was the best plan I had."

The Captain puts her hands on her hips.

"So now it's up to me to find a place to put you," she says. "You have money left?"

"I do," Nyssa says.

"Okay. After I figure out a place, you and me will discuss how much of it you're going to pay."

The Captain then moves next to me. She stares directly into my eyes.

"And you, my young friend…"

I'm so caught up in wondering what she's going to do, I don't feel Salvadore slip the "crown" over my head. I don't notice it at all until I hear the click as it closes.

I reach up to touch it and hear someone say, "I wouldn't do…"

I don't hear the rest of the sentence because I immediately pass out.

1.2.4

"...and so the readings show that he'd been..." Baldi is saying as I come to.

"He's awake," The Captain says.

They both turn to look at me.

The Captain says, "give us the room." Baldi presses a few more buttons then leaves.

Once he's gone, she stares at me without saying anything.

A part of me thinks about how odd it is that I keep waking up in a bed with people staring at me.

The Captain sips from her coffee cup. Then she presses a button on the bed and it slides into a position where I'm sitting up. I notice that I'm not restrained. She hands me a bottle of water. She notices that I'm not taking it.

"Drink," she says.

Even though I don't want to, I take a sip. It's flat but good. I sip some more.

I reach up to touch my "crown."

The whole world feels muffled...distorted.

"Did you ever hear of what they eventually called 'The Nine Days War'?" The Captain asks.

I shake my head no. She nods.

"Hardly anyone has," she says, sips her coffee and leans back in her chair. "Even though I've come to accept that fact, every time I find out how little anyone knows about something that had such a huge impact on my life, on the lives of people I love dearly, it stings a little."

All I can think about is the "crown" and how much I want it off. It's very hard to stay calm.

"My home world was called Hasturmas. Not a pretty name, really, as far as worlds go, but when you come from a place, that place's name takes on a kind of poetry. At any rate, we were a nothing little planet full of farms and fisheries. Everything was all backwater bliss until we discovered that a war had broken out between two other planets in a system close enough by that our solar system was almost exactly halfway between theirs using all the direct routes. We discovered this because broken hulks of star cruisers started falling from the sky and destroying our land, and in some cases wiping out whole cities." The Captain takes another sip of her coffee. With her eyes, she indicates that she wants me to take another drink. I do.

"We had a small defense force. A handful of rusted out Scorpions that we'd bought third hand after the last big blowup out that way, and a couple of Yamar three-twenties. Our 'grand fleet,'" she says and laughs in that way that people do when they don't think what they just said was funny at all. "Still, I signed up immediately. We asked, then we warned, but they wouldn't stop their skirmishes in our solar system. We did our best to protect our own gravity well, but we were overwhelmed very quickly. Enzen, one of the worlds, landed a strategic force and claimed our planet as theirs for a forward staging ground. Compared to their pilots, I wasn't much, but I was better than almost anyone from our world, so they put a gun to my mother's head and told me to fly for them. So I did."

The wall beeps and The Captain leans forward and flips a toggle. "Go ahead."

Max says, "Coming up on your mark. Sweet Caroline says we're all clear. Salvadore confirms."

The Captain nods to herself, "Okay. Drop us to sublight and let Eli go to cruise on the reactors."

"Course?" Max asks.

The Captain looks at me for a moment, then back at the speaker, "Ragent 256c."

"Got it," he says, and the speaker goes dead. She flips the toggle down.

"So," she says, sighing at the same time, "I fought for them. It took me all over the galaxy. I saw things that to this day I still can't believe. I hated them for making me do it, but I also loved it. It was during that time that I first encountered people like you. See the other side, they just happened to have a population that had a higher potential for mental…powers…than the Enzenites did. Certainly higher than any of us from Hasturmas. They knew that, so they put together a few squads of very high testing ESPers. They would show up in their all-black uniforms and they would cut us to bits because they could make us see things that weren't there, press the wrong controls, hear incoming messages that didn't exist…drop things on top of us without even having to be in the room. Worse, though, some of them were extremely accurate about predicting what we were going to do next. We thought they had some kind of future-sight, but it turns out it was…more horrible…than that." She closes her eyes and shudders.

After a moment, she opens them again. "It turns out they were reading our minds. Deep diving into every corner they could find. Nothing was safe from them. They started using what they found there against us. Making us…see things…people we knew, loved, being tortured or…" The Captain stops. She takes a breath and her shoulders square.

"At every encounter, we barely made it out alive. Because I'd survived so many times, the Enzenite high command brought me in and their research division went over me with a fine-tooth comb. Turns out there was nothing special about me, I was just lucky. While I was there, though, I met a guy about my age. He was the one person they could find that they thought had high enough ability with all the…headstuff…that they could maybe make him into a weapon to use against these telepathic murder squads.

They sent me back home, but he and I stayed in touch on the sly. After the war ended, he contacted me. It turned out he'd been through hell and come back but he was alive. He couldn't tell me where he was for a long, long time. Said that even after the war, there were 'things to do.' I suspect he was out there hunting down the last of these killers and putting them out of their misery.

The second I knew what you were, I contacted him," The Captain says.

"If..." I start to say but stop.

"Go ahead," she says.

"If you're so afraid I'll read your mind, why tell me all that?" I ask.

Something in her eyes shifts. "You're a lot more sharp than you let on."

I don't say anything.

"Baldi says that from everything he can tell, your...ability...is always on. Background noise. From the research he and Sweet have been doing, and what I can remember, that's fairly rare. My friend said the same thing. He says that you're something of an odd duck. He says that me putting that on you," she says, pointing at my neck with her mug, "is going to cause you to feel cotton brained. Stumbly. He actually..." she drifts off. After a moment, she continues, "He actually made me feel sorry for you. So, sitting here, I made a decision."

"What was it?" I ask.

"Not to kill you."

The words hung there in the air between us.

"Everything in me is screaming to get rid of you as fast as possible," she says.

"But why? What have I done to you?" I ask.

"You yourself? Nothing. But I know what you're capable of."

I know what I want to say next will make her mad, but I can't stop myself, "but you just said your friend has the same...abilities...and he's a friend. Why would you assume that I am—,"

"It is that thought and that thought alone which has kept you alive," The Captain says. "Well, I should say that thought and Eli's pleading on your behalf." She swivels the screen from the wall so that we can both see it. On it is a room I've never seen. She and Eli face one another:

94

"...thinking about your question. You wanted to know if there was some other way, some other solution." The Captain is saying. "And I agree."

I can feel Eli relax.

"So where are we going?" Eli asks as the captain comes in and sits. He puts aside the small tree he was trimming with tiny scissors.

"You keep cutting away on that thing and it'll die eventually," she says.

"It hasn't yet," he replies. "Where are we headed?"

She crosses her arms over her chest and says, "Gros Morne."

His brow crinkles. "That's pretty far out."

"Yeah," the captain says and closes her eyes.

The quiet stretches between them.

"What for?" Eli asks.

"There's a monastery there. I think they can help the boy."

"Help him how?" Eli asks.

"You got a lot of questions today," the captain says.

"I know," he responds. "Help him how?"

"Peace. Quiet. I don't know. However, people get their...you know...." she says, making a gesture toward her head.

"Ah," Eli says. "I see. And until we get there?"

"He wears the headband."

"And if he doesn't want to wear the headband?"

She doesn't say anything.

"Come on," he says. "Look, you don't kill an animal simply because it doesn't want to obey a command. You don't put it down because it won't wear a leash."

"This isn't some scruffy kitten we found on the street like Milo," she says. "He *is* dangerous, whether you want to admit it or not."

"He isn't," Eli says.

"He is. The fact that you can't see it makes it worse," she says and puts her feet up on the table, then sighs.

"So, what?" Eli asks. "We're just going to, what, drop him off on someone's doorstep?"

"No. Yes. Kind of. Look, it's complicated. I need you to…I need you to trust me."

"I do trust you," Eli says.

She pauses. Then asks, "Do you? Because it doesn't really sound like it."

Eli leans forward, "I always trust that you believe you're doing the right thing. I wouldn't have followed you in to so many hellholes if I didn't. Thing is, though—what if what you think is the right thing turns out to be the exact wrong thing?"

They stare at each other for a moment, then she gets up and walks out of the room.

The Captain presses a button and the screen goes blank.

"So," she says, "here are the rules. You will wear that headband until we arrive at the monastery at Gros Morne. At that point I will hand you over to my…friend. Once we've left the planet, what happens to you is entirely up to him. It would be in your best interest to get him to help you to learn to live with…," she says and gestures toward her head.

"Do I get any say at all?" I ask.

"You get to live," she says. She gathers her things and walks out.

1.2.5

I've been lying here looking at the ceiling for a while.

I'm not restrained—I could get up and walk around if I wanted to.

The problem is that I can't *feel* anything, and the numbness makes me dizzy.

I can't feel anything except my "crown," that is.

I'm continuously aware of it.

Just then, Milo jumps up on the bed. He stares at me for a moment, his tail moving back and forth, then quirking into a question mark. He kneads the covers as if he were making dough, then lays down and closes his eyes.

The door to the med bay opens and Eli comes in. Milo opens one eye, then closes it again and goes back to sleep. He leans against the raised door jamb and the door slides closed behind him.

"Hi," he says.

I don't say anything.

Eli moves over to sit in the chair next to me. It's hard to see someone I care about sitting in the same place someone I dislike so much just was.

"Other than knowing you must be mad, I can't imagine how any of this feels for you," Eli says. "Look at it this way, though; we'll be at Gros Morne soon and then The Captain will take the...headband thingy...off and you'll be safe."

"From her," I say.

I can tell it stings him to have someone he cares for so much talked about that way, but he allows it.

"You'll like Gros Morne," Eli says. "It's gorgeous, especially the site of the monastery where you'll be. They're in the middle of their growing season."

"Grand," I say. For a moment I wonder at it, though; I don't think I've ever said that before, but it came without effort.

He sighs.

"How long?" I ask.

"Just a few days at present speed. We could go faster, but we put a hurt on the reactors blasting our way off Saberhagen like that. We're babying them some until we can put down for a while."

"You're not going to stay?" I ask.

He doesn't say anything.

"Oh," I say.

"The Captain…she won't let any of us stay with you. She says that opens up a window for trouble to get in."

"And you are staying with her?" I ask.

I watch as a wave of pain passes over his face. I feel the instinct to jump into his head to know fully what he's feeling, but the numbness is all that's there.

"This is my crew," Eli says. "I care about you…so much…but…this is my crew."

I'm feeling low, and miserable, and so I do say it, but I regret it before I'm even finished saying it.

"And I'm not," I say.

I don't have to be able to reach into his head to see the sting of the slap hit home.

Eli stands.

"Your bags and everything are still in the bunkroom with Nyssa and Ardra. I can move them in here if that's what you want."

"Whatever," I say.

He doesn't move for a moment, then nods and walks out.

I didn't notice, but while we were talking, Milo has gotten up, jumped off the bed, and disappeared, too.

Baldi keeps inviting me to go to the galley for food, but I spend most of my time just staring out the single window in the infirmary. He brings trays back for me and I eat them alone.

I want to tell him how I'm not ignoring him. I'm just numb.

I can't feel anything.

I wake up. I stare at the ceiling. I eat. I go back to sleep.

All around me, people are talking. Making decisions. Plans.

I know I should be listening, but I can't focus.

"Hey," Eli says, waving his hand in front of me. I put down my spoon, just now noticing that I was eating. "I said we're going to be landing in a few hours. Are you listening?"

I nod.

"It sure doesn't feel like it," he says. His tone is sad. I can tell he wants me to engage with him. To feel something back.

I can't.

The only thing I feel is this tightness in my throat.

He nods.

I wander back to the infirmary and lie down.

I wake up to the sound of a siren.

It stops.

"Belt in, kiddo," Baldi says, buckling his own belt.

I fumble with the straps next to me until he gets up from his chair and comes over to belt me in. I know I should say thank you, but I can't feel anything.

He belts back in just as the ship starts to shudder and shake. I think for a second that I should panic, that something must be wrong—then I remember that we're landing.

There's something I know I should feel about that, but I can't.

The shaking lasts for a few moments, then things go calm.

"Get him ready," The Captain says over the speaker.

Baldi comes over and unstraps me from the bed.

Eli comes in and gestures for me to follow. I stand up and walk behind him.

"...and remember that we're just a few days away if you need anything. A week, tops. All you have to do is tell this guy to call us and we'll..." I can hear in Eli's voice that what he's saying is important. I know I should listen, but I can't.

We go to the room where Nyssa and Ardra stay.

They are concerned. They say some things. I know I should ask them why they look so sad, that I should care that they do, but I don't. It's all I can do to actually hear what they are saying and not have it just drift away into background noise.

They hug me.

The Captain and Salvadore show up.

She looks mad. He looks calm. His hand is always on his hip where his gun is.

Eli puts the bag he gave me over my shoulder. His eyes look wet.

I know I should care about that, but I can't.

They all walk me through the hallways. We come to the end of a hallway and The Captain presses a button on a control panel nearby. Eli's hand squeezes my shoulder.

The wall in front of us starts to slide down, becoming a ramp.

I guess we're here.

Part 1: A Hole In The Ground

2.1.1

The ramp whines as it lowers. Air rushes in past from the outside. At first it smells foul, but in a second or so that goes away, just as Baldi said it would.

I have to squint to keep from being blinded. My eyes take a moment to adjust to the harsh sunlight.

Standing at the foot of the ramp is a short man with brown skin. He's wearing a single bolt of cloth draped and tucked in such a way that he's completely covered.

The Captain walks down the ramp. I start to move forward but Eli puts his hand on my chest. I notice The Captain has her hand resting on her pistol.

She says something to him. He shakes his head, then takes from one of the folds of cloth a metal badge. It's in the form of a circle with a five-point star inside that has an arrowhead in the middle. She takes it from him, looks at it a moment, then hands it back.

She gestures over her shoulder without looking. Eli puts his hands on my shoulders and then pulls me into a hug. He squeezes me so tight I can't breathe.

I know this is important, and that I need to pay attention, but I can't.

Then he lets go and turns and walks back to the top of the ramp. Salvadore steps up next to my shoulder and gestures for me to walk in front of him.

We get to the bottom of the ramp, then we're standing next to The Captain.

"This man's name is Valkar," she says. "He's going to take you to the man we spoke of. You will do everything he tells you to do, is that clear?"

I want to be mad. I can feel that.

I want to say something mean back, to spit at her for doing this to me. That's all miles away, though.

"As soon as we're gone, Valkar will take it off of you." With that, Valkar shows me that he has a small metal tool in his palm.

"I don't want to go," I say. Even I'm surprised that words have come out.

"What was that?" she asks. For a second I wonder if she actually didn't hear because of the noises the ship makes around us, or if she means it as a challenge.

"I said I don't want to go." They escape me again.

"We're all burdened with things we don't want to do," The Captain says. "Now, hear me." She bends down just a bit so that we're eye to eye. "If you do what you are told and complete whatever the man Valkar is taking you to asks of you, then he will contact me, and we will come back for you." My heart skips, and I try to hide my smile. "Give him even a moment's trouble, and that's it—we're done. Do you understand me?"

I look back at the ship. There, on the ramp, through the front windows of the ship, are the only people I've ever known. Sweet Caroline, Baldi, Max. And there is Eli, holding Milo and crying.

"I understand."

The Captain nods. For a moment, I notice Salvadore relaxing his hand off of the butt of his own pistol.

Was he going to shoot me if I'd said or done something different?

Without saying anything else, The Captain turns on her heel and moves back to the ramp, Salvadore following close behind. They walk up the ramp.

Eli makes a small gesture of goodbye, but the ramp is already closing.

Valkar gestures for me to follow. I want to watch the ship lift off, but he's right—this close, we might be burned by the thrusters. It takes everything I have not to turn around as I hear them whine then roar behind me, the wind whipping across my back. I do take a small glance as I hear the deep rumble of the ship shifting to it's main thrusters to leave the atmosphere.

Then they are gone.

Valkar is quite a way in front of me when he stops. I rush to catch up.

When I get there, he motions for me to stand still. He takes the metal tool in his hand and does something to my "crown." The second it falls away I feel the release physically. I also feel the world go back into sharp relief from the muffled distance I'd been feeling. It was as if I could suddenly hear again.

It's overwhelming and I start to cry.

I almost fall over.

Valkar catches my shoulder and holds me up.

Valkar smiles. "That has to feel better," he says.

"Thank you," I say.

He looks at the device for a moment, and I could swear I see him shiver. "Nasty bit of work, this," he says. "I'd fling it as hard as I could right here and now if there wasn't a danger someone else might find it. Brother Hieronymus will know what to do with it, though, you can bet on that."

"Is that who we're going to see?" I ask.

Valkar nods. "Yes. And we'd better get a move on if we want to make it there before dinner."

He tucks the device into the folds of his robe, and we start moving.

As we walk, everything is so bright and colorful, and my eyes are welling up constantly at every little thing. I can *feel* everything.

"Hey," Valkar says with a bit of a grin. "How about you back it back down a bit." He taps the side of his head with a finger as he walks. "Man, are you loud."

I smile because I can feel his amusement that also has a bit of fear in it. I'm broadcasting without meaning to and it's stronger than he's used to.

"I'm sorry," I say.

"It's okay," he says. "They put that damned thing on you and then made you wear it while they said goodbye. Everything that you've been numbed out for is coming back to you all at once," he says. "I hope you don't mind me saying—I'm not super impressed with your friends."

For a second I am mad that he said it. Then I'm not. And that makes me a little sad.

We keep walking.

It takes us about an hour to come to the top of a hill. The path winds down from where we stand to a small town below, then up again. Just over the crest of that next ridge I can see the top of something. Valkar stops us and takes out his water bottle. He offers me some and it's the best water I've ever tasted—at least, I think it is.

"That's where you're headed," Valkar says. "The Temple."

"To meet The Captain's friend?" I ask.

"To call them friends is a bit of an overstatement, but yeah. That's where Brother Hieronymus will meet you."

"Oh," I say. We start walking again. "What's he like?" I ask.

"Hieronymus?" Valkar asks. He tilts his head to the side a bit, then says, "He's funny. Reverent when he should be. Wise in that way that people who have seen too many terrible things often are. You'll like him. You'll love his wife; she's the best. The training will be good—like stretching your legs after a long time sitting. At least at first." At that, Valkar laughs a bit.

"What does that mean?" I ask.

"You're here to learn from him, right?"

I nod.

"When was the last time you knew anyone who got along with their teacher once the work got hard?"

"I don't know. My memory is a little..." I drift off.

Valkar nods. "I know. That's one of the things that's going to be difficult. But don't worry. We've met others with similar problems."

A half an hour later or so, we are in the town. The houses are made of a kind of mud paste over wooden frames.

The people all have brown skin and dark eyes. I notice that I look a lot more like them than the people on the ship, but we're not the same. After the relative stillness of the ship, the activity in the streets is overwhelming. They all know Valkar and everyone says hello and waves. The children run up to look at me and smile.

It feels like the word welcome.

One young woman says something to Valkar and gestures. He smiles and nods at her. I feel their connection.

"Is she your wife?" I ask.

He shakes his head a bit. "I'd like that, but I won't be staying," he says, looking back at her as she walks away.

We follow the street to a market. People are just now starting to pack up their stalls as the sun is beginning to arc toward the horizon. The smells are powerful and wonderful.

We come up to the last stall in one of the last rows. A tall man with light skin and dark hair like the people on the ship is talking with the man who behind the stall.

"Well, who knows. I mean, for all we know, he may hate bread," the tall man says. He stops, though, and stands up straight, then turns around.

"Do you?" he asks me.

"Do I...?"

"Like bread?" he asks.

"I...do?" I say. I honestly don't know if I do or not. I mean, I can remember eating bread. I've ate bread on the ship. But the question is whether or not I like it and when I think about it, I honestly don't know.

The man behind the stall laughs.

"Hieronymus, this is..." Valkar starts.

"Akari," the tall man finishes. He extends his hand. I go to shake it, but there's still a loaf of bread in it. He looks down, notices, shakes his head, and shifts the bread to the other hand. "Hi," he says. "I'm Hieronymus."

We shake hands.

Then we just stare at each other for a moment.

"Oh!" Hieronymus says. He turns back and hands a coin to the man who owns the stall. Then he puts the bread in the bag he's carrying.

Something tickles at the front of my brain and then I hear his voice.

Can you hear me alright?

For a moment, I just blink. Then I respond, *yes; can you hear me?*

He laughs. *Yes, but you don't have to yell.*

I'm sorry, I say. *I didn't mean to.*

I can hear him laugh. *I know. It's okay. We're going to help you get control of that thing.* As he says this, he pokes my forehead with his index finger. I can't help but laugh, too.

Valkar says goodbye, and I sense the deep feeling between them. Hieronymus and I leave the town headed up the other side of the valley toward the structure I saw before.

"We're headed for The Temple," he says as we walk. *You won't believe it when you see it.* I hear in my head. There's a brief picture of a massive structure but it goes away before I can focus on it.

"Did they" *really blast their way out of Saberhagen?* He starts off talking, then switches to telepathy. There's a brief feeling of ducking and hiding.

Yes. I respond and I let through a few flashes of what it felt like.

He whistles and shakes his head.

She told me a bit about you, but I told her not to give me too much information.

Why? I ask.

"Because I want to get to know you, myself. Not through her prejudices," he says.

I don't say it, but this feels so good. Like exercising your legs after sitting for far too long.

"Is this how people like us usually" *do things?*

"You mean" *back and forth between head talk and mouth talk?*

I nod. We're this far into the conversation when I realize that I've never talked like this with anyone before.

"I've been told it's" *pretty much just how I do things. Others tend to* "do all one or the other. Which do you prefer?" he asks.

"I don't know," I say.

He laughs. "Okay. How about we just stick to one or the other for a bit, too, then."

Then it hits me—this whole time he's been gauging me, seeing how strong I am.

He laughs. *Yes, but not like an enemy. I just want to get to know you, who you really are. Yell for me.*

What? I ask

Yell. Yell your loudest yell.

Are you sure? I ask.

Trust me, he says, *I'll be okay.*

So I stop, close my eyes, and in my head let out the loudest sound I can think of.

I see insects leap away from where I'm standing.

A few birds on a tree near the top of the ridge fly away.

Hieronymus' eyes get very wide.

That's…that's not too shabby.

Are you okay? I ask.

I'm fine, he says. He turns and starts walking again. I follow him.

When we crest the top of the hill, I have to stop.

Down in the next valley is the largest structure I have ever seen.

It's a pyramid with the top flattened. Instead of being smooth, the sides are huge steps. There is moss growing all over it.

It's so big, the ship could have fit inside of it at the base.

Takes your breath away, doesn't it? Hieronymus says.

I can't think of anything to say. I just stare at it.

111

"Come on," he says. "We have to get there soon or we'll miss dinner."

He's right. Already the sun has drifted down far enough that it's almost touching the top of the massive structure.

Hieronymus starts to move. I shake my head to try to get back to my senses, then I follow him down into the valley.

2.1.2

The steps are covered in moss. I can see the worn places where people have gone up and down them for centuries. Up at the top, I can see boys going by in bright orange robes.

When we reach the top, the yard seems huge. Long rows of columns line the area. They aren't holding anything up.

"They used to," Brother Hieronymus tells me.

I keep forgetting that he can hear me.

"I know you're not used to it. You'll get there, though," he says out loud.

At the far end of the yard are more steps leading up to the entrance to a temple. The columns and the temple are covered in pictographs.

"Their history," Hieronymus says. "Going back five thousand years."

Around us are hundreds of boys my own age and younger. The setting sun makes their bright orange robes and shaved heads look studious, noble. I look down at my own shabby clothes. They helped me fit in on the ship, but here I stand out.

"We'll get you robes as we get you settled in and press on for home tomorrow."

"Should I be reading your mind back?" I ask.

"You can try, if you like. But I didn't have to read you for any of that," Hieronymus says. "I've been helping young initiates get settled in for a long time, now."

I nod.

A group of boys go racing past, kicking a ball around between them, and almost collide with us. One yells something back that I can tell means "sorry."

"It's a game they say goes all the way back to the mother planet," Hieronymus says.

"What do they call it?" I ask.

"Scur. It's a word that doesn't have any translation in their language. They think the name also comes from the mother tongue," Hieronymus stops us before we start up the steps to the temple. "Imagine that," he says and shakes his head.

We start up the steps. Again, I can see the worn places where millions of feet have first polished then carved away at the stone. We're about halfway up when a bell starts ringing deep inside.

"Dinner," Hieronymus says. The courtyard, already a riot of movement, becomes absolute chaos. The boys swarming up the steps make it hard for me to keep track of Hieronymus.

When we reach the top, before I step onto the floor of the temple, he stops me. We wait for the thunder of the other boys to pass us, then he says, "Shoes." He toes out of his and I do the same. My feet touching the stone make the whole thing, all of this, seem more real.

I'm standing on a planet, the cold stone of an ancient temple seeping through my heels.

"In time, you may even come to call it home," he says. "This will be all there is to eat until sunrise in the morning, so make sure to take enough to fill you. After, we'll go to the hotspring."

The temple is half open space defined by columns and different levels of floor, and half thick walls of stone. There are sudden openings that make unexpected interior courtyards and long closed off hallways with soaring ceilings. Throughout, the walls are covered with the pictographs of these people.

We follow the smell of the food, my stomach rumbling. Solemn faced boys near my age are lighting torches along the walls while others, slightly older, are herding the little ones along a main hallway that opens up into a huge open space. On the far side are recessed pits along the floor where huge pots are steaming.

"I know that it's customary on many planets and on many ships to have meat as a meal, but here they do not indulge in that practice. I hope you're okay with that," Hieronymus says.

I search myself and find I don't have a preference either way.

"They are especially fond a root vegetable that grows very easily here. It's a kind of potato that is quite sweet. I've come to like it very much," Hieronymus says as we get in line for stew. Boys along the line hand each of us a wooden bowl as we pass. The bowl is filled to the brim with an orangey-golden mush that smells amazing in a way that the ship's food never did.

We follow the flow of people to the open area and sit. Another boy a bit shorter than me comes over and sits with us. He nods to Hieronymus and then to me. "This is Zan. Zan, this is a new boy who will be staying with us for a time. His name is Akari."

Zan says something I don't understand.

Hieronymus laughs.

"What?" I ask.

"You aren't reading him?" Hieronymus asks.

"Should I?" I ask.

"It'll make things a lot easier, unless you feel like you can learn their language quickly."

"Do you think he'll mind?" I ask.

Hieronymus nods, "ah, so you do understand that some people might not approve. Interesting," he says, and then eats.

"But what did he say?" I ask after a few bites. The mush makes my stomach feel warm and full.

"He thinks you look a bit like they do, but he's never seen eyes like yours. He wondered which clan you were from," Hieronymus says and laughs a bit.

Already some boys have finished eating and are moving out of the hall. I catch Zan watching me from under his eyebrows. I try to smile to let him know that it's okay. He says something to me. I can tell it's a question from his tone, but I don't know what he said. Slowly, I open myself up to him and reach out. His thoughts are peaceful, calm.

Hieronymus chuckles.

"What?" I ask, closing myself off again.

"He likes you. He was wondering where you'd be sleeping."

"Oh," I say. Then it hits me what that might mean. "Oh," I say again.

"You'll find they are very open, very warm. Very little time wasted on any of our prudish hang ups, especially when it comes to sleeping arrangements," Hieronymus says. "Do you want to sleep with him?"

"I...I hadn't thought about it." I realize that, in fact, I hadn't thought about it with anyone as far back as I can remember. "What should I say?" I ask.

Hieronymus says something to Zan who smiles, nods, and finishes his mush. He gets up and leaves. I make myself look at him closely. His skin is dark, like mine, and his eyes are a pretty shade of brown. I like the way he has wrapped his robe.

"What did you say?" I ask.

"I told him that you were still cold from being in space. That you would likely warm up soon," he smiles. "It's an expression they have."

"Have you ever...?" I ask.

"Me? No. I was already married when I came here, and my wife is more than enough for me," he says and laughs. "Come on, finish up so we can get you settled before evening meditation call."

I finish the rest of the mush, wishing there was more. I look toward the pots, but I can see that the fires have already been put out, and the pots no longer steam.

Hieronymus stands, his joints popping. He groans. I stand, too.

We follow the stream of people moving deeper into the temple, down a huge well of stairs. I notice that it's getting warmer as we go deeper. I can also feel more moisture in the air.

"It's been a long day," Hieronymus says. "This is going to feel incredible."

I try not to look down, but at the bottom of the immense stair well there is a huge painting of a sun with tendrils radiating toward the four walls.

At the bottom, the group separates into four different lines following the flares coming off of the sun.

"North, East, etcetera," Hieronymus says. "We're directly over a major geothermal front. That's what makes heating such a huge temple possible without any power. Also what makes these possible."

I follow him through the enormous archway into a room with a huge pool. It's large enough that even with this number of boys and men disrobing and getting in, no one is less than half an arms length away from one another.

Hieronymus strips off his robe and leaves it on a table nearby. I try not to look at his body, though I notice that no one else is in any way trying to be so modest with one another. He's covered in scars. No part of him is without the remnants of cuts or gouges. There are also tattoos, but I am not close enough to understand them.

There isn't any sexual energy in the room, though; just comfort and ease.

I take off all the clothes that Eli gave me, wondering what will happen to them.

They are my last connection to the ship, to the only people I've known.

A kid younger than me takes them away immediately.

I hesitate at the pool's edge, but I'm filled with a strong desire to not wind up the last one standing there.

I step into the pool to find the water is much hotter than I expected. It's almost too hot to bear. Far hotter than the water was on the ship. Still, around me I see boys younger than myself move from the edge into the water with no problem. I don't want anyone to think I can't handle it, so I step all the way in and sink to my neck as everyone else does.

In that instant, a memory flashes across my mind.

Like the first time, again, looking through water at someone. This time the face is more clear; it's like mine, especially around the eyes. Whoever he is, he looks in at me, and he smiles.

I come back with several pairs of hands on my shoulders and lower back. They are leading me through the pool. Their sense of peace and the sense of order pushes through and the panic that was coming dissipates just as fast.

All is well is all I can feel. It's more than a thought, more than a song, it thrums through everything like a heartbeat. It is all I can feel.

All around me, people are scrubbing themselves in the same way, starting with the head and going down. They're all also slowly, almost imperceptibly, moving from the front of the pool where they stepped in, toward the back wall. I watch, side-eye, to make sure that I do the same thing as everyone else.

As each person finishes and gets out the far side, they take a robe from the stacks of them along the wall. More are brought out from a smaller arch on the side wall constantly. I notice that those who are bringing the robes are those who have just recently finished bathing.

When I get out, I take a robe from one of the stacks and put it on. The fabric is rougher than I expected, but still softer than the things I had on earlier. I follow Hieronymus' actions folding the robe in a few different ways to make it stay on. I then shadow him through the arch on the side wall, pick up a stack of robes and take them out to the main room again. We set them down on the table for the next group.

He then leaves through the huge arch at the back wall. We walk back up a long set of steps to another large archway that leads us down a huge hall. Every thirty feet or so there is another smaller arch. Inside I can see that these are open rooms with windows cut in the walls. Hieronymus takes us to the third such room.

Far off down the hallways, a set of chimes are rung. I look over at Hieronymus.

"Final meditation call. I would normally recommend it, but you have had a very long day already. I think maybe we should just grab some sleep."

I nod as old men stream one direction past the doorway while younger men and boys stream the other. The chimes stop and the hallway quiets down a bit.

Against the far wall are stacks of blankets. He takes two, like everyone else is doing. I see that each person lines themselves up in long rows and then almost as one they put one of the blankets down on the stone floor. That's when I notice that the stone is warm under my feet.

"Just high enough up to be above ground for windows so the breeze keeps things cooled off, but not so high that the warmth from the springs below dissipates," Hieronymus says as he sets his blanket down. I set mine next to his.

He lies down and drapes his other blanket over himself. I do the same. All around us, the room is settling in. The last boy standing goes to the lamp and turns a knob on it, dousing the flame, then gets settled into his own corner near the far wall.

Where it was just coming on sunset when we landed, it is now full night outside the windows. A calm breeze comes in through them, moving the air just enough to feel but not so much that it takes attention.

There is some soft conversation in the room, but people drift off to sleep fast.

All except me.

I have so many questions.

"Don't worry; the answers will come in time," Hieronymus says. "For now, just know that you're safe."

"Are you sure?" I whisper.

Hieronymus is quiet for a moment.

"They weren't always like this," he says. "A thousand years ago, they were warlike. They had an empire that stretched for lightyears. Huge warships hovering over the poles of the major planets ready to rain down destruction at a moment's notice."

"What happened?" I ask.

He shifts a bit. "A leader came from their poorest ranks preaching kindness and compassion. Like all leaders who try to tell us how to be kinder to one another, he was assassinated. His followers kept his message alive,

119

though, and it spread and spread until one day the last soldier put down his weapon and took up the cause of peace."

The quiet settled around us. In another room someone coughed. "They dismantled all of their machines, their weapons, and they started ministering to the needs of others. It took a long time, but eventually they became what you see here. Throughout this whole quadrant, everyone knows that if you're in trouble, if you need help of any kind, find the orange robes."

"Is that why you're here?" I ask.

"Get some sleep," he says. "Tomorrow is going to be a long day."

2.1.3

My eyes pop open as the bluish light comes through the window. From the hum in the background of my head I can tell that I'm not the only one awake.

I sit up and see many of the other boys are already doing the same. We're all reluctant to leave our blankets, but bowing to the inevitability that we must.

Awake? Hieronymus asks. He hasn't opened his eyes or even moved from the position he fell asleep in.

Yes.

"Good," he whispers, and sits up.

Again, I notice the scars. He stretches and yawns, then stands up, letting the blanket fall away. His bones creak and pop.

I stand up, too.

It's as if his standing was the signal everyone was waiting for, because they all start moving, standing, yawning, stretching.

It's a custom they have. In each room, whoever is the eldest in the room is the one everyone waits on. "Did you dream?" he asks as he slides back into his robe.

"Not that I remember," I say.

"Do you normally remember your dreams?" he asks.

"I...I don't remember if I do or not..."

He smiles.

"Okay—morning chores while we wait for breakfast. Then, after we eat, we'll head for my place," Hieronymus says.

"We're not saying here?"

"I wish we could," he says. "But no—while they're happy to have guests, our presence here for too long might interrupt their routines too much. My cabin is in the next valley over, and with it my comfortable bed," he says and laughs. "We'll be back, though, from time to time." He turns and walks out the door and I follow him.

Zan and I are handed brooms and we're told to sweep a particular set of steps. All up and down the massive structure, boys and men are doing similar tasks. Hieronymus was given a hallway to sweep with several other men close to his age (I'm guessing), but he and I continue to talk telepathically.

Zan asks me about the ship, and about Eli, and about Milo. I can feel how awkward I am around him and I don't want to be, but I don't know how to act. He says something and I shake my head to let him know I don't understand. He says it again, slower this time. I shake my head again, then remember what Hieronymus said. I concentrate for a second on Zan and when he speaks again—

"It's okay," he says.

I wrinkle my eyes a bit.

"That you're awkward—I don't mind. I was like that when I first came here, too."

"You weren't born here?" I ask.

"No. Some of us boys are brought here by our parents and left for a time. I'm one of those."

"Why?" I ask.

"Because we need to learn about our history, and how to be better people. Everyone in my family comes for a few years, then we go back home."

"Where is home?" I ask.

"On the other end of the continent. I'm from a town called Zalor. I imagine you don't know where that is," he says. I shrug a bit. I find myself admiring how his muscles look on his arms, and the way his robe drapes around him. I think about shaving my hair off like his.

The bell is rung, and we go back through a very similar process for breakfast as we did for dinner. Only, instead of going down for a bath, the boys all scatter in different directions.

Hieronymus finds me. He's wearing clothes much more like those the people back on the ship were wearing. He has a bag over his shoulder, and one in his hand. He holds that one out to me.

Over there, he says, and I can feel him point even though this is all in my head, which is new. I look over and there are some empty rooms. *Go get changed back into your clothes and we'll start out.*

I slide back into the clothes Eli gave me, which I can't seem to think of as mine, for some reason. They've been cleaned, and smell of something nice.

It's called ginger. It's an ancient root from far back in our ancestral past. It grows very easily here, so they use it for many things.

I catch up with him and we start away from the temple. "Did they build more of those," I ask, gesturing toward the pyramid with my head, "on the rest of the planet?"

"No," he says, and I hear something in his voice.

"Zan said that he's from a different city here on this continent—will we be visiting any of the other cities?"

"We might, but it's unlikely. How did you understand him?"

"I did what you said," I say, and tap the side of my head, copying the gesture he makes.

He nods, then says, "Remember, like them, you're a guest here, and you've got a job to do."

"They're guests? What does that mean?"

Hieronymus says. "This isn't their home world. It's a world that they conquered long long ago. It's within the stretch of what used to be their empire, but it isn't their home world. That temple?" he said, pointing back the direction we came. "They built that over the site of one of their worst atrocities from that time period. See, they developed a weapon that could burrow to the center of a planet. A world burner, they called it." He adjusted

123

the straps on his pack, and we continued walking. "Pulled up into orbit around the equator and dropped it. It bore down into the crust and then set itself off. Cleared a hole all the way down to just above the core layer. Not just the explosion, not just the dust that covered the sun and made the surface almost unlivable for centuries, but also the magma that came spilling out. Extinction level event, they called it. Made this planet an example to all others that thought about resisting."

"And the temple?" I ask.

Hieronymus is quiet for a while. Our footsteps, the only sounds.

"When they came to their senses and realized what they'd done, they decided to build one of their largest temple monasteries right on the site of one of their worst crimes. That's how it stays heated and how the springs are warmed. The floor of the monastery is the bottom of the shaft that planet killer weapon they dropped cut into the planet." He wipes the sweat from his forehead. "Every day they have to wake up, live, and sleep in the place where their people made their worst ever decision. Committed their worst crime. Parents send their young here to study, to live, so that they will never forget."

We're both quiet for a long time.

"Taren will have the place ready for all of us by now," Hieronymus says as we walk.

"Have you not been there in a while?"

"No," he says. "Taren and I were away on…business, and Alee, my wife, was on her medicine walk."

"Medicine walk?" I ask.

"She's a doctor, among other things. So once a cycle of the moons she goes out to visit the campsites and villages to see if they need any help. A lot of births, the odd tooth to be pulled, that kind of thing."

"Was Taren in the war, too?" I ask.

"No," Hieronymus says. "He's too young, like you, and not from the same star system as I am. He came here to learn, as you have."

124

2.1.4

We come over the next ridge and far down this next valley I can see a home. It's surrounded by a large fenced in area and there are animals roaming the yard.

Before I can ask, though, we pass by a large almost perfectly smooth opening in the rocks along our route. Hieronymus stops. It's as if someone has taken a cave and made a perfectly smooth stone arch leading into it.

"What is that?"

He looks at the door then back at me. "When you're ready, that will be the door you go through."

"Where does it lead?"

"When you're ready, you will find out," he says. "Come on; we're almost there."

"What about when I'm done?" I ask. "What happens to me then?"

"What do you want to happen to you?" he asks.

"Do I go back to them? Eli, The Captain, and the others?"

"Is that what you want?" he asks.

"I…I don't know."

He stops walking and turns to me. "Why did you come here?" he asks.

"This is where The Captain said I had to go."

He grins. "And you didn't think for a second that a telepath as powerful as yourself could have found a way to stop them from bringing you here if you had wanted to?"

"My crown…I mean…the device…" I stammer.

"You were with them an awful long time before they decided to do that to you. At any point you could have asked them to go anywhere...or made them take you. But you didn't. Why?"

"I...don't know."

"Akari, you're free right now to do whatever you want. You could leave if that's what you wanted to do. I'm not keeping you here. No one is."

That's when it all clicks—there haven't been any guards of any kind, no walls, no demands. I had noticed but not noticed all at the same time.

"You wouldn't try to stop me if I left right now?" I ask.

"Do you think I could if you truly wanted to use force?" he asks. "Are you here because you want to be, or because you were told to be?"

"I'm...I'm not sure," I say.

"Well," he says, "how about this—why don't you stay here with me, learn what you can, and when you want to leave," he gestures toward the sky. "All I'm saying is—what happens to you is entirely up to you, not me, and it always has been." With that, we start walking again.

We round a bend and we're at the opening to wooden fence that comes up to my waist.

Even if Hieronymus wanted to hide his feeling of relief, I don't think he could. He radiates the word *home*. I wonder what that would be like, to have that feeling.

In the middle of the area the fence marks off is a large building made with the same white mud and clay as the buildings back in the town were. There are a few smaller buildings surrounding it. A tall, thin young man with bright red hair who I assume is Taren is coming from one of the outer buildings toward the front door. He stops to wave at us.

In the fields behind the house I can see a few animals moving around.

"My little flock," Hieronymus says.

"It's about time you guys made it. I was starting to get worried," Taren says when we get close.

"We slept in," Hieronymus says. "Is she back?"

"Not yet," he says.

126

Inside is a large open area. Off to one side is a kitchen and the other are a few couches and chairs. From there a hallway goes to the back of the house.

I follow Hieronymus down the hall. One of the rooms has technology in it, a few small computer stations humming away to themselves. The end of the hall has four rooms, each with a bed and a desk. All of the furniture looks sturdy but somewhat last minute.

Yours Hieronymus says, gesturing to one of the rooms. As I go in and set my bag down on the bed, I see that the two rooms across the hall are lived in. Hieronymus goes into the larger one and starts to unpack.

How long had you been staying with them? I ask him as I begin to do the same.

A week. Around this time every year I like to go and spend a week or two with them. It helps to ground me out, get me back to zero, he responds.

"You guys all settled?" Taren asks from the hallway between the rooms.

"Just about," I say. He smiles.

"Come on," he says. "I'll give you the tour."

2.1.5

"...so, it's a little farm ecosystem, just large enough to sustain three people or so," Taren says as we stop near the back fence, the furthest spot from where we entered. A sheep butts up against my leg and I hand it another of the carrots Taren and I pulled from the root cellar building.

"It's just you three?" I ask.

Taren nods. "Though, soon it'll be just *you* three."

"Huh?" I ask.

"My time here is almost done. It's time for me to go back home," Taren says. I can feel his happiness and sadness at the same time.

"How long have you been here?" I ask.

"Four years now," he says. "Four years," he repeats more softly.

"Why do you have to leave?" I ask.

"I was sent here to learn how to control my gift by my people. I'd become...a problem," he says.

"Like me," I say.

He nods. "Hieronymus is one of the few people in the whole galaxy who will take us in, help us."

"Why do you think that is?" I ask. The sheep butts against me again. I feed it another carrot.

"Male telepaths are dangerous," Taren says. "I mean, female telepaths *can* be dangerous from time to time, but often they just aren't. But us males..." he drifts off. "And we're so rare that really no one knows what to do with us, anyway. It's by luck that one of us gets sent here instead of..."

"Does that happen a lot?" I ask.

Taren nods. "A lot more than you might think. Everyone hears the horror stories of one of us using their power to become a king then an emperor then…something worse." Taren leans back against the fence. "Didn't it ever cross your mind?"

"No," I say. "But I'm…maybe something different."

"Like how?" Taren asks.

Before I can answer, Hieronymus sends a thought: *Lunch*

"Did you show him the trick to the pump at the back fence?" Hieronymus asks over a mouthful of stew.

"Yeah. And I made sure to mention the way the door sticks to the cellar so he doesn't accidentally get locked in," Taren says and they both laugh.

"Worst first day any kid every had here," Hieronymus says.

Taren shakes his head.

"Will he be going through the door?" I ask.

The room grows incredibly tense all of a sudden.

Hieronymus stops his spoon halfway to his mouth. Taren tries to hide how intensely he's looking.

"Tomorrow," Hieronymus says.

"So he saw the…"

"Yeah," Hieronymus responds.

"I'm sorry," I say. "I didn't mean to…"

"No," Taren says. "It's okay. I already knew."

Hieronymus nods.

I send a picture of the cave-like entrance and a feeling of fear as a question to Taren. Taren shakes his head and sends back a picture of sunlight and a feeling of warmth on my face. I smile and send a feeling of warmth on the face back. It's an entire conversation about feelings and thoughts that takes place in seconds and I marvel at how fast we and freely we can communicate.

"Out loud," Hieronymus says.

*I was just wondering if…*I start, but Taren shakes his head.

129

"Out loud," Hieronymus says.

But why don't we just talk like this? It's much faster, I say.

Lightning fast, he smacks my knuckles. I pull my hand away.

"Out loud," he says.

Why?

He smacks the knuckles on my other hand. I pull it away, too.

"Out. Loud."

"Why?" I ask.

"Because that's part of what you're here to learn," he says.

"But you and me, we're faster than that," I say.

He nods, "yes, but down that path lives all kinds of horrible thoughts—that we're faster than them, which means we're smarter than them, which means we're better than them, which means we can destroy them."

"I wasn't thinking that," I say.

"Not yet, but you would. You still might, which is why we have to work quickly."

"Is…is that what she's afraid of, The Captain?"

"It's one of the things, yes," he says.

Through all of this, I can see and feel Taren dealing with a lot knot of emotions. I get the feeling he's seen this all before and been on my side of the table more than once.

We finish eating lunch in silence.

After lunch, Taren asks me to come help him check the fence line and draw in some more water.

"I'm sorry," he says before I can start my apology. I hadn't realized it, but I'm rubbing my knuckles still.

"I guess I just don't understand," I say. "It's just…it's really exciting to be able to talk with other people like this. It feels like it's the first time I've ever been able to. He and I had already been talking like that and it's so much faster…"

130

"You will understand, eventually. Trust me, he has a point," Taren says. Almost every step the pump system goes through is automated, but the first cycle must be done by hand and watched. Taren shows me how and then asks me to perform one full cycle to make sure I have it. "It's just that we can't even start down those paths because it moves so quickly," Taren says.

"How does he know?" I ask. I realize after it's out of my mouth that the words sound more accusatory than I mean them to.

"He lost a student early on is what he told me," Taren says without looking at me. "Kid just would not come to understand that our most important role is helping others. Got caught up in the whole, 'we're better than them' way of thinking that he warned you about." Taren then leans back against the fence. "Apparently the kid went on a rampage, and eventually Hieronymus had to put him down."

I want to say something to express how upset that idea makes me, but I don't have any words for it. Taren just nods.

"Just...remember that, ok?" Taren says. "We're here to help. That's what these gifts are for. Always keep that in mind," he says, and laughs a bit at his little joke.

I smile, too, and we both watch the afternoon pass by for a while.

2.1.6

We're both standing there when we see a figure coming along a barely cleared path toward the back gate.

"She's home," Taren says.

"His wife?" I ask and Taren nods. He walks over to the pump and pulls water into the basin.

"Hello!" she calls as she pulls back her hood starts down the hill.

"Hello," I call back.

She's the same height as me, and her eyes are a fierce green that I haven't seen from anyone else. I open the gate, and she walks through. Her blonde braid touches her waist. She walks over to the basin and says, "Thank you," to Taren as she splashes water onto her face and arms. "You must be Akari," she says.

I nod. She smiles. "A bit quiet, huh? That reminds me of someone," she says and Taren laughs. "How is he?" she asks, jerking her head toward the house.

"Good," Taren says. She nods, then smiles back at me. "How long have you been on planet?"

"Two days," I say.

"Eaten already?" She walks over to me and looks deep into each eye, then pulls first one wrist to her, looks at it intensely, then the other. "I know spaceflight sometimes makes people queasy."

"No," I say, then "I mean, no to being queasy. I feel fine. And I have eaten."

She nods, then pulls me in close and puts her ear to my chest. I stand there a moment. "Heart sounds okay, breathing normal," she mutters. She pulls away and looks at me again. I feel almost like she's looking through me. "Give me about twenty minutes to get in and get settled, then come in so I can run the machines on you."

"The machines?" I ask.

She turns and walks toward the house. "Twenty minutes," she says over her shoulder without turning around. I look over at Taren and he shakes his head with a laugh.

"Okay," Alee says, taking her earphones out and putting down the small device she's been holding over my chest. Next to her, the screen is giving her lots of different kinds of information that I don't understand.

Something about all of this feels very familiar, though.

VERY familiar.

"Will he live?" Hieronymus asks with a grin.

"He will," Alee says. "You can put your shirt back on," she says to me.

"What is it?" Hieronymus asks, seeing the look on her face.

"Maybe we should…" she starts to say.

"No," he says, looking at me. "Anything you need to say about him should be said in front of him."

Her eyes shift from me back to him.

"Physically, this body is about fifteen years old. It shows all the markers for that."

"Why 'this body' and not 'he is'?"

"That's what I'd like to know," she says. She looks at me, "Cells degrade, hormones can be distributed unevenly, especially during puberty, growth happens in starts and stops…in other words, there is no such thing as textbook growth for a humanoid. Except…"

"Tell me. Please," I say.

"Your readings aren't just normal for someone your age, they are perfect. Across the board, you hit all the benchmarks that we're taught don't actually exist. It's as if…"

133

"What?" Hieronymus asks.

"As if someone made him."

My mind flashes to the things I've been told and overheard. The tube, the people watching me, the video Sweet Caroline found. All of it.

"We have a lot to find out," Alee says, "but...you...let's go," she says to Hieronymus. He growls. "Come on, we don't have all day."

"Out," Hieronymus says to me. I leave the room but look back just before she closes the door. That's when I see the latticework of scars that cover his entire torso and upper arms. I turn away quickly before he can see that I've seen.

Who did that to him? I wonder.

And who did this to me?

I follow the smells to the kitchen. Taren is stirring a large pot.

"Here, try this," he says and holds the spoon out to me with his other hand just under it.

I didn't know that the ship's food was so bland and awful until I had the mush at the temple and now this stew. My stomach came alive immediately.

"If there's one thing I know, it's this: no matter how good the technology is, food never tastes as good as it does when it all comes from your own back yard," Taren says. He continues stirring. "I'm going to miss it."

"Is there nothing like this where you come from?" I ask.

"There is, but not where I live. My family are all in a very large city on my home world. This," he says, looking all around the kitchen and the house, "this has been something very special."

"What will you do now that your training is over?" I ask.

He puts the lid back on the stew. "The whole idea was for me to join our diplomatic corps. I can use my...abilities...to help ambassadors to make peace. That's all I've ever wanted."

"Is your planet at war?"

"Not when I left, but that's the idea—to help things stay that calm. My home world is at a kind of crossroads. If war breaks out anywhere in that whole quadrant, there's the chance we'll be drawn into it…or…"

"Or?"

"Or that we could become collateral damage, a footnote of some accidental incursion during a battle," Taren says. He reduces the heat on the stove. "What about you?" he asks. "What will you do when you're done?"

I don't have any answer to give him, so I shrug.

"Don't worry," he says. "Hieronymus will help with that."

"With what?" Hieronymus asks just finishing tucking his shirt in and coming around the corner. Alee is right behind him, her braid not quite as tightly kept as it was before. I feel Taren blush, but don't understand why.

"Dinner is ready," Taren says with a laugh.

"Good," Hieronymus says. "I'm starving."

There is very little talk over dinner because of two things; one, the food is very good, and two, there is a nervous tension. No matter how much Hieronymus and Alee congratulate Taren on how good the food is, I can see the worried looks they give each other.

After dinner, we all go out to the back porch where Hieronymus starts a fire and we sit around it on wooden chairs. A long but pleasant silence stretched over us for a while.

"Your ship should arrive tomorrow morning," Hieronymus says to Taren.

"I'm ready," he says.

"We're going to miss you," Hieronymus says.

"Very much," Alee says.

Taren smiles but doesn't say anything.

Hieronymus sighs, then says, "So that just leaves one more thing."

Taren nods and stands up. Hieronymus puts his hand on Alee's knee. "Will you help Akari get settled in?"

"What's happening?" I ask.

"Yes," Alee says. Hieronymus stands up with a groan. Taren has already

135

gone inside and returned with two coats. He hands one to Hieronymus.

"What's going on?" I ask, alarmed.

"The final trial," Taren says and sends me a picture of the cave-like opening back along the path. He shrugs into the jacket and comes over to me.

"Chances are we won't see each other again. Just know that I wish you good luck," Taren says, pulling me into a hug. He pushes me out to arms length and says, "do good in the universe."

I've hardly known him a day and yet I'm very sad at all of this. I feel like I should say something, or do something, but I don't know what to say, and I don't know what to do. Before I know what I'm doing, I lean in and kiss him quickly on the lips. He smiles and puts his hand on the side of my face. "Thank you."

"Say 'good luck,'" Alee says to me.

"Good luck," I say.

Taren smiles one last time, then turns and goes with Hieronymus out the gate and down the trail back toward the temple.

2.1.7

Alee helps me get settled into what she calls "the guest house," which is just the other bedroom. Taren had already shown me where I could do my laundry, but Alee shows me again. Same for the fresh linen and blankets.

"Over dinner, you were worried," I say as we smooth the new blanket across the bed.

"You should already know it isn't polite to read other's emotions without permission," Alee says without stopping.

"I didn't," I say. "I didn't have to."

She stops. Without looking up, she says, "The final trial is…dangerous. It involves the culmination of everything one has learned. If he's not careful…" Alee comes around the bed and puts a hand on my shoulder. "Well, we'll see." Her smile doesn't touch her eyes, and she leaves without saying more.

I lie in bed for hours trying to sleep.

The next morning, I wake to the sounds of someone cooking. Cabinets open and close, plates clink, etc.

I close my eyes and settle into the halfway state. *In the kitchen, I can see Alee and Hieronymus. They move around one another in a dance that seems long practiced.*

"Will you tell him?" she asks Hieronymus.

"No," he says. "There's no reason to start his training off on a negative note."

I snap myself back to my own mind and open my eyes.

I remember what Alee said last night and sadness rushes over me.

I hardly knew Taren, but I could feel in him someone like myself.

I wondered if something terrible would happen to me.

"Good; you're awake," Hieronymus says from the doorway. "Breakfast is ready."

I slide on some of the loose drawstring pants that Eli packed for me and try to smooth down my hair.

"Did you sleep well?" Alee asks, spooning eggs onto my plate. She hands over two large squares of toasted bread, as well.

"I did, thank you," I say.

"Second night sleeping on our planet. Did it have an affect on your dreams?" Hieronymus asks.

"I don't remember dreaming," I say.

He stops eating. "Do you ever?"

I nod.

I can tell something very important has just been revealed, but I don't know what. I see that Hieronymus and Alee exchange a look.

"Is that bad?" I ask.

"No," he says. "Just…interesting."

Quiet stretches between all of us for a time. As soon as Alee finishes all of her food, she says, "I'm off once more."

Hieronymus makes a sound low in his throat.

"Can't be helped. The lake region. Several births coming in the next few days. I should be back in a couple of weeks," she says.

"But you just…" he says, then growls again.

She smiles, stands, kisses him on the forehead, and takes her plate into the kitchen.

"I hope you're a decent cook," Hieronymus says.

"Why?" I ask.

"Because I'm lousy at it."

We help Alee get her equipment packed up and see her to the head of the trail. She hugs and kisses Hieronymus, then hugs me. In my ear, she says, "you two take care of each other, okay?" I nod.

Once we can't see her anymore, Hieronymus turns to me.

"Today, we begin your training. Do you feel ready?"

I nod.

"Okay." We walk back into the house

"Sit," he says, gesturing toward the floor in the front room. I start to sit on the couch.

"On the floor," he says over his shoulder. I do.

He goes into the kitchen and I see him putting tea and then water into the kettle, then setting it on the stove.

"A man I knew once told me that the difference between females who have the gift and males that also have it, though most often they call it the curse, or some variation of that, is that girls and young women who are first manifesting their power have to be shown how to build their power," Hieronymus says. He leans against the counter.

"Young men and boys, as rare as we are, tend to show a...different pattern."

The kettle begins to whistle. He nods and walks back to the stove.

"This is why you are here," he says.

"I'm not sure I follow," I say. I reach out to scan him to see if I can better understand what he is thinking, but I run into a wall. It's so sudden, so unexpected, that I flinch.

He pours two mugs of the tea and walks back to me. "And just like that, the problem is revealed."

He hands one to me. For a moment, I'm surprised by how heavy, how thick the mug is. The tea immediately clears my sinuses.

"For females, the problem is how to open themselves. They hear whispers...a thin, dribbling stream from others. For you, though," he says, sitting. I try to pretend I don't hear his tendons creak. "As with all boys who have the ability, our task is different."

139

"Drink," he says.

I sip the tea, its strong, dark flavor washing over me.

That's when I feel the wave of relaxation flow through my shoulders, down into my limbs. Something in my mind relaxes.

"And that is why I'm going to have to ask you to forgive me," he says.

"What is…" I say but then my senses, my ability to speak, get away from me.

"Don't worry, it's meant to act quickly."

I'm so far behind that it only occurs to me that he has drugged me with the tea after he's already said it. I try to set the mug down. He reaches forward and takes it from me, setting it aside.

"There's no reason to be alarmed. The tea is simply meant to help you relax so that we can get to work. Don't worry; you're in no danger," he says. Then I see him take several gulps of the tea, himself. He sets his own mug aside and closes his eyes.

"Do I have your permission?" he says, touching his fingers to his temple.

"I don't know if…" I try to say, but I can hear that it's coming out garbled nonsense.

"There are defenses that you have in your talent. Things that spring up to stop someone from simply walking into your memories, your innermost thoughts. This is a good thing, except that right now, you have no control over anything you do, including those same protections, those barricades. You could consciously say that you welcomed me in, but right now those defenses, like so much of what you do, are instinctual…they are automatic, and beyond your conscious control. The tea will help us get past them."

Then I feel him in my head.

"Close your eyes," he says.

I don't want to, but I feel them closing.

"Don't be alarmed. Try to breathe," he says.

A moment later I realize I've shut my eyes.

I'm standing on a flat surface that seems to be made entirely out of the purest, clearest crystal I've ever seen. Not glass; there are flaws in it, but nearly that clear.

The sky is a hazy pinkish-gray.

Just behind me, a palace rises up, made of crystal as well.

There is a buzzing sound that grows steadily louder.

In seconds, I'm surrounded by what seem to be huge wasps made of the same crystalline material.

As I bring my hands up to protect myself, I see that I'm made out of the same thing.

I wonder why the wasp-things aren't attacking me as they swirl around my shoulders and head.

"Think of them like dogs. Dogs you command," someone says. "You have to get control of them."

Past the swirl of wasp-things, I can see Hieronymus' head sticking up just above a trench in the ground. He, too, is a figure of pure crystal.

"What are they?"

"Your defenses," he says. "You have to get control of them. If you don't, very quickly they will realize I'm here and they will destroy me."

Already I can hear their buzzing growing louder, angrier.

"How do I...?" I trail off. I can sort of feel them. Their buzzing, their swirling, it's all the same thing. As one passes, I can see a shard of blackness in its belly. I start to notice that they all have one. I think about that darkness and I feel myself start to vibrate as well.

When I do, their pattern shifts from a spiral to a ring around me.

"Whoa," I say.

"There. You can control them; they are you and you are them."

I think again of those dark shards and feel something in my chest change its vibration again. The wasp-things go from a circle to aimlessly floating in a cloud around me.

"Reduce the vibration," Hieronymus says. "Like turning down the volume."

I think about making them quieter and their buzz starts to reduce.

"There," Hieronymus says and pulls himself up out of the trench.

As he does so, though, the wasp-things once again grow loud and snap into a circle around me.

"Quiet them," he says and stops moving toward me.

I think about quieting them, but they grow louder.

"Akari," Hieronymus says taking a step backward.

The wasp-things stop circling and being to hover in place, their heads pointed directly at him.

"I...ummm...I can't..." I mutter as I try again and again to think about them growing quieter.

"Akari, you must get control of them," he says. I hear the fear in his voice, and some part of me likes that. The buzzing grows louder.

The wasp-things start to move slowly in his direction.

"The energy that flows between you and them, you have to master it," he says, stepping backward again.

A part of me knows he isn't fast enough to make it to the trench before the wasp-things get to him.

A part of me likes that.

It likes his fear.

"Akari," Hieronymus says.

The buzzing grows louder.

I know that it is mere seconds before they cut loose and destroy him.

A grin comes to my lips without me putting it there.

"Feel the current of energy flowing between them and you," he says taking another step back.

Like a million million darts, they launch for him. He turns and runs for the trench. I know he won't make it.

In that moment, though, I *can* feel a current running between me and the wasp-things. It's in the sound, the buzzing. A river running from me to them.

I feel myself struggle against the flow of energy, like trying to tread water against a vast current.

Hieronymus has seen that he won't make it, and around him, a sphere of darkness has erupted. The wasp-things attack it again and again, smashing themselves into it. It is cracking faster and faster.

"Think of the resistance as something you control, that comes from your will alone," Hieronymus yells. The panic in his voice is unmistakable, and a part of me wants to focus on that, but I keep myself from it.

"Akari!" Hieronymus yells. His sphere of darkness is spiderwebbed with cracks. It won't last much longer.

2.1.8

Finally, with one last push, I grab the current like a rope. It snakes and writhes trying to get away from me, but I'm holding it. The second I do, I see that I can pull the wasp-things back.

"Hurry!" Hieronymus yells. One more attack and he's done for.

I pull as hard as I can.

Almost immediately, the landscape shifts, the wasp-things melt into pools on the ground and then I am standing in the middle of a large pack of dogs, their leashes all connected to my hand. They look as though they are made of gemstones.

"Command them to sit. Make them bow to your will," Hieronymus says, the sphere of darkness around him disappearing. He puts his hands on his knees and breathes heavily.

I send the command along the leashes and the dogs sit.

"Good," Hieronymus says, out of breath. "That's…good." He stands and comes toward me.

As he does, several of the dogs begin to growl.

I send the command to quiet down along the leashes.

They stop growling.

He comes up to them. I can feel them wanting to growl but they don't. Inside each, I can see the same dark shard of crystal that every one of the wasp-things had.

"Good," Hieronymus says.

"What is all this?" I ask.

"People have a lot of names for it. It's both you and not you. Think of it sort of like the shore between things, the place where you meet the larger spaces that minds and spirits share," he says. "I was taught to call it the astral plane, but, as I said, people call it different things."

"So, this is my mind?" I ask.

He pets the head of one of the dogs. I feel them relax a bit more.

"Yes and no. It is both your mind and every mind. The dogs are you, you are you, that palace?" he says, pointing to the palace behind me. "That's you, too."

"But you are you?" I ask.

He nods. "This is the part of me that can leave my body meeting the part of you that can leave your body in a space in the astral plane that is closest to you."

"This sounds like it should be confusing but it makes sense to me— why?" I ask.

"Because you already know a lot of this without having to be told. These," he says, gesturing to the dogs, "are your mental and spiritual defenses. Like white blood cells, they immediately attack anything that comes too close."

"Even if I don't want them to attack?"

"Well, that's the lesson we just learned. And, again, I'm sorry—I had to drug you to give me the few seconds I needed to show you how to get in control." He scratches one of the other dogs under the chin. "They were even faster and stronger than I thought they might be, though. If I hadn't, they would have killed me before you even knew what they were doing."

"It was still not okay," I say.

"We can talk more about that once we're back out in the physical world. For now, since we're here, do you feel like you have a good hold on them?" he asks.

I nod. "Good. Remember that in the future—they are tethered to you, no matter what form they appear in. The form, though, is usually quite specific. Any idea why wasps or dogs?"

I shake my head.

"Well, that'll be part of our journey, too. For now, the important thing is this—you have these defenses and you are in control of them."

"Will other people try to get into my head?"

"Other telepaths, yeah. We just met, but I'm betting you've actually already gone into other people's astral space before and hurt them. You're a little brute."

"What's that mean," I ask.

"Let's head back. Chances are the tea is about to wear off, anyway."

"Okay, how do we do that?" I ask.

"It differs for people. For me it's a door," he says and makes a gesture. Next to him, a wooden door, the kind you'd find on the front of a house, appears. "On the other side of that door is my body. I just walk through and come back. Take a second and—,"

As he speaks, I think about my body and immediately wake up.

I'm slumped onto the floor.

Across from me, still sitting upright, is Hieronymus.

The light coming in from the window had been vibrant and yellow when we sat down. Now it's dark, and there was a cool breeze coming in through the windows.

Seeing him makes me feel upset and angry and defensive all over again.

His eyes open. He blinks a few times, and I see him touch each of his fingers to the tip of his thumb quickly.

"I know you are angry, that you feel mad at me for not warning you about the tea ahead of time. You're not wrong to feel that way, and I apologize for it. While it *is* wrong to administer a drug to someone without their knowledge, though, had I warned you, those defenses you saw, that you felt, would have worked fast enough to make what we accomplished impossible. So, feel angry at me. I don't begrudge it. But please try to also understand," he says.

"I don't want you to do that again," I say.

"And I won't. Now that you have the rudimentary beginnings of control over the door, I won't have to. But, in that, the true struggle begins. You've just become aware of a muscle, and now we must make it stronger," he says.

"There must have been other ways to do that," I say.

"There might be. The problem is that I don't know them," Hieronymus says. "Remember, I'm not a teacher. I don't train generations of telepaths. I'm a stop-gap measure. Don't worry, though; I don't go around just drugging people." He sits down. "Had I not, you would have shredded my mind in an instant. Even in your relaxed state, you nearly destroyed me anyway."

"I doubt that," I say.

He sighs. "Akari, you are...powerful. And because of that, we have to be very...cautious," he says.

We're both silent. The fire crackles.

"Why does it scare you? I wouldn't hurt anyone," I say.

"You already have."

"Just in self defense," I say.

"Maybe," he says. "Maybe. But maybe there were other things you could have done that wouldn't have hurt them at all. There are many ways to use strength, and only a few of them are brute shows of force."

"Why does it scare you?" I ask.

"Because you have almost no control over your talent. All that raw power, no governor on it. A hurricane."

That stings. And I'm surprised by how much. I've only just met this man, but for some reason, I care deeply about what he thinks of me.

"I can learn control," I say.

He nods. "Maybe," he says. "Maybe."

We stare at one another for a second.

He stands, his knees creaking. It's only then that I realize that I'm exhausted and slick with sweat. I try to stand but falter a bit.

"Will it always be this exhausting?"

"For the first while, yes. Eventually, no," he says.

Is that how they trained you? I ask him.

Yes, he says, *but that's the only one of their techniques that I'm going to use in helping you.*

Why? I ask.

Outside the window, far off down the valley, the wind shushes through the leaves.

Because what they did to me was his voice stops and I get flashes of pain, yelling, the color red, and crying.

Neither of us say anything for a while.

"I'm sorry," I say.

You don't have to be, he says, *but just know that at no point from now on will I be anything like they were.*

"Come on," he says. "Let's scrounge up some food and then get some sleep."

Later, in the bath, my leg muscles slowly unknotting, I try to imagine him at my age. I find that I can't. I dry myself off, dress, and barely make it down the hall and into bed before I slip from awake to asleep.

2.1.9

I'm hovering right at the edge of dreaming when I hear the first *ping*. In my mind, a bird with a glass beak taps on the window of a huge castle. The second *ping* is an enormous finger tapping against the window of a starship's observation port empty of everyone save me.

The third *ping* wakes me up.

I sit up in bed.

It takes me a second to orient myself because nothing is humming or moving. I'm not on a ship, I'm on a planet. I'm on a thick, soft mattress, covered by a blanket that someone made with their own hands.

With the fourth *ping*, I look at the window where it came from. Behind the curtains, I can see someone moving.

There is someone at the window.

I creep from bed and flatten myself beside the window. I can see someone moving outside, but I can't get a look at them because of the angle.

I slowly pull the curtain aside.

Zan is outside my window.

Even though I was afraid a moment before, I cannot help but smile.

He smiles back.

He motions for me to open the window.

The moon reflects off the window and then off his eyes, giving them tiny glowing stars.

"Hi," I whisper.

"Hi," he says.

For a moment, neither of us says anything.

"Come out," he says.

"I…shouldn't," I say. I want to, but something tells me that Hieronymus would be upset by it.

Zan rolls his eyes and then leans in close. "Come. Out."

He reaches across pane and puts his hands on my wrists, pulling on them.

I pull myself up and over the pane, my bare feet landing on the grass.

I feel the planet against me for the very first time.

Zan smiles and pulls me away from the window. We go to the fence line.

He pulls himself up onto the fence, then holds out his hands. I let him help me up. He's very strong.

"How are you doing?" he asks, leaning in close.

"I'm okay," I say.

He shakes his head, then taps his finger against my temple. "No," he says. "How are you *doing?*"

"Oh," I say. "You know about…all of that?"

"I pay attention. I know what Brother Hieronymus is. I can guess why you're here."

"Well, we only just started, so…"

Zan nods. I look back toward the house, convinced that I'm going to see Hieronymus coming toward us. We're still alone in the field, though.

"How did you know which room I'd be in?" I asked.

Zan shakes his head, but at the same time takes my hand. "I pay attention," he says. I like the feeling of my hand in his, the warmth of it.

I'm trying to think of something to say because the quiet is stretching out between us longer and longer.

And that's when he leans in and kisses me.

I have never felt less prepared for something, and yet completely ready at the exact same time. His lips are soft against mine, the closeness of his body is exciting and calming all at the same time.

He leans back and smiles at me, still holding my hand.

I smile too.

"I will come again tomorrow night," he says as he lets go of my hand and slips down off the fence.

I want to say something. Something to let him know how happy he's just made me, and in some way thank him for it.

Nothing is coming to me, though.

And just like that, he's gone into the woods.

The world seems far larger than it did just twenty minutes ago. The whole universe does.

I'm alone on the fence in the middle of a field on a vast new world.

"Interesting dreams last night?" Hieronymus asks as I sit down at the table.

I don't say anything. I start fixing a plate.

Hieronymus smiles. "It's perfectly okay, you know. We didn't get a chance to talk about the house rules, but that sort of thing is perfectly alright."

I am both mortified and happy that we're talking about it.

"You can invite him in, in fact, if you like. Zan is a nice kid, and I'm glad he's your friend." He seems to finally sense that I don't want to talk about it and smiles. "Okay. Eat up; we have a lot to do today."

When we've finished and cleaned our plates, we move to the sitting room at the front of the house.

"Sit like this," he says, crossing his legs over one another.

I mimic him.

"This hand over the other," he says, putting his non-dominant hand over the other one.

"Close your eyes," he says.

I do.

"Breathe in through your nose," he says, "then breathe out through your mouth. Imagine it like a big circle inside of yourself. In," he says, and I hear him take in a big breath. "Then out," he says, and I hear him exhale."

I try to match his breaths. On the very edge of my mind, I can feel that this makes him happy.

"Begin thinking about your littlest toe," he says. "Imagine it in your mind. See it very clearly."

I do.

"Now imagine relaxing it."

It's a strange sensation to be so aware of a part of me that I normally don't think about at all, but soon I can feel my toe relax.

"Next, think about your next largest toe," he says, "and relax it."

In this way we go through all our toes, our feet, our ankles, our hips, our shoulders, our elbows, our wrists, and all of our fingers. All the while, I can feel the breaths that I'm taking go deeper into me than I feel I have before.

"Now think about that same part of your mind where we were before. Think about the long plain made of glass. The distant mountains of crystal. Imagine it as a space right next to you and…"

I don't hear the rest of what he's saying because I'm standing in that space. Again, I see myself as if I'm made of glass, as well. My hands, my feet, all of me, somehow a being of crystalline form. Again, too, I see the long umbilical cord stretching from me off into the distance.

That's when I notice that I'm not alone. At a far clip stands another person. I feel myself bristle and find that I'm surrounded by the glass wolves from before. They snarl at the newcomer, but don't move.

"It's me," the person yells across the distance, and I realize that it's Hieronymus.

"Just like before, concentrate on calming them down."

I think about them curling up at my feet and it takes a moment, but they do.

"Now think about them being on leashes, leashes that you hold in your hand," he yells. I do, and the leashes appear.

Slowly, but deliberately, Hieronymus walks across the space between us to me. When we're standing about an arm's length apart, he stops. Through their leashes, I can feel the wolves wanting to snarl and snap, but they stay still.

"Excellent," Hieronymus says. "Now imagine yourself floating back to your body along this," he says, gesturing toward the umbilical.

"What is that?" I ask.

"Exactly what it looks like. This is the umbilical cord attaching your body to what you are right now."

"But can't we just jump back into our bodies? I did that before," I say.

"We can, but floating back requires far less energy. It's easier on you. Try not to jump back if you can help it. Save that for emergencies. Here, like this," he says and takes a hold of the umbilical snaking away from him. He then starts to slide away from me. After a moment, he's disappears.

I take hold of my own and think about my body. Soon, I'm sliding along the glass and then I'm back in my own body, waking up.

He's right; it feels much more pleasant and calm.

"Good," he says as I open my eyes. "Let's do the whole thing again."

By late day, our bodies are sitting safely in the main room of the house, and we're both standing on that long crystalline plain that is both in my mind and not. Off in the far distance there are what look like mountains made of glass. The wolves, my defenses, don't even come unless I call them.

"Float," Hieronymus says.

"Float?" I ask.

He nods back. Then he lifts into the space above us. As soon as he does, I can see the long umbilical reaching from him back across the miles behind us.

"How?" I ask.

"Remember that everything that seems physical here is just a metaphor for something going on in your mind. Therefore, the weight holding you to the plain under your feet isn't gravity, it's the heaviness of your thoughts," he says. "Think of something that makes you feel light, as if you could fly."

153

Immediately I think of the kiss, and my body lifts away from what I had been thinking of as the ground. I can see my silver umbilical snake far away into the distance.

"There," he says. "You move by manifesting a desire. Want to travel and you will begin traveling." As soon as he finishes saying that he floats away from me. I feel a desire to be closer to him and fly at him unbelievably fast. He catches me by the shoulders and laughs. "Good," he says. "Now, modulate that desire some."

Again, he floats away from me.

Again, I move toward him, but this time I think about it more as a desire to shake his hand rather than hug him. I move slower, and he catches my shoulders much easier.

"Good," he says. "Now, try to keep up." With that, he lets go of me, turns, and flies off. I think about playing tag and catch up to him easily, our umbilical's floating off behind us.

"How am I doing?" I ask.

"Faster than anyone I've taught before."

Later that night, after a long bath to soothe joints that both ache and don't from the level of the day's mental exertion, I'm just about to nod off to sleep when I hear the bedroom window open.

Without opening my eyes, I smile a bit.

I can feel that it's Zan. Not just with my mind, but oddly enough, with my body. I already know his sounds, his slight burnt-wood scent.

"Hi," he says as he climbs in the bed behind me, his arms already circling my waist.

I scoot closer into him.

Hi I send, feeling the warm, clear waves of his mind in response.

He kisses my neck, then my shoulder, and I turn so that we're facing each other.

The rest of the night is filled with hands, and lips, and a million things

I never knew were possible, and we fall asleep in each other's arms. I find out more about myself in those few hours than in all the lessons from all the teachers in all the universe.

When he sneaks back out the window the next morning, I open my eyes to watch him go, marveling at his body and at him and at my luck for finding him.

2.1.10

Days later, I'm floating high above the crystalline valley of my mind, my tether drifting behind me lazily in the wind. Suddenly, A huge shard, sharp as a sword, juts up from the floor below me. In a second it will slice through this body that represents me, here.

As we've been working on, I think of the feeling of being safe. Hieronymus said to think of a place where I have been happy.

Yet again, I'm left wondering where that place is as the shard stops millimeters before my forehead.

I am still shield-less.

I can feel Hieronymus' disappointment before he even floats up to me.

"Still nothing?" he asks.

I shake my head.

"Okay," he says. "I really thought surprising you like that would do the trick. It did with me when I was training."

We've been over it and over it—giving me as much time as I like hasn't worked. Surprising me hasn't worked. Talking me through it hasn't worked.

"Maybe I'll never be able to make a shield," I say.

"I don't accept that," he says. "You shouldn't, either."

"But it still might be true."

"Or it might mean that we have to manufacture the experience. Search for a place now, with the specific intent of finding a place that makes you feel safe." He descends to the floor of the glass valley below us and I follow.

He returns to sitting with his legs crossed, mimicking our bodies in the real world. "Okay, let's head back for some dinner," he says. I sit beside him and copy his pose. I think of returning along the tether to my body and in the next moment, I open my eyes back in the living room of Hieronymus' small house.

"Maybe I'll never be able to make a shield," I say to Zan as he slides back into his underclothes. "It's been over a week," I say.

"Maybe," he says, "but you've always found a way to do the things that Hieronymus has asked before. If he says it's a thing that's possible, then it would be strange for you to not be able to do it." He slides back into bed, and we pull the covers up to our chins to save the warmth.

"I feel so stupid that I can't just do it," I say. "He says that I need to find a spot that makes me feel safe."

"Where would that be?" he asks. Already the warmth of us has me feeling sleepy.

"Where do you feel most safe?" I ask.

Zan nuzzles further into my shoulder. "Besides here? When I was little, and there was a bad storm, I would get under the kitchen table."

I laugh a bit at the adorableness of that. "Really?"

"Yep," he says, laughing a bit, too. "That's where mom would find me. She would crawl underneath with me, and we would lay on our backs, and she would tell me stories about Uncle Ezuel the sailor, or Aunt Vees the pilot, about how they got through horrible storms. She made it seem like that stupid table was the greatest shield that had ever existed."

"I don't have anything like that," I say.

"Well, you do now," Zan says, pulling me closer to him.

We drift off to sleep together like that.

The next day, when it happens, it seems so obvious that I feel stupid.

It had just never occurred to me before that very moment.

Hieronymus is what seems like a thousand feet away in the mindspace, hurling crystal daggers at me. I'm dodging as many as I can, as if my body is physical, and growing exhausted. More of the mind daggers are hitting me than missing. Hieronymus has blunted them as much as he can, but the sheer number of them hitting me still hurts.

I'm about to give up, again when it occurs to me.

Zan. The blanket on that guest bedroom bed.

The warmth of us, together.

It feels so obvious that I almost waste time berating myself.

The last glass-like dagger is headed straight for my face.

Rather than try to dodge it, I think of that specific warmth, so similar to something I don't even have a memory for, but also completely new and powerful, of Zan and I together under that blanket.

Instantly, a bubble forms around me just in time to shatter the last crystal dagger before it can hit.

I feel Hieronymus' joy.

I let go of the memory and the bubble falls away.

There, he sends, with the feeling of pride.

I feel both exhausted and ready to take on the universe.

"How come we don't ever meet in your mindspace?" I ask as we eat lunch.

"Because there are things in there you aren't ready to see, yet," Hieronymus responds, taking another bite of his sandwich. The wind is up around the house, and the shutters bang against the wall.

"I'm strong; I can take it," I say.

"You are strong, that's true," he says. "But sometimes strength has very little to do with readiness."

"When will I be ready?" I ask. Already I've been here months, and I've learned so much.

"Yes," he says, "you have learned a great deal. However..." he lets that sentence trail off. "The most dangerous thing that a telepath can ever do is go into someone else's mindspace. In here," he says, tapping the side of his own head, "I'm in complete control, if I have the training and the willpower. If you enter with anything less than that same level of control, then...disaster..." He finishes the last bite of his sandwich and wipes his hand on the towel in his lap. "The only thing that could possibly be more dangerous is entering the head of someone who has power but absolutely no training."

"Like you do with me?" I ask.

He nods. "That first day, your defenses, especially as powerful as they are...you could have killed me. That's why the drugs were necessary."

"Why do you do it, then?"

He stares off into the distance for a moment, then looks back at me. "You know how few of us there are," he says. I nod. I don't know exactly, but all anyone has ever said to me about male telepaths is that we are rare in the universe. "All of the cases of a telepath hurting people on a large scale, all of the stories of the monsters that have destroyed and rampaged through the universe bending whole populations to their will...those were all male telepaths." He takes a swig of water. "Yet, at some point, like you, like me, those monsters started out as boys who had a gift. If...if maybe someone had just gotten to them to help them learn about their power, to learn how to use it before terrible things happened to them...maybe some of those tragedies could have been avoided."

I finished my own sandwich.

"Once I had that thought, I couldn't shake it. Worse, I started wondering why no one else seemed to have had it. Or, at least, why they weren't doing anything about it. Then I stumbled upon the temple, here. Zan's people, they showed me that you have to stop waiting. That you have to make the changes in the universe that you want to see. No one else is going to do it for you," Hieronymus finishes. He sighs. "Okay, let's get this cleaned up and get packed."

"Packed?" I ask.

"Yep," he says. "We're going hiking."

As we hike the long trail, Hieronymus hums. It's not a song I've ever heard before, I think, but then I catch myself.

I wouldn't know if I'd heard it before or not.

It sounds incredibly familiar, though.

I want to ask him about it. I want to reach out and listen to his thoughts to see what he's thinking about it, but I don't. I have a sense now of those boundaries. I feel pride in myself for having them, too.

I've come a long way.

The sun is starting to go down when he says we should stop for the night. Setting up camp goes quickly.

"The locals call it Ezeda Urul. That doesn't translate directly into standard, but it sort of means, 'the place where the bad parts fall away,'" he says as the water in the pot comes to a boil. He empties a few packets of dried meat and spices into it. "You're going to love it," he says.

"What is it? A river? A cave?" I ask.

He grins. "Yes," he says.

We climb into our sleeping bags after eating and cleaning the pots. Night falls very quickly. As the sleeping bag warms itself up, I stare up at the stars, wondering if Zan is looking up at that moment. I reach out to him but can't feel him. It must be too far. I fall asleep slowly with the sound of the river.

"There it is," he says, stopping at the top of the ridge. He has to put a hand on my shoulder to stop me from falling.

"Where, beyond that river?"

"It *is* the river," he says. "This stream comes down directly from the top of the tallest peak over there." He points to the mountain range that has dominated the landscape no matter where I'm standing. "Unbroken, never dammed up…it may be the purest water on any inhabited world. It may also be the coldest."

"Coldest?" He's already moving, though.

"After the third time the locals brought me here, I brought a thermal monitor with me once just to see how cold it actually was," he says.

"And?"

"It broke in seconds."

"And we're going to drink from it?" I ask.

We're starting down the ridge into the valley, heading right for the river.

"No," he says. "We're going to swim in it."

Just over our heads there is a screech. We both look up. A bird with a huge wingspan flies off toward the mountains.

"It's huge!" I say.

"Valka bird. Pretty rare, anymore. Majestic in flight, but those huge wings are ungainly on the ground. They have a tough time getting away from predators."

We both watched it hover on an updraft for what seemed like forever.

"One of the first things my father ever taught me about flying," Hieronymus says. "'To get a feel for the wind' he said, 'watch the way birds move—they don't try to fight the wind, they try to become one with it. Jet engines, faster than light drives, it doesn't matter—if you don't learn to get a feel for the wind, you'll never master flying.'"

"You miss it," I say.

"Flying?" he asks, "yeah. I do."

"Why don't you do it more often?" I ask.

"It doesn't just bring back the good memories," he says, his eyes growing darker. The quiet stretches out between us for a moment. "At any rate," he says, "I know you're just stalling so that you don't have to go in the cold water."

"I am not!" I say.

It takes longer than I thought it would to climb down to the river. By the time we make it to the riverbank, I almost welcome the idea of climbing in no matter how cold.

With no warning whatsoever, Hieronymus is already stripping out of his clothes.

"Whoah," I say, turning away.

"What?" he asks.

"You're almost naked," I say.

"What does that matter?" Behind me there is the sound of a splash. Then he makes sounds as if he's in pain. I turn to see him waist deep in the water and walking further out into the stream. He seems so awkward, like a bird trying to fly for the first time. Eventually he makes it to the middle of the stream, resting against a rock that rises just above the current. He wipes his hands across his face and pushes his hair back.

"Okay," he says. "Your turn."

I hesitate.

"What?" he asks.

I send him a quick snapshot of how I feel exposed and embarrassed.

"Akari," he says, and in that moment, I realize how little he has ever used my name. "It's just a body. Everyone has one. If it helps, remember that I'm not attracted to males at all. The important thing about this experience is the river. Besides, we already shared the communal bath in the temple."

I know he's right, but up to this point, the only person who has seen me naked when it wasn't an accident, is Zan. I had no hesitation about showing myself to him. For a second, though, I wonder if that might have been because he had so little concern about me seeing him with no clothes.

I strip out of my clothes and pile them on the side of the river. The second I step into the water, my body begins shouting that this is a mistake and demands I turn around. I've never experienced cold like this before. Once I make it in up to my knees, I start making sounds as though in pain, but not consciously. In fact, I try to stop myself from making them, and I can't.

Up to my waist, and I can't feel anything lower than that.

The current pushes against me, and it is all I can do to stay upright.

When the water reaches my chest, the current is strong enough to push me up off my toes, and I'm floating free.

In that split second, I feel elated, like what I've imagined flying to be like when I do it in the mindspace.

162

It is also in that second that I realize I don't know how to swim.

Immediately, I go under, and I can't find my way back up.

The current is sweeping me away from Hieronymus.

I'm under the surface of the water. Somehow, up to my chest very quickly became far over my head. Some tiny part of my brain that can still reason keeps saying that I should be able to just stand up, but my feet can't find the bottom.

My lungs scream for me to get air, but I can't find the surface.

Across the surface of my mind, I see myself looking through water. This time, it is less distorted. The man comes close to me, and I see that he is like me. His skin is the same color as mine, his eyes shaped like mine. I see that he is wearing a long white coat and there is something on the left side of his chest. Something with writing on it.

That's when something grabs me and pulls me to a stop. I snap back to reality. I can feel the water rushing around and over me, like the rock that Hieronymus was standing against.

I still can't get air, though.

Whatever it is that has me pulls me up to the surface, and I lose control, gasping huge lungfulls of air down into myself.

A part of me notices that where I expected there to be Hieronymus holding me up, there is nothing. Still, I'm above water and slowly moving toward the bank of the river.

Calm, Hieronymus sends, *calm. I have you.*

The invisible hands set me down on the bank of the river with me still coughing and sputtering.

"I'm sorry," Hieronymus says as he arrives, putting a towel around my shoulders. "It didn't even occur to me to ask if you knew how to swim or not. I just assumed…I mean, with the memories that…"

I didn't know either, I send.

He sits down next to me and rubs my shoulders and back with the towel to get me warm again.

163

Once I finally stop sputtering, and the shivering subsides, he says, "We need to teach you to swim."

"When we come back," I say.

"No," he says. "It has to happen right now. Already, in the back of your mind, there is a fear growing of the water. If we wait at all, it will take root."

"No," I say. "I can't."

"You can," he says. "And you have to. And I'll be here, this time. I'll keep you safe."

I groan.

"And as a reward for being brave enough to get right back in the water, I'll teach you how to move objects with your mind."

"How *did* you do that?" I ask.

"I'll show you. But first, breathing."

Here, where we've gotten out, the river is far more calm. One small area here near the bank has almost no current at all, like a tiny pool, almost.

For the next few hours, he teaches me to calm myself and take in a big gulp of air before going under, and then how to let it out slowly though my nose while I'm under, each time finding the spot where the amount of air I'm holding feels equal to the pressure outside my body.

He shows me how to move my hands, making big flippers out of them, or pulling my fingers all together to make little blades. He shows me how to kick figure eights so that I can control how fast I'm going.

"It's a lot like flying; catching the current, working with it or against it, using arms and hands to control movement," Hieronymus says, and that sticks with me.

By the time the sun is going down, and we pull our clothes back on and start a fire to cook dinner, I feel almost embarrassed that I was so easily pulled under. Already, it seems like a laughable thing that I was so easily pulled under.

We say very little over the rice and beans that Hieronymus puts together. "Watch carefully," he says. "Tomorrow, you cook." I nod.

I'm almost asleep before I can even get my sleeping bag zipped up.

The next day, I am anxious to get back in the water.

I still feel the cold, but now instead of pain, it makes me feel that what we're doing here in the water is important.

Once we're both out at the rock in the middle of the current, Hieronymus says to go through the meditation steps. With the power of the water rushing against me, and the cold numbing my body, I don't know if I'll be able to make it.

"What if I can't?" I ask.

"You will," he says. He closes his own eyes, and I can feel him calming his energy.

I try to do the same and am swept off my feet. I catch myself and swim back to the rock.

I try again, and the once more am swept away in the current.

I swim back and try again. Again, I'm swept away.

Finally, though, I have an idea. What if I turn sideways, and use the rock to break the current?

It takes a few more tries before I find the spot that works, but eventually I can stand, get my body to be still, and get my breathing under control.

It is in that moment that I understand what Hieronymus has been talking about, what those who live here must have felt—there is something very special about the river and being connected to it in this way.

The peace surpasses anything I've felt in any of my previous meditations.

For a split second, I feel connected—the river, the water that seeps from it into the ground and goes into the grass, the trees, the bodies of the animals that take it in, me…all one thing.

I can't stay in that state too long, though; eventually, my body does get my attention and brings me back to find myself shivering, my teeth chattering. Hieronymus comes out of his trance at the same time. He smiles at me, and I try to smile back, but I have no control over my face. We both race for the shore, and immediately into our sleeping bags. I mash the "emergency heat" button.

Still, though, as the bag brings itself up to almost my body temperature, and the muscle spasms slowly subside, I keep thinking that I want to go back into the water. To find that peaceful place again.

Now you see, Hieronymus sends.

Yes, I say. Yes.

I mimic what I've seen Hieronymus do to make the rice and the beans. I burn the bottom layer of both, even though the top layer isn't completely done. Hieronymus laughs. I'm about to throw the pot of beans down and walk away, but he holds up his hands. "I'm just remembering the first time I tried to cook," he says. "It was a disaster. You at least haven't started any fires, so that's good."

My anger goes away quickly, though, and I laugh, too.

We don't say much as we eat.

"Tomorrow, we'll pack up and head back."

It's strange, but in that moment, I don't want to go. I came here with no feeling about this place whatsoever, but now I don't want to leave it. I want to build a house here so that I can go into the river every day.

"You can, though," Hieronymus says when I tell him that. "It's in your memory, now," he says. "You can come here whenever you want."

"But when can we come back?"

"I try not to come here more than once a year. That way it never becomes ordinary. It stays special," Hieronymus says.

I nod.

After sundown, we both climb back into our bags. As it warms up, I think about how, even after I leave this planet, I will want to come back here at least once a year.

Again, the stars above me, and the sound of the river, lull me to sleep.

166

2.1.11

"One of the most important tricks that we have is to disguise ourselves," Hieronymus says. "That's not easy. It involves convincing the other person that you aren't who their eyes can clearly see. But because the information the eyes give must be interpreted in the mind, we can control that."

"So I could be..."

"Standing right in front of them the young person that you are and convince them that instead they are seeing something else, entirely. That starts in your mind, though. You have to convince *yourself* that you are someone else, first."

In the weeks since our trip to the river, we seem to have hit a new level of practice. Things are more intense, which is makes them more exhilarating. He's taught me to move things with my mind, and slowly I'm getting stronger at it. When I showed Zan, he was afraid, at first. Since then, though, it's become just part of who I am.

We've spent a lot of time talking about the difference between a mind that is trying to defend itself and one that is one the attack.

Here, sitting across from one another, I can feel that we've grown closer. That Hieronymus takes me seriously, and that he approves of my growth in power and control. It's a feeling that makes me want to push even harder.

To make him even more proud of what I can accomplish.

He makes a motion that I've come to know means to meet him in astralspace.

I do the quick breathing exercise and soon I'm there, surrounded by the diamond mountains. For just a moment, I remember the flower opening visualization, and how long that used to take. He appears next to me. A troop of crystal dogs appears at my heel, ready to spring at him. I silence them with a gesture, and they sit obediently.

"Think of someone else. It's easiest if you know them, have been around them. Picture someone you know well. So well you can easily hear their breathing pattern, the ways that they walk."

I think for a moment, then nod.

"In your mind, listen to them breathe. Listen to the way they walk. Hear the way they sound when they say the word, 'home.'"

Out of sheer force of habit, I lean my head down to concentrate.

"Got it?" he asks.

I nod.

"Okay," Hieronymus says, "Go!"

I concentrate on the idea of looking like someone else. Feeling like someone else. Sounding like someone else. The picture I hold in my head is familiar to me.

"Ah," he says with a laugh in his voice. "And, who is that?"

"It worked?" I ask.

"Yes," he says. "Who is that?" He calls up a mirror from the raw dreamstuff around us.

Looking back at me is Eli.

"Someone I knew. From the ship," I say.

"One of The Captain's men, eh?" Hieronymus says and laughs again.

We practice for a few more hours, then we test it out on the boy who brings the order of vegetables up from the town. When the door opens, he says, "Good morning, Hieronymus!" because that's who he saw open the door.

I nod to him and take the package, then pay him.

As soon as the door closes, the real Hieronymus comes from the back bedroom to stand beside me, and he pats me on the back. "Good job," he says.

"Tell me about your family," I say as Zan is slipping his clothes back on.

"My mother is a math teacher," he says. "She's very good. My father works on a freighter that hauls cargo back and forth between our third moon and home."

"You must miss them," I say.

"I do, but it's nice to be away, too," Zan says and lays back down. He pulls me over and I lay my head against his chest. "I have two sisters and a brother. He's older than me and works with dad on the freighter. He hopes to captain a ship someday. I think he might just be smart enough to do it. My sisters are younger."

"Did your brother come here to learn from the monks?"

"Yes," Zan says. "He hated it, though."

"And you?"

"I love it. I…I haven't even told the head abbot this, yet, but I think maybe I want to stay. I want to spend time helping people find peace."

For some reason, that makes me smile.

"What will your parents think about that?"

"Mom will love it. I think my father is sort of hoping I will come work on the freighter, too. I think he hopes that someday we'd buy it, and it would be our own family business. It still can be, though, even with me not there." He waits a few moments. "I'm sorry," he says.

"For what?"

"To be talking about my family when…you know…"

"It's okay," I say. "I asked."

"Do you think that maybe there was a family?"

"There would have had to have been. At very least, someone that they took the cells from that grew me. No matter what," I say, "somewhere, out there, there are people I'm related to. Still, though, I miss Eli and the people on the ship."

"You're my family, now, too," Zan says, pulling me even closer. He kisses me, and then sits up and starts putting on his shoes.

"Stay. Hieronymus already knows about us and he said it was fine."

"It's not just that," Zan says. "I have temple duties. Things that have to get done." He stands up, and I see his face in the moonlight coming in from the window. He's so beautiful.

"But I want you to stay," I say.

He leans over and kisses me. Then he kisses me again.

"I'll see you tomorrow night," he says, and then is off out the window.

I fall asleep dreaming of walking hand in hand with him through the tall grass fields beyond the back fence.

"Can I ask you about something?" I ask one day as we're taking our midday break. We've been sparring in the mindspace all day, Hieronymus teaching me about offensive strategies, and ways to slip in to someone else's mind when they aren't paying attention.

"Okay," he says, splashing some water on his face.

"The boy that died," I say.

"The what?" Hieronymus asks, scrubbing the water away from his face.

"There was…Taren said that there was a boy who…"

"Oh," Hieronymus says, and nods without looking at me. "I should have known he'd say something about that."

"What happened?" I ask.

Hieronymus looks off into the distance for a while, then says, "I made a grave mistake and it cost him his life."

"What mistake?"

He looks directly into my eyes, "a test he wasn't ready for. I thought he was, and I was wrong." He sits down across from me. "What brings it to your mind at this particular moment?"

I gesture around us.

"Oh, well, yeah," he says. "It is a pretty obvious topic for us to broach. I had hoped maybe to bring it up some time later, when you were stronger."

"What test?"

170

He sighs. "At the end of your training, there is a final test. One last test that will determine what happens to you."

"And someone can die from this test?"

He nods. "You need to remember, always, that what we're doing here is important. That there are consequences. This...this is how it has to be."

"Do you regret his death?"

"Of course," he says. "I used to be a horrible person. I may still be, who knows," he says. He leans back in the chair and rubs his forehead for a second. "But I'm trying very hard to not be one anymore."

"How is that working out?" I ask.

"I'll let *you* know when *I* know," he says and takes sip from the bottle. Then he gets up and walks to the chest near the window. From it he pulls a book. He walks to me and opens to a page that is well-worn.

The picture is of a knight in full armor with a huge shield.

"That," Hieronymus says.

"A knight?" I ask.

He nods. "This is what we'll practice tomorrow morning. You becoming that."

"Making armor?"

He sets the book down on the table between us. "Your defenses are now under your control, and that's good. But we have to plan on someone, somehow, eventually getting through them. If they do, I want you to be as tough as you can possibly be."

When we go back into the astral plane later that afternoon, on the diamond plane of the mindspace, I try to imagine myself covered in those thick plates, carrying that enormous shield. Hieronymus makes a mirror out of the crystal stuff that surrounds us and shows me what looks to be a half-melted version of the picture from the night before.

"You can't just picture it. You need to *feel* it. Make it a manifestation of how you feel about yourself."

"Do you have an armored form?" I ask, still trying to shape the armor around me and failing.

"I do."

"And what do you feel in order to make it work?" I ask.

"Righteous indignation," he says with a laugh.

"What is that?" I ask. The half-formed crystal armor falls away.

"It's a feeling of 'how dare you?!'" he says. "I make myself believe that they are in the wrong for even thinking of attacking me. How dare they? Who do they think they are?" he says. "Do you ever feel that?"

I shake my head no.

"Give it a try."

I think, how dare you?

Nothing happens.

I try to think louder, how dare you? Who do you think you are?

Nothing happens.

"Anything?" he asks.

I shake my head no.

He nods. "Well, you always were a loser, anyway."

"What?" I ask.

"You. I guess it's time to tell you that you're the worst student I've ever had. I mean, I can't keep up this charade any longer. You're terrible," he says.

"Why…why would you say that?" I ask.

"Because you are. The worst. Period. I mean, I've seen little boys who could master this first day. You? Not even after all these months. Pathetic."

I feel sadness welling up in me. "Do you really mean that?" I ask. Somewhere off in the distance I hear bees.

"I wish I didn't. I'd like to have a decent student. When I think of all the work I've put in to making you better and this is the half-assed level of effort you give me?" As he says this, he steps closer.

The sound of bees grows louder.

"No, no," he says gesturing behind me, "don't rely on them. Don't threaten me with them. I'd say stand here and take it like a man, but you aren't capable

172

of that, are you? Are you?!" He steps closer.

In that moment, somewhere in my chest, the anger starts. I can't believe that after everything I've done, he thinks I'm somehow unworthy.

I *am* worthy.

I *have* worked hard. I've done *everything* he's asked.

"Are you going to stand there and cry or are you going to get to work and show me what you can do?!" he yells and steps closer.

"Stay back!" I hear myself yell.

"Or what?" he asks and grins. The grin makes me even more mad. "You're too pathetic to do anything about it if I decide to come at you. A child half your age could stop me easier than you." He steps even closer, just a few inches from me.

"Stay back!" I yell. Who does he think he is, to berate me when I am so much stronger, so much more powerful?!

In that instant, I feel it. It doesn't look exactly like the picture, but in that moment I am covered in armor plates. A shield covers my right forearm.

Hieronymus takes several steps back and smiles.

"There it is," he says. "Outstanding!"

I'm about to start yelling at him when what he did becomes clear to me.

"Oh," I say.

"I didn't mean any of it," he says. "Not one word. I just had to get you—,"

"I understand," I say.

"Do you?" he asks.

I nod. The armor drops. A second later I call it back by remembering that exact feeling. This time, both the plates and the shield are larger.

This time it wasn't his attack I was thinking of, though.

I was thinking about The Captain.

As we have done every morning for the last few months, Hieronymus and I meet in the astral plane.

"So far," he says, "we've focused on defensive moves. Getting you built up to withstand an attack." He moves toward me and puts his hand on my shoulder. I know that physically, in the real world, nothing has happened. We're both still sitting on the floor across from one another. However, here, in this place, I feel the weight of his touch and it's comforting.

"Now it's time to start talking about attack," he says. "Or, at least, being aggressive rather than reactive. We're going to start with the easy stuff and work our way up to the really nasty parts. Thing is," he says, "instinctively, you've already had some experience with the absolute worst techniques. I wish I knew how, to be honest. Once we get there, though, if we've done this all correctly, you'll have more control."

I nod.

Right next to us, an arched doorway appears.

I can't help but take a step back.

"It's okay," he says. "This is the first part. Learning to create this doorway into someone else's mind."

"What's through it?" I ask.

"Me," he says. "Take a second and look at that doorway. See how, when you get close to it, it's made of fibers? Like little ribbons?"

I step closer to it. It's humming.

"The noise," I say.

Hieronymus nods. "It vibrates differently than anything else in here because it's not you, it's me. Do you understand?"

"I think I do."

The doorway is made of millions of little diamond ribbons, just like he said. There's a pattern to them. "Memorize the pattern. Commit the hum, that specific sound, to memory. Take as long as you need," he says.

I think for a moment that this will take forever, but almost instantly there's a vibration in my head and another doorway appears right beside it.

I look over at him. He takes a step back and his eyes go wide. He shakes his head.

The initial doorway that he made disappears. I notice that mine is identical to it.

"How…" he starts but stops himself.

"What?" I ask

"I guess I should have known; nothing about you ever takes as long as the others."

"Was that fast?" I ask, already knowing the answer.

"No one else I've ever trained has been able to duplicate the doorway in less than a few months." I sense from him that this is something that puzzles him and at the same time scares him. "Erase it and do it again, this time without the example."

I'm just about to ask him how to do any of the things he just mentioned when my head vibrates again and the copy doorway that I made goes away. Then I hear that specific hum again, and a new doorway appears where the other one had been.

"Again," he says.

Again, the doorway disappears and reappears.

"Okay," Hieronymus says. "It's time." He steps to the doorway and waits. I step up next to him. Inside the doorway, energy swirls. "Through this door is my head. My memories. I've picked one specifically and called it to the doorway. Eventually, though, you'll be able to enter and pull memories to the doorway by yourself without the other person knowing. Eventually, not only without them knowing, but without them cooperating."

"That sounds…awful," I say.

"Yeah, it's not great. It's the main reason so many societies across the galaxy fear and hate telepaths. But secretly they use guys like us in their interrogation rooms…" he says trailing off.

"How can you cross into your own memories?" I ask.

His eyes go wide, again. "I can't. Tell me something—how did you know that would be a problem?"

"I dunno," I say. "It just seemed like it would be."

Hieronymus shakes his head. "Unreal. You're right, I can't cross into my own head. So, I'm going to disengage and meet you on the other side. All you have to do is walk through that doorway. I'll meet you on the other side."

I nod and he disappears. I'm left standing next to this humming archway in a desert made of crystal and glass.

I step through the doorway.

2.1.12

Immediately on the other side, we're in an exact replica of the living room back in his house. I know we can't be, though, because that's where our physical bodies are. Nothing here is made of crystal or glass, though.

"How...?" I ask.

He smiles. "It takes time, but before long, you'll be able to do more with raw astral space than just make shapes. Eventually you can make it take on color, and warmth, and other things. We'll work on that. I thought for this first visit to someone else's mind...or, I should say, this first *intentional* visit, I thought it'd be best for things to be familiar."

As he mentions it, I can feel the warmth of the space. I hadn't realized it, but my own astral space is always cold.

"Here," he says, and turns. When he turns back, he's holding a box in his hands. It chimes a song that sounds at once familiar and strange. I feel like I've heard it before, but I know that I haven't at the same time.

"What's that?" I ask.

He starts. He stops the song quickly, as if caught doing something he shouldn't have been.

"This?" he gestures to the box. "It's a sort of an heirloom. In my culture, we make them for children. It's a clockwork that plays a song."

I step closer, hoping he won't put it away. The box is made of wood with beautiful geometric designs on it.

"Who made it?"

"This one? I have no idea. Some families have those kinds, made by some long ago ancestor and passed down. This one," he says, putting it up on the shelf. I realize that I've seen it many times before but never paid any attention to it. "My mother bought. I don't know where, maybe a street bazaar. There would have been many of those near our home at the time. It's the kind of thing someone would have for sale fairly cheap." He rests his hand near it. "I imagine her, pregnant with me at the time, her first child, passing by a street vendor, maybe someone who worked wood themselves, and seeing it. Hearing it chime its little song. Deciding it was the kind of thing she wanted in the nursery." Without looking, one of his hands goes to his belly. "The song is a lullaby she used to sing around the house."

"I don't have anything like that," I say.

"It's just a thing, in the end," he says.

"No, I mean, the memory. The story you think of when you see it," I say.

He thinks for a moment, then reaches out his hand.

"Here," he says, and I feel his mind touch my own.

I still don't trust him fully, but I take his hand. I let down my guard and am swept into a vision, blurry in that way that memories, especially the happy ones, I'm learning, can be. I'm walking along a row of stalls in a street market. The vendors are talking with customers, trying to get them to buy trinkets, or dried herbs, or fresh honeycomb in jars. Or they are calling out to those of us walking past to catch our attention with "fresh milk!" or "wouldn't this be lovely on a neck like yours!" I feel myself smile. Then I see the stall with the wooden boxes and windchimes. I stop because I hear the song my mother used to sing to me as I looked up at her from my crib. I feel the sadness as I think of her, gone many years now, having died giving birth to my youngest brother. The person sees my interest in the box and my swollen belly and says, "help to make the nursery even brighter with song!" It's enough to make me reach for the little money I have with me. I take the box, running my thumb over the carvings on the lid, and give over the money without even attempting to bargain.

Then the memory shifts and I know that I am now him rather than her. I hear the song chime through the air as I look up at her. She smiles down at me like the sun itself, her eyes the whole universe. She sings along with the chimes and her hand touches my face. She radiates safety and warmth and acceptance, and the song weaves itself into that feeling.

The memory fades and I come back to myself. When I do, I'm crying.

He lets go of my hand.

"Okay?" he asks.

I wipe away the tears and try to get myself back together.

"Okay," I say.

He nods. "You can come listen to it whenever you want."

"It's real?" I ask.

He nods again. "Yes. You must have never paid much attention to it, but this exact box is on the windowsill in the living room."

I finish wiping away my tears. "How...?"

"Did I copy it so exactly? Objects that remain in your life for a long time tend to find their way into your mental space. Especially if they are powerfully sentimental," he says. "Somewhere around in here, you'll find the first Sparrow glider that I ever flew." He shakes his head. "Man, I loved that thing."

"So why weren't there any things like that in my head?" I ask.

"That," Hieronymus says, "is a *very* good question. One that I have been trying to answer for a while, now, without much luck."

Right next to me, the arched doorway appears. This one hums differently, though. "Is that me?" I ask.

"That specific sound is you, yes. Mem..." Before he can even finish his sentence, I've examined the doorway and another stands beside it. The first one disappears. "Okay, again," he says. The first doorway I'd made fades, and another appears two feet to the left of it. "Again," he says. Once more, a doorway vanishes and another sprouts in its place.

I step through. Again, the vast emptiness of smooth mirrorstuff, raw astralspace.

He appears next to me.

I let the doorway I'd made slip away and it dissolves.

"I'm going to have to stop being amazed," Hieronymus says.

"Was that fast, too?" I ask.

"I think you already know the answer to that. Somehow," he says, "somehow this all comes almost...instinctively...to you. I've never seen anything like it."

"Is it okay, do you think?" I ask.

"It is what is," he says. "Come what may, you're the single most gifted telepath I have ever encountered," he says, and I wish I didn't know that he felt both pride and fear at the thought. "Come on, let's get back to the real world," he says, and we do.

"Armor, huh?" Zan asks. We lay together on top of the covers as the weather has warmed. The breeze through the open window brings with it fresh leaves and new grass mixing with the smell of us, together.

"And how to disguise myself in other people's memories, and...so much. Just so much. But mostly," I say, "control. He's taught me so much about controlling my gift that I never would have guessed was possible back when this all started."

"He is a good teacher," Zan says. He runs his hand over my chest. "It means that sooner rather than later, you'll be going."

"Going?" I ask.

"Like all the other students that have come here."

"Oh," I say. I hadn't thought about it in quite a while.

"Where do you think. you'll go?" Zan asks.

"I don't know. I hadn't thought about anything but day by day learning to get control over myself for so long." I kiss his cheek. "Maybe I can stay here."

"I'd like that," Zan says, "but none of the others ever have."

"Were...were any of them...with you?" I ask and wonder why I hadn't thought to ask before.

"No," Zan says. "I don't think any of them were interested in other males, for one, but also, I just didn't like any of them. Taren was nice, but from the moment he arrived, all he ever talked about was going off to save the galaxy. Most of the rest weren't here very long, or they were just arrogant jerks."

"Really?"

"Yeah. I'm not sure, but at least from what I've seen, you're one of the youngest that's ever come here. So many of them had already had their powers for a long time before they arrived. They were used to people bowing and deferring to them."

Something about that makes me happy for some reason.

"I really would like to stay if I can," I say.

"I'd like that, too," Zan says, and we fall asleep like that, together.

"I'd like to talk about what happens…after…" I say a few days later over breakfast.

"Ah," Hieronymus says. "I've been thinking about that, myself."

"Could…could I stay here?"

He thinks for a moment. I see something hard set in his jaw. I already know the answer is no.

"You have bigger things to accomplish," he says.

"But I like it here. Learning from you, being with Zan. Maybe I could go live at the monastery, help people find peace in their lives."

"You have bigger things to accomplish," he says. "I've been thinking, in fact, that you're…you're close to finished with your studies."

"What?" I say before I can stop myself.

"There are more things I could teach you, yes, but those would just be finishing things. Polish on a sword that is already sharp, if you see what I mean."

"So…so what now, then," I ask, "if I'm done?"

He sighs. "It's time to call The Captain and have her come pick you up."

I try to hide my disappointment, but I can't.

I want to see Eli. But I don't want to see her.

181

"Why not?" Hieronymus asks, my thoughts so surface he can't help but hear them.

"Because she hates me," I say.

He inhales slowly, then says, "she doesn't...hate...you."

"Yes, she does," I say.

He shakes his head. "It's...it's much more complicated than that. If the only issue we were dealing with was that a grown woman for some reason hated a teenage boy, this would be fairly simple. We could dismiss her as an extremist. But this...this is something much deeper." He stands up. "There are a lot of things you don't know."

"Then tell me," I say.

"I'm not sure where to begin," he says.

"She said you were an Enzenite," I say.

"Okay," he says. "Do you know what that means?"

"No."

"Fair enough. What else did she tell you?"

"That because she'd managed to survive so many times, your high command brought her in to study and..."

"Is *that* what she told you?" he asks. Then he starts to laugh. I don't say anything. "Of course that's how she'd put it," he says and shakes his head.

"Well?" I ask, more than a little mad.

"She was shot down over a moon that we were all fighting over," he says. "It was my group that found her, barely any oxygen left, trying to build an airtight shelter from her emergency kit."

"Oh," I say.

"Yeah," he responds. "She had maybe fifteen minutes worth of air left and at least two hours before the shelter would be anything close to airtight. She was in a real rough spot."

"But wasn't she the enemy?" I ask.

"That was a sort of gray area at the time. We know that the Hasturs— that's what we called her people—that the Hasturs had gotten involved, but they weren't who we were really fighting. When we found them in situations where we could take them in and return them to their planet, we did," he says, staring away. "They were just a bunch of farmers, really, caught up in something much much bigger than themselves."

He's quiet for a long time, so I ask, "why didn't you do that, then? Just take her home?"

"I didn't know that, either, for a long time. Turns out, she had some information that the higher ups wanted. And don't ask me what it was. We're not ready for that conversation, yet."

"So why did you two become friends?" I ask. "She may not have been an enemy or whatever, but she was fighting on the other side."

"We were both pilots. And pilots always recognize pilots," he says.

"How so?" I ask.

"It's a thing. I can't even explain it. It goes deeper than any telepathy, though."

"And you recognized it in her?"

"Immediately," he says. "Just like I recognized that you are something very special. Believe it or not, so did she."

"She hates me," I say.

"Her feelings are a lot more complicated than that," he says. "At any rate, it is time to call her, and for you to get ready for the door."

"What's the door?" I ask.

"Graduation day," he says. "The final test."

2.1.13

Alee has returned sometime in the night. I can hear her voice mixed with his down the hall. I wake and roll away from Zan. He must have crawled in the window sometime in the night without waking me.

"But all the others had so much more time," I hear her say.

"They needed it. I know you can't feel it, but not a single one of them had a tenth of the spark he has," Hieronymus answers.

"Is the test just one of brute mental strength?"

"That's the thing...not only does he have far more..." Hieronymus starts to say but then stops.

It's rude to eavesdrop he says in my head. *Come get some food.*

"He's awake," I hear him tell her at the same time.

"You're awake," Zan mumbles, stretching.

"Yes," I say.

He rolls over and cuddles against my chest once more.

I would love nothing more than to lie here for the next few hours cuddled and warm, but the door lies ahead.

"I have to get up," I say, picking his arm up off my chest. I try to slide out of bed without moving the blankets off him, but they stick to me and suddenly there he is—very naked and very beautiful in the morning glow.

He snatches the blankets back from me. "Cold!" he mumbles, his eyes not open.

I can't help but smile.

I slip into my clothes. He sits up, rubbing at one eye.

"Today is the day of my final test," I say.

"I know," Zan says. "Alee came to tell me so I could be here this morning." His eyes open and I melt a bit. To think that someone so beautiful and smart and funny thinks of me as worthwhile nearly knocks me over.

He pats the bed next to him.

I sit down.

"Remember this," he says, taking my hand in his. "No matter what happens, I will love you. You will be important to me."

We kiss for a moment. Then the door opens.

"Come get some food, boys," Alee says, then turns and leaves. The door stays open.

Zan puts his forehead against mine for a moment, then stands and begins to fix himself into his robe. The orange catches the morning light and the whole room flashes gold.

The mush has spices I don't recognize in it this morning, sweet and warm.

"It's called cinnamon," Alee says. "From a planet far away from here. We get a tiny bit of it every once in a while when merchant ships come through. I make sure to buy it because it makes toasted bread taste so wonderful."

Hieronymus isn't talking. I catch him staring at me a few times.

"Thank you! It's wonderful!" Zan says, well into his second bowl. How he stays so thin at the ankles and wrists with his appetite is a mystery. Just as he finishes his last spoonful, Hieronymus stands.

"It's time," he says.

I nod, and stand, too.

Alee looks at me and I can feel her trying to hide her worry.

Zan looks at me with pride.

For a second, I wonder which one is right.

We're very far up the trail before Hieronymus stops. There's a small boulder next to the path, and he sits, gesturing for me to do the same.

"So," he says, but then stops.

185

So I repeat back to him.

"I'm sure you're wondering what the final test will be," he says.

"It involves the door, the one I saw on the day I arrived, right?" I ask.

He nods. "The door is locked," he says. "The final test is that you will have to pick the lock."

"But I don't know how to pick a lock," I say, looking at my hands.

"Do you remember how I told you that there are some people in the the galaxy who have learned to marry technology with telepathy?"

"Yes."

"That kind of technology is incredibly rare. Leftover from races long gone from here. They are relics, some of which are very dangerous because we don't understand them." He waits for a moment, then says, "This door has that kind of lock on it."

"How dangerous?" I ask.

His mouth forms a straight line. "It's a technology that we barely understand."

"I saw you shake your head when your wife asked about Taren."

Again, Hieronymus goes dark inside. I feel it.

"It wasn't just that he failed the test, was it?"

He shakes his head.

He puts his hand on my shoulder.

"You're ready."

"Was he?"

"As ready as he was ever going to get," Hieronymus says. "More training wouldn't have helped him."

"What will happen to me if I don't make it?"

He doesn't say anything for a minute. Then he sighs and says, "Not everyone who tries and fails dies."

"But most do?" I ask.

He doesn't say anything. He stands. "Let's go," he says.

186

We round the bend and there it is. The small pathway that leads off to the cave with the almost perfectly smooth entrance. We both stop.

"Here we are," he says. I nod.

We both stand there saying nothing for a moment.

I nod and walk into the cave.

The temperature changes instantly when I step inside the mouth of the cave. The level of light, too. I wait for a minute to see if my eyes will adjust to the darkness.

They don't.

I step forward anyway.

The floor of the cave has a slight downward angle to it. I keep feeling like I'm going to fall over but I don't.

It grows colder with every step. I imagine that I can see my breath.

After what I feel is a very long time, I stop. I should have reached whatever it is I'm supposed to reach by now. I turn in a circle, wondering if I can see the mouth of the cave behind me. I can't, and I have to stop myself from panicking.

I'm completely alone in the dark.

I stick out my arms as wide as they'll go, thinking that I might touch the walls or outgrowths from the ceiling or *something*.

There is nothing there.

If it weren't for the feeling of something beneath my feet, I could be floating.

Then, in the darkness, I feel something nearby.

It is huge, and somehow, I can tell it hasn't noticed me yet.

The way a night swimmer might feel a whale nearby.

"Hello?" I call out.

I expect that there will be an echo, but there isn't.

Whatever it is out there in the dark does not respond.

I feel it turning lazy figure eights in the vast gloom, content in itself.

"Hello?!" I yell louder.

Still, nothing.

A part of me already knows what I need to do, and what will happen when I do it, but I'm afraid. I think about Taren and the other boys who must have come through here. I wonder how far they made it.

Am I already at this very moment standing in the bones of some other kid who tried?

I want to turn and run. I want to curl into myself and give up. But then I think of Hieronymus. I think of how losing yet another boy to this test will hurt him.

I have to try.

Hello? I call out with my mind.

The thing in the dark stops. Not all at once, but slow, turning its bulk to face me. I feel it drift in my direction, the space all around me being taken up with its enormousness. I feel as if I should duck or find a rock to hide behind.

In my mind, I hear it respond wordlessly. It isn't shouting, but just by virtue of its giganticness, the voice feels as though it booms through me, vibrating the bones in my skull, though no sound was made.

Hello, I say, this time as a greeting not a question.

There is a shift out there in the dimness and the vast shape shrinks to become something closer to my size. It no longer soaks up all the space around it.

Hello, it says in return.

I can feel it circling me. Though smaller, it still radiates far more power than I generate. I can feel its curiosity moving around and through me.

Where do you come from? it asks. *I haven't met one like you before.*

I honestly don't know, I say. I wonder if it can take in pictures and understand them, so I give it what I can remember—a flash of a glass tube filled with backlit clear fluid, the feeling of panic, fire, then waking on the ship.

I feel it take in the information and consider what it has seen in the long pause that follows.

Why have you come? it asks.

I am about to say that I have come to open a lock, but then I think that if this is a lock in and of itself, it might not respond very well to the idea of being picked. By virtue of its nature, it would want to protect whatever is in here.

Before I can answer, it asks, *would you like to play a game?*

I would, I say.

The darkness goes away gradually enough that I don't have to blink.

Standing before me is a person with the same physical build as me and nearly identical clothes. However, when I try to look at its face, there is only a blur, and a strong urge in me to look away. Every time I try again to look at the face, my eyes shift away as if they aren't under my control.

Between us is a chessboard.

I found this in your mind, it says.

I step closer to the board.

Some part of me recognizes the game and remembers the basic rules.

I notice that he has already made a move.

Before I can stop myself, I make a countermove.

Over the space of what seems instant but also an eternity, we move and countermove again and again. It all happens so fast I can't recall which move leads to the next to the next. There is only the general sense that he is more defensive than an attacker. He seeks to keep me from advancing further than the middle board. He is also better than me, and I lose piece after piece as my attacks smash against his defenses.

Unless I do something to change the game, I am going to lose.

I keep thinking to myself that there must be some weakness. There has to be some tiny corner he's forgotten, some slight movement that will suddenly open up a corridor to winning, but I can't see anything. His defense is thorough.

Worse, I can feel that he truly is having a good time. This is enjoyable for him. Not in a gloating way, but simply that he hasn't had company in a long while.

Not since Taren.

Unintentionally, I flash on a picture of Taren.

In that instant, I feel some part of the other's self flinch as if cut.

While I make the next move, I also picture Taren again. Again, some distant part of the other player winces as if pinched.

For that split second, there is sorrow.

It makes the next move and before I countermove, something occurs to me.

It must be sad to be here alone so long, I say. I try to make the tone casual.

Without pausing the game, it responds, *I am sufficient.*

However, off in that distant part of itself that isn't here as a boy, I feel a reaction, a sadness seeps through.

I don't have many pieces left. This game is almost over.

Still, it's nice to have a game with someone, isn't it?

It is, he agrees. I notice that there was a pause before the next move.

Five pieces left.

Before I make my next move, I say, *it would be nice if the game could go on forever, wouldn't it?*

But then it wouldn't be a game, it responds.

I make my next move and then it easily sweeps that piece aside.

Four left.

Then, a tiny sliver of a thought drifts across my mind.

Could it work?

But it could be, I say. I put my finger on the next piece, but don't move it. *We could agree on new rules, ones that we like. If we agreed, pieces could come back after a certain amount of time, maybe. Or something like that,* I say.

I feel it considering my proposal. In that same stretch of time, I'm wondering how I might be able to pull off the small glimmer of an idea that is forming in the very back of my thoughts.

Create our own rules? it asks.

Yes, I respond. I know that I can't beat it. But can I play in such a way that I keep it from winning long enough to allow pieces to come back if we agree to that as a new rule? Can I play to keep it at stalemate?

With it tied up in the game, could I in some way sneak past it?

I make the next move. It easily bats aside my advance.

Three pieces left.

It's an interesting idea, it responds. It doesn't make a move. *You would agree to stay and play until the game with this special rule in place ended?* I sense something behind its question, as if it's asking two things at once.

Still unsure how to do what I'm thinking of doing, I say, *I would.*

I make my next move.

Then I nearly fall over when, instead of taking the piece, which it could easily do, instead it makes almost the exact same move on its side of the board. As if there were a mirror there.

Then it hits me: a mirror.

I have to work very hard to hide my sudden excitement.

A mirror!

Very well, it says. *I consent to the new rule.*

I picture a large mirror in the darkness behind me. I step backward through it.

It feels as if something is being ripped out of my chest and my head at the same time. The pain is excruciating, but only for a second.

Then I am standing in a fairly dim cave. There isn't much, but there *is* light. I collapse to my knees and gasp. Even though it is just the memory of pain, it feels as though something huge has been taken from me.

"No," Hieronymus says from behind. "Not huge, but enough."

He puts his hand on my shoulder, and the other one under my elbow, and helps me to stand.

"Did…did I do it? Did I beat the lock?" I ask.

He nods, and I feel pride and happiness stream from him.

He helps me to lean against the wall of the cave. It is so nice to be warm, and to see, that I don't even care about the damp slime on the rocks.

"Give yourself a second."

Looking back, I see that we're not more than twenty meters inside the cave. I can clearly see the mouth of it from here.

"The darkness is part of the effect of the…the lock," he says. He sits down on an outcropping. "The only way anyone has ever found to defeat the lock is to give something of their self to it."

"You did it, didn't you?" I ask.

He nods. "Since the moment I figured it out, you're the only other person to beat it."

"You mean…all the other boys who…"

He nods. I feel the weight of it on his mind.

"If you don't mind telling me…" he says.

"It wanted to play a game. I figured out that it was lonely. So, I figured out a way to leave a part of me there to play the game with it forever, or at least a very, very long time. I made a mirror. One that would never try to win but only ever play to stalemate."

He nods.

In that moment, I could feel a part of myself was gone.

2.1.14

"So," he says, standing, "time to show you what you came here to see."

I stand and follow him deeper into the cave.

We reach a metal wall. After what I've been through, the keypad that he punches a few numbers into seems quaint. I can't help but give a scoffing laugh.

A door in the wall opens and he gestures for me to step through.

On the other side is a large hangar bay, the lights flickering to life.

In the center of it is a ship.

It is low-slung and its profile is mean. Everything about it screams aggression, even its black and gray paint which seems to eat up the light.

Across the midsection and part of one wing is a tarp that I can tell used to cover the whole thing but has moved over time.

At the back of the cave there is a vertical shaft that opens onto the sky. The rain that has come in for centuries has made a shallow pool.

He walks to it and rests his hand against it for a moment.

He looks at me.

"The technical term is 'two-seat tactical interceptor' but we always just called them 'headhunters.'"

I can see that, even though the tarp has enough dirt on it you could plant a garden, underneath the ship gleams. It's been lovingly cared for.

"But...you could leave any time you wanted," I say, gesturing toward the ship. "You don't have to wait for supply ships or whoever to come here."

"Oh, yes," he nods. "Any time."

"So, then why stay? Why choose to spend all this time away from the rest of the universe?"

He runs his hand along the lines of the fighter. "Because I've done horrible things. Truly terrible things." He pats the wing as though comforting a resting pet. "Things there is no coming back from. Only," he says, finally turning to me. "I hope that there is."

"I don't understand," I say.

He nods.

I walk up to the ship and put my hand on its long, sleek nose just ask he did.

I can almost feel the anger vibrating off of it. It is a bird that wants to kill. In my head, I can hear the scream of the engines.

I take my hand off.

"So that's the question," he says, leaning back. "Is a life lived trying to help others, to help them through the difficult parts of what the universe has thrown at them…is that enough to undo my own mistakes."

"Do you think it is?" I respond after long silence.

"I don't know, yet," he whispers. "I don't know. But I know that I want to try," he says. "When I came here, almost two decades ago…when I parked this ship in this little cave and locked it, I wanted to leave everything from out there," he says, gesturing toward the roof of the hangar, "behind."

"Do you feel like you haven't?" I ask.

"I did, for a long time. I found these incredible people and learned peace of mind from them. Then I found Alee, and I didn't have to struggle for that peace of mind, it was just…there," he says.

He leans into the cockpit and flips a few switches, then there is crackling sound. Then there is a beep and I hear Sweet Caroline's voice. "Go ahead."

"Tell her he's ready."

"Okay," Sweet Caroline says. "When?"

"Come now."

"Roger that," Sweet Caroline says, then, "Out." The crackling goes away. Hieronymus flips a few more switches.

"So, they're coming now?" I ask.

He nods. "It'll take a few days, most likely. I doubt they were very close. Come on, let's go back to the house. We'll make a special meal. You can have Zan over."

After the huge meal that Hieronymus and Alee cook, and after a long night of Zan and I touching and kissing and holding one another, eventually he and I are just left staring at the ceiling.

"I made you something," Zan says. He gets up out of the bed and rummages in his pants pockets for a moment. When he comes back, he hands me a small carving.

"It's a bird," I say.

"A Valka bird," he says. "You mentioned how you saw one at Ezeda Urul when you learned to swim."

Something in me melts in that moment. To have remembered such a small thing that I mentioned so long ago. I hold it up into the moonlight. It's perfect.

"They hover over the temple toward sunset, coasting on the updrafts. I like to look at them, too," Zan says. "Maybe," he goes on, his voice going softer, "when you're away out there, you'll look at it and remember that we might have once looked up at the same time and saw the same bird."

We fall back into one another, kissing and holding and touching long into the night.

Zan is gone in the morning when I wake.

Goodbyes are just too hard, so you'll just have to come back to me his note reads. The little bird sits on the windowsill where he left it as I get dressed.

As I open the bedroom door, Hieronymus is standing there just about to knock. In his hand is a watch that is pulsing red.

"They're here, aren't they?" I ask.

He nods. "I have no idea what they must have done to get here so quickly. You'll need to get packed."

Neither of us say much as I gather my things.

"Where is Alee?"

"Another village trip. She's not very good at goodbyes."

"You didn't go with her?" I ask.

"No," he says.

As we walk to the front door, all of this feeling too rushed, the tension growing with each moment, I notice another bag near the door.

Hieronymus picks it up.

"Are you going somewhere?" I ask.

"Yes," he says. "But first, here," he says. He hands me the little wooden music box.

"No," I say. "I couldn't—,"

"Take it," he says.

I take the box and put it in my pocket next to the bird carving.

"You're coming with us?" I ask.

He nods. I want to ask why and a million other questions, but he opens the door and starts walking at a brisk pace. Again, everything seems to be so rushed.

I close the door to the house behind us and hurry to catch up.

We see the fire of the ship entering the atmosphere before we make it back to the same place where I was dropped off so long ago. I think back, counting the days, the weeks, and that was almost a year and a half ago.

Hieronymus doesn't say anything, and his entire demeanor has changed. It's like I'm walking next to a complete stranger.

Once we make it to the landing field, the ship is already here, the ramp already down. The Captain stands at the bottom of the ramp.

"Akari," The Captain calls. "It's time." Her face reveals nothing.

I can see Eli at the top of the ramp, though, holding Milo.

Hieronymus walks past her and up the ramp without saying anything.
As I reach the bottom of the ramp, The Captain turns and walks up.
Never forget, I hear, *you ARE ready* Hieronymus sends.
I wait a moment longer, then turn and go up the ramp, myself.

Part 2: The Run

2.2.1

After we lift off, I notice that everyone is just staring at me, but no one will talk. I'm sitting in the galley alone when Eli walks in. I was wondering if he was going to come see me.

He sits down with a bit of space between us.

"Are you mad?" he asks.

"At what?" I ask in return.

"At me," he says without looking at me.

"No," I say.

His eyes meet mine. "Really?" he asks.

"Yeah."

He smiles. "Good," he says. "'Cuz I didn't want to. The Captain said we had to, and…"

I smile back at him. "It's okay."

Milo wanders in, comes about halfway to me, stretches, then starts grooming himself.

"Did you learn lots of cool stuff?" Eli asks.

"Yeah," I say and nod.

"I thought so," Eli says, "because you seem different."

"Different how?" I ask.

"More grown up, but not just the way time makes everyone more grown up. Grown up like more calm."

I nod at that. He stands and goes to one of the lockers along the wall. He comes back with a package.

"Here," he says.

"What's this?" I ask as I take it from him.

"It's a tart that you can have for breakfast. You can eat them cold or warm them up," he says. "This one is strawberry, my favorite flavor."

I open it and, finding two tarts inside, I give him one. He smiles, takes it, and bites into it almost immediately.

"I really like to eat them when it's early and I can't sleep."

Just then Hieronymus comes in. He goes directly to the counter and pours coffee into a mug. He takes two large drinks before he even looks over at us. Milo notices him, turns, and leaves the galley.

I can tell from his expression that something is wrong. Slowly, though, his face smooths itself. He doesn't sit, though.

"Okay," Eli says, "I should get back to minding the reactors. The Captain has us burning so hot they could go nutzo on us."

"I'll catch up with you later," I say.

Eli walks out.

"Can't sleep?" I ask Hieronymus.

He nods, then finishes the coffee with one gulp. He sets the mug down on the counter and walks over to where I am.

"So," he says as he sits down next to me, "it's time for you to find out what you've been working toward this whole time." He removes a pad from his jacket. When it lights up, on the screen is a long cylinder made of some dark material that somehow glitters at the same time. It's as if it is trying to hide but also trying to shine, as well.

"What's that?" I ask.

"This is the goal," he says. "Something that the Enzenites discovered a long time ago and tried to keep hidden from the rest of the galaxy." He presses the button on the bottom of the screen and the object begins to rotate. At the same time, dimensions and measurements are listed. My eyes go wide—it's enormous.

"It's enormous!" I say.

He nods. "Over a mile long, half a mile wide. That surface is a material that has never been found anywhere else in the galaxy. Can't blast it open, can't melt it, can't liquify it…it is indestructible."

"So, what is it?" I ask again.

"The Enzenites believe that it is a weapon of almost unlimited destructive power. A weapon maybe even capable of destroying an entire planet in one shot," Hieronymus says. His eyes never leave the screen.

A chill runs down my spine.

"No," I say. "That's…something like that isn't…"

"It *is* possible," he says, then turns to face me. "And The Captain wants it. Or, to be more precise, she want to get it so she can make sure no one else has it."

I don't say anything. The look in her eyes makes me freeze.

"And you're going to help me get it," he says.

"I don't understand," I say.

He presses another button on the pad and a list of information appears. I can't bring my eyes to focus on it.

"There have been three different crews that have tried with varying degrees of success to penetrate the device, to gain control of it." He shakes his head one time decisively. "None have succeeded."

"Then how could I…?"

"The best information that money can buy says that there are a series of…of locks, you might call them…that someone has to pass in order to gain entry, and only a single person is allowed to attempt them at any given time. Meaning that the person who tries to go in has to be able to do all of them by themselves," he says. "They say that the weapon itself scrambles any nearby communication, as well, meaning that the person who makes the attempt cannot get any help from the outside." He shakes his head, again. "Alone."

"But, again, I am not…"

"The information says that some of the…the locks…are telepathic, in some way. That only a trained telepath can work them."

"But, I mean…there has to be a more powerful telepath out there somewhere…"

"The information also says that, for some reason only the designers of this thing know, the telepath who attempts entry must be male," he says, then walks away.

The look in his eye is what I imagine a mouse feels when it sees the eagle's eyes at the last second before the talons tear into him. It is so different from the way I'm used to seeing him that for a moment I feel alone in a huge universe.

I still can't sleep. After trying for a few hours, I get up and walk. Ship's time morning is almost on us, anyway.

I find Salvadore sitting alone on the flight deck. One the main screen, he has the same schematics that Hieronymus was showing me cycling. I walk to the front of the room and stare out at them, too.

"Someone explain it all to you?" Salvadore asks.

I try to hide my shock that he has spoken to me, but I can't. For so long, he was the gun to my head. I'm not even sure how I feel about it.

He's the one who put the band on my head.

I nod. Then I realize that he's sitting at an angle where he couldn't see me nod, and I say, "Yes."

"For what it's worth, I'm sorry."

I once heard Eli say that you could knock him over with a feather after something shocked him so much, he could barely speak.

That's where I'm at.

He sighs. "You're a kid. Kids shouldn't have to…" he trails off.

I nod, again.

"The information we have cost us a lot," Salvadore says. "*A lot.* So you'll be going in with the best intelligence that money can buy."

I can tell he thinks that will make me feel better.

"All the reports are that this is a very bad thing to have lying around. You'll be helping us get it away from other people who might actually do

204

something with it."

Like me, I think.

"What do *you* think it is?" I ask.

Salvadore says, "A planet-cracking device. Doomsday. My people, we called the idea of a weapon like this a worldburner. The reason is fairly obvious. We never made one, though." He cocks his head to the side. "I've been all over this galaxy and I've never seen anything like it. I suppose that's encouraging, in a way."

"Why would someone ever make something like this?" I ask.

"That's...that's a very good question," he says. "I guess the idea in some minds is that it matters who dies last. That..." he sighs one of his huge sighs, "that somewhere, someone is keeping a running tally, and that they'll clap the one on the back who killed the most enemies."

I turn to him. "Do you think that?"

He blinks. "I did. At one time. I can remember a time, when I was young, I was so angry that I wanted something like that. For the entire world to burn. To have the satisfaction of watching, alone, from orbit, as every living thing on the planet and then the planet itself was destroyed. There were nights when a thought like that brought me a lot of comfort." He shifts a bit in his seat. "Like so many young people, I believed whatever I was told to believe. Very often, that involves thinking of an us and a them, and hating the them as a way of making the us better, somehow."

"But you don't anymore?" I ask.

"No," he says. "Vengeance is a comforting thought to those who feed only on anger." I can see the panel prompt him with a question and he presses a few buttons in response. "It's taken a long time, but I've turned away from that path."

I turn back to the screen. The worldburner rotates there. For a second, my eyes blur, and it and my reflection are the same thing. When I turn back to him, I feel his eyes on my neck.

"Would you have? Killed me?" I ask.

He looks at me for a long moment. Then nods. "If the captain had ordered it, yes. Without hesitation."

"And now?" I ask.

He's goes quiet. After a too long a moment of silence, I leave the flight deck.

I'm playing with Milo in the bunk they've assigned me the next day when Sweet Caroline comes over the com saying, "We're here."

I reach up under the pillow and put the bird carving in my pocket, then head toward the flight deck.

I nearly run in to Eli.

"I'm excited," he says.

Hieronymus joins us. *Ready?* he sends.

I think so I send back.

When we walk on to the flight deck, everyone else is already gathered there, including The Captain. The tactical screen is put away, and we're all gathered at the front window.

Out there, in the darkness, is the same huge cylinder that I saw in the simulation on The Captain's desk. However, seeing it, really seeing it, changes everything.

Pitted and scarred, the light of the distant stars reflected off of it, the massive hulk exudes menace at us. I almost have to look away from it. It's truly massive, and I fear that at any moment it will open up and swallow our ship whole. Not just swallow, but somehow make it so that we never existed at all. No memories would remain of this ship or anyone on it.

"There," The Captain says without turning around to face us. "That's the goal. That, ladies and gentlemen, is our target."

I try to pretend that everyone is not looking at me out of the sides of their eyes.

All I want to do is run away from it.

I look up at Hieronymus and even with just a cursory feel at the edges of his thoughts, I can tell he feels the same.

"It's time," The Captain says to Hieronymus as she turns and passes him, leaving the flight deck.

"Okay," he says. *Come with me* he sends, and I follow him. It's hard, though, to take my eyes away from the object. I feel as if it's watching me as I turn my back on it and leave.

"Okay," Hieronymus says, gesturing for me to sit down at the table in the galley.

I sit.

He looks at me for a second, sighs, then sits down, too.

"Time for us to talk," he says. "That thing out there is the biggest bomb in the universe. It could crack a planet in half easily. There are tales of there having been more than one of them, once. As far as anyone can tell, though, now this is the only one left."

"You said," I say to him.

"I told you that once we got to the place, I'd let you know what your part in all of this was going to be," he says. Then he stops and just looks at me.

"Am I supposed to guess?" I ask.

He grins, but it disappears fast.

"No," he says. "It's just...it's a lot. And you're just a kid. Or, at least, you appear to be just a kid when people...some people...look at you."

"You?" I ask.

He nods. "Even after all the training, after all the time we've been together, when I look at you, I still just see a kid. It makes this next part hard."

"Okay," I say because I don't know how I'm supposed to respond to that.

"Akari, you are the only person that we've ever found who I think can disarm it."

"I don't know how to disarm a bomb," I say and sit up straighter.

"We're going to help you," he says.

"Will you, though?" I ask.

"What do you mean?"

"You've changed. It's like…it's like the second I passed that last test, the second you stepped onto this ship, you've become someone else."

"I know," he says, "and I'm sorry. It's because…the second you passed that test, I knew that this moment was going to come. What that was going to mean for you."

"Why me?" I ask, my heart racing.

"The people who built it, they had…fearsome technology. It combines physical as well as telepathic locks, somehow."

"Have you been there? How do you know?" I ask.

He nods. "I know because, as far as I can tell, I was the last person there." He waits a moment. "I didn't succeed in…disarming it…but you're stronger than me, and you will."

"Disarm it," I repeat.

He nods. "Disarm it. It's a tremendously dangerous object, and someone has to."

"But why me?"

"Like I said, the technology combines both physical *and* telepathic locks."

"But why me? What not Taren or one of the others?" I ask.

"Because none of them had the raw power," Hieronymus says. "Do you remember when you asked me what had happened to that earlier student—the one who died?"

"Yes," I say.

"It *was* my fault that he passed away. But it didn't happen back on Gros Morne. It happened here. Right where you're standing."

The danger I felt amplified. I stopped moving and my breath went shallow.

"It was our first attempt. We didn't know…well, there were a lot of things we didn't know. One of them was just how powerful the device really is," Hieronymus says. "Just like we talked about, there are locks. Safety devices built into the system. The very first lock is that someone has to be a male telepath, because of how rare that is. The second lock is that they have to be over a certain amount of power just to access the system without being burnt out."

"And…and he wasn't?"

The pause grows into a gulf between him and I. "No," he says finally. "He wasn't."

"And you think that I am?"

"Akari, no matter how you came to be, no matter who you might feel you are or aren't, there is one thing about you that you need to acknowledge," Hieronymus says. "You are the single most powerful telepath I have ever encountered. The Captain thought that might be the case after you downed that police cruiser. All our time together proved it." He pauses and we stare at each other for a moment. "By making a system with these requirements, they thought they were making it inaccessible to anyone but themselves. The truth is, though, that they were making it tailored to you, like a glove. They just didn't know that, yet."

"Me," I say, "and whoever built it."

"Yes," he says. "It means there would have to be at least one other person out there who was…like you. If they're still alive."

"If they're still alive," I say under my breath at the same time he does.

"So," Hieronymus says, but doesn't finish his thought.

"Yeah," I say. "So. Your…your student? Was he the one you got the…"

"The person who made it the farthest? No. *That* attempt was nearly a hundred years ago. My former student didn't…he didn't make it nearly that far."

"How long ago?"

Hieronymus looks up at the ceiling for a moment, then back at me. "About twenty-five years ago."

I do some quick math. "About the time you and The Captain stopped talking and you moved to Gros Morne?"

He nods. Pieces of the puzzle click together.

"And you think…you think I'm going to…"

"Do better than either of them? Yes, I do."

"Why?"

The intercom on the wall beeps. "Hieronymus," The Captain's voice says.

He waits a moment, looking at me. Then he gets up, walks to the wall, and taps the button. "Go ahead."

"Would you and the boy join me in my office."

"On our way," he says, then gestures with his head for me to follow him.

Neither of us says anything as we walk down the hallway and then head up the two flights of ladders. I can tell we're nearly at the top of the ship. Hieronymus stops in front of a door that says "Captain" on it. He raps on it with his knuckle.

"Enter," The Captain says from inside. The door slides aside and we walk into a cramped room. On the far end is a desk where The Captain sits. Just behind her is a large bubble window.

Out that window is the object. At this distance, from this angle, it just looks like another ship. Still, the hairs on the back of my neck stand up.

The door slides closed behind us.

"Have you told him about the run?" she asks.

Hieronymus nods. She looks at me. "And?"

"I am sure that he understands," Hieronymus says.

Her eyes never leave mine.

"So, will you do it?" she asks.

I feel a bit uneasy for a moment.

I didn't now that I had a choice.

"If…umm…" I start, but the words won't come.

"Go on," she says. I know she means it to be comforting, but it just makes me feel even more like crawling into a hole somewhere.

"I was just wondering…you know…" I hate how I'm stumbling but I can't stop. "What if I were to…maybe…to say no?"

Her eyes become even more cold, even more hard. I didn't now that was

210

possible.

"Is that what you're going to say?"

With each passing second it seems less like I have any kind of choice.

"You're a weapon, Akari, and we are asking you to turn that around. To be more than that."

"I don't understand," I say.

She looks over at Hieronymus. For a second, I wonder if they are talking, having a completely separate conversation without me while I'm in the room.

It's in that moment that I realize I *don't* have a choice, and that I never did.

"You are a creature manufactured by a very dark minded scientist to be the greatest male telepath that the galaxy has ever known. That they planned on making more just like you the instant that they were sure that their experiment had worked. A little army of incredibly powerful telepaths with which they could do just about anything they wanted. Topple world governments. Assassinate leaders from great distances. They had it all mapped out," Hieronymus says.

"Wait, what?" I ask.

"You said you explained," she says to Hieronymus.

"I did," he says. In that moment, I see that even he is intimidated by her. "But there were some parts of it that I thought…"

"What is she talking about?" I ask him.

"Oh, Akari," Hieronymus says. "I spent almost a year with you, rooting around in that head of yours. Do you think that at some point, I didn't find all of this out?"

Shock hit me.

"I knew three days after I met you. I wouldn't be a very good telepath if I didn't."

"But…"

He looks at her. She nods, and I see his eyes grow distant.

He sighs. "Okay," he says. "The whole thing. Kay," he says and then thinking for a moment says, "The Captain and I knew it before she and her crew ever entered the system, in fact. You were the reason they were there. She didn't tell her crew anything, though, in case they got caught. And they nearly did," he says. The Captain nods. Both of them looking at me.

"That's when the accident happened. That patrol ship showed up out of nowhere and in the fight, we wound up destroying an awful lot of the facilities on the surface," The Captain says. "What we're pretty sure happened is that stray fire hit the building you were being kept in, damaging the life support and the power supply. Somehow this woke you up," she says. "The shock of waking up and the panic of being in a tiny tube filled with liquid so you couldn't breathe, or at least thought you couldn't…you panicked, as best we can tell. And when you panicked, you reached out to the nearest scientist, mentally. Somehow, you copied a huge amount of his memory into your own head. It must have happened very quickly, too, because the video that we recovered show him coming over to the tube you were in, going limp, and collapsing all with in the space of about thirty seconds."

"That's that head of yours," Hieronymus says. "Always big swings."

"I…killed him?" I ask.

"The shock killed him," The Captain says, "you did it out of reflex. But…" she says.

"You were afraid I might accidentally do it again," I say.

She nods.

"You see?" Hieronymus says. "I told you Kay didn't hate you. That it was far more complex than that."

"I treated you with all of the caution I would an unexploded bomb, because that's what you were," she says.

"We're pretty sure that Akari was that scientist's name."

"Then do I…?" I ask.

"That's the level of horrible these awful people were. They didn't even bother to give you a name. Maybe they would have, eventually, but nowhere in the data we got initially nor anything later in the ruins suggests that they

212

were headed that way," Hieronymus says. "They were likely just going to assign numbers. That's usually how assholes like that think."

I sit down.

It was as if the last puzzle piece was put into place. Everything became so clear, now.

"We decided to get to you first; to take what they had made and use it for a better purpose," Hieronymus says, kneeling down in front of me.

"The...thing," I say, gesturing vaguely in the direction of the screen and the mass destruction weapon on it.

"Yes," The Captain says.

There is quiet for a moment.

"But you were going to let me go with Nyssa and Ardra?" I ask.

The Captain looks away for a second, then back. "I...hesitated...for a moment."

I feel frustration from Hieronymus.

"Why didn't you, then?" I ask.

"The attempt on their lives made an...impression...on me. I knew that there was the possibility that if you went with them, you might wind up just as dead as they were. Or worse, captured by some stupid ridiculous backwater dirtworld government and used in their petty little war for land or water or whatever. I...couldn't let that happen," she says. "I came to my senses."

We might all be in the same room, but in that moment none of us were thinking about each other.

Hieronymus grows even more frustrated. That's when it dawns on me. He didn't know that part until very recently. I look from him to her. She had deviated from their plan, even if only for a moment, and he was still upset about it.

His quiet meant that things were fully back on track.

"What we're asking you to do is more important," he says.

"Will you do it?" she asks. "Will you make the run?"

213

"Do I actually have a choice?" I ask in return.

"Yes," Hieronymus says. "There is always choice."

2.2.2

"Okay," Hieronymus says, "let's go over it again."

I sigh. This will be the fifth time.

"There are eight ordeals you must go through in order to access the device," The Captain says.

"How do we know that?" I ask again.

"We have very...reliable...information from the last person to ever try."

I let the sink in for a minute.

"At least, the last person *we know* ever tried," Hieronymus says.

"The ordeals function like locks. The person attempting to gain access to the device must pass them before they will be granted entrance," The Captain says.

"Before you even start, it will tell you that," Hieronymus says.

"The eight ordeals are separated into four physical tests or tasks—," The Captain starts.

"—and four telepathic or empathic tests," Hieronymus finishes. Then they both stare at me for a second.

"Okay," I say, not knowing what else to do. I already know all this.

"That's what you've been training for," Hieronymus says.

"Oh," I say.

"That's the thing," Hieronymus says. "Only half of the...the locks...are physical."

"What?" I ask.

"That's why this particular weapon is so difficult to disarm. The AI that holds the whole system together is...partially biological. And that biological part is telepathic."

It hits me: "so only a telepath can disarm the weapon."

Hieronymus nods. "It's designed that way. What's more, it's designed to be even more impossible to break…the telepath attempting to crack the other half of the locks must be male."

"How would it know something like that?" I ask.

"I have no idea. It just…does," Hieronymus says. "So, since only something like one percent of all telepaths are male, and the particular male telepath attempting to crack this thing open also has to get through the physical tasks…"

"And you think that could be me?"

Hieronymus nods.

"How do you know all this?" I ask.

"Huh?" he asks without looking.

"How do you know all of this. I'm assuming there isn't just some manual lying around that says, 'here's how to crack this thing.' So…?"

He stops what he's doing and looks over at me.

"Because you already tried," I say.

He nods, looks away, then looks back at me. He takes a huge breath in then out. "One of the…mental…locks…has to do with power. Not logic or cunning or…just sheer power. And I…"

I nod.

"In fact, no one else that I've met in the time since I started training telepaths."

"Is this why you started?" I say, gesturing toward the thing.

"No," he says. "No. I started for the exact reason that I told you—to teach peaceful use of power in order to reduce the number of us that were being used as weapons. But I'd be lying if I said that I wasn't also looking for others who might have the ability, the raw strength that I knew it would take since the moment that Kay approached me with the information she'd gotten."

"So, when she tells you that she's not only found me, but that I'm in her…custody…"

He nods but says nothing.

"But she almost let me go with someone else," I say.

"Last minute guilt, she told me. You have to remember that you appear to be a kid to us. In that skull of yours, you have the memories of a full-grown man whenever you want to access them. You also have the power of…I don't even know what. Any comparison I could make would fall flat. But to just look at you, you're a kid. She said she hoped for a minute that maybe the universe would let you have a normal life. So, she was going to let you off with the royals, there. She said at least that way, she'd know where you were. Maybe we'd pick you up later."

"But then…"

"Yeah," Hieronymus says. "Then that bounty hunter showed up and things worked out the way they did."

"The universe doesn't want me to have a normal life," I say.

"I don't know," he says. "All I know is that whatever the plan was in that moment she tried to let you go, it didn't work out, and now you're here."

I sigh. "Now I'm here." He nods.

I close my eyes and step backward out of the airlock.

My brain reaches for something to compare it to, but there is nothing. I have never experienced anything even remotely similar to zero gravity. Especially not like this—hanging outside the hull of a ship, unprotected. The only sound is the sound of my own breathing. Without telling myself to, I wrap my hand around the long umbilical rope leading back to the airlock.

"Okay, Akari," Hieronymus' voice comes over the com in my earplug. "What I want you to do is to turn yourself around very slowly so that you are facing the object."

I breathe in and count to ten in my head to calm myself. Then I twist at the waist the way The Captain told me to. Slowly. Carefully.

I start to spin too far the other way, so I have to stop myself by spinning a bit at the waist again.

I immediately close my eyes because, without our ship taking up most of my visual field after I turn, I'm now looking at mostly empty blackness. It disorients me so much that I can feel the tickling in my stomach that means I'm seconds from throwing up.

With my eyes closed, I take a big breath in and count backwards from ten.

"Okay, Akari," Hieronymus says, "I can see you've turned in the right direction. That's good. How are you doing?"

"You can see my vitals," I say without opening my eyes.

"Yeah, I can. But I want you to talk to me. And out loud," he says, knowing that I might switch to telepathy if my physical body stays too unsteady. "It'll help keep you calm and grounded."

"Okay," I say.

"Okay. Just like we practiced, I want you to use the pad on your wrist to program your visor display so that it will detect the object."

I press the sequence of buttons that we practiced, and the blackness comes alive with the greenish-blue hulking tube that is the whole reason we've come out here. It's another jolt to my system because I felt so tiny and overwhelmed in the huge gulf of blackness that I saw. Now I feel almost crowded because of how close it was the whole time.

It's enormous.

That something that huge could have been sitting this close to me the whole time without me knowing it shakes me.

"Oh," I can't stop myself from saying out loud.

"Got it?" Hieronymus asks.

"Got it," I say and work to get my breathing under control.

When you're sitting at a table, comfortable and safe, and someone says that something is miles long, and miles in circumference, you say to yourself, "I understand what that means." It is quite another thing to be faced with the reality of such a behemoth.

"Okay, so reach into the hip pocket and pull out the line thrower. Remember that the magnetic anchor is in the other hip pocket."

I reach into my right hip pocket and pull out the bulky gun, then into my left hip pocket and pull out the box that, when I press the button on top, expands into a four-pronged claw as large as my chest. I slide the tube that comes out of the top of the claw into the barrel of the gun and feel the click just as when we'd practiced.

"Anchor attached," I say.

"Good," Hieronymus says. "Now you have to unhook yourself from the line that attaches you to the ship. The most important part is to not panic. You're not too far away; if something happens after you're untethered, we can still come get you."

I know he can't see me, but I nod, and unhook the line from the clip on my belt.

Even thought he just said everything would be fine, a part of my brain now knows that I am not attached to anything.

I'm floating free in open space.

"Alright, now you've got to get over to the surface of the object. Just aim for the object and pull the trigger, remembering to hold on tight. There won't be any count down or anything—it'll just start pulling the second you pull that trigger." I look from the gun to the surface of the object. "Just like I told you, when you get about two body lengths away from the surface, you need to let go of the trigger—your momentum will bring you to the surface. If you keep going at full speed, you'll hit the object too fast, and you might hurt yourself."

"Okay," I say.

I tell my finger to pull the trigger, but it won't obey.

I close my eyes and concentrate on my breathing.

I open my eyes, steady my hand and whisper, "okay."

Then, I pull the trigger.

The line doesn't do anything for a moment. I just see the puff of gas escape from the barrel and the line reeling away into the blackness. Then there is the tiniest of pulls on the gun. I flip the switch on the side like Hieronymus told me to, and then pull the trigger again.

I barely have time to get my other hand around the handle as I'm yanked toward the object. As big as it was in my view, it grows larger every second.

"Akari, get control of your breathing," Hieronymus says.

I try to but can't.

In my viewer, the object grows larger and larger. It now takes up my entire view. I'm starting to discern details—antennae, contours of the hull plating, windows.

I realize that I can't clearly figure how far I am from the surface because of just how massive the object is.

I'm going to have to guess when to stop pulling the trigger.

Then I remember that there is a distancing feature in my display. In order to activate it, though, I'm going to have to take one hand off the gun and tap a command into the pad on my wrist. I'm sure there is a voice command that would activate it, but I didn't bother to learn it.

Telling my hand to move off of the gun while moving at this speed, the object growing more enormous in my view every second, is incredibly hard. Worse, once I get it to release, and realize that I'm only tethered to anything at all by one hand; I have to then turn my arm a bit to get to the pad. This makes my whole body change positions, and I start to spin a bit.

I clench my teeth and press the contact that tells my viewer that I'd like a display of my distance from the nearest object.

Immediately I see that I'm much closer than I thought I was and moving far faster than I feared I was.

"Terrain. Slow. Terrain. Slow," the computer starts to repeat in my ear.

Five meters. Three meters. I let go of the trigger. The motor stops pulling, but my momentum doesn't stop.

"Pull up. Pull up," the computer hammers at me.

Two meters.

One.

I bend my knees like we practiced and suddenly I have stopped moving.

"Contact," the computer says.

Zero the range finder says.

I'm standing on the surface of the object.

"I'm down," I say.

Hieronymus' voice comes back with static, "Good job, kid!"

I think about The Captain sitting there, next to him, and wonder if she maybe smiles at all.

A metal forest of antennae of all sizes and shapes stretches off in every direction. I bend backward to look back at the ship. It seems to fly above me.

"Okay, kid, time to focus up," Hieronymus says. "From where you're standing, it's a few meters over to the hatchway. Can you see it, there, off your right?"

I can. The raised lip around the doorway into the object comes up to about my ankle so it sticks out from the tall, slender antennae all around me.

"Just like we practiced, you need to disengage the magnetic anchor, respool the line, then shoot it over at the hatchway and pull yourself over. Got it?"

I nod, then remember he can't see my nodding, and say, "Got it."

It takes a moment to remember the right commands to tap in to release the anchor, but I get it turned off, then the line winds back up into the gun. I fire it over at the raised lip around the hatchway and pull the trigger once more. This time the yank and then stop is much more violent because it's shorter.

I'm now looking down at the doorway into the object. There is writing on it, pitted, faded, and scratched nearly away. I know that I wouldn't be able to read it even if it were brand new, but still my brain tries to puzzle through it for a moment.

For some reason, chills run down my back.

Right next to the door, as Hieronymus told me it would be, is a small panel with six buttons and a tiny screen.

"Now, remember," his voice comes to me, the static increased, "the panel is a decoy. It's a trap that immediately separates out those who know what to do from those who don't. Don't fall for it."

I nod.

"Be polite," Hieronymus had said when telling me about this, the first of the traps. "Some of the snags…the traps…that these people designed into the machine are almost jokes. *Their* idea of humor, at any rate. This first one is an example of that." He sat down across the table from me and rapped his knuckles on the table three times. "In their culture, for instance, we've been able to piece together that politeness, at least their concept of politeness, was at a premium. So, if you were entering a building or a room, you had better know to knock first."

I pull myself closer until I'm resting my feet on the raised lip around the door. I have to reorient myself from thinking of this as down. Now, I have to make myself see this as forward. I glance at the panel, again, its buttons lit up so inviting even after all this time.

Against all logic, I make a fist and rap my knuckles on the door three times.

Nothing happens.

I think, this is crazy. Hieronymus has lost his mind, and this won't work.

I'm starting to turn myself around and grab for the anchor gun again when the door slides open.

"Enter," a voice I've not heard before says over my speakers.

"Door is open," I say.

"Great!" I hear Hieronymus say, but faint; almost completely drowned out by static.

I look inside. The airlock is wide, with lots of rounded corners to make it safe for space suits, and it's about three meters to the other door. I expected dust and cobwebs, but inside it is shiny and clean, as if new.

"Okay," I say to myself, and step through the hatchway. It's hard to turn around, leaving an unknown room behind me, but I do. As I'm searching for the handle or button to close the outer door, I see our ship in the distance.

Something in me feels like this will be the last time.

As I'm thinking this, the outer door closes. I'm startled, of course, not just because I didn't make the door close, but also because there are no lights in here.

"Welcome," the voice says over my speakers.

The clean white lights in the airlock come up. Outside my helmet, I can hear the hiss of the air being pumped in.

Over my speakers I hear the new voice say, "78 percent nitrogen, 21 percent oxygen, 0.9 percent argon. Trace amounts of carbon dioxide, methane, water vapor. Is this correct?"

"Um," I stumble, "Yes?"

"Please remain suited until the inner environment has been adjusted accordingly," the voice says. The hiss continues.

I turn to face the inner door of the airlock.

"Hieronymus?" I say over the coms.

There is no response.

A part of me knew this is what would happen. Still, it's a bit of a shock.

The hiss stops.

"Safe to remove your suit. Enter," the voice says, and the inner door opens.

I check my wrist pad the way Hieronymus told me to.

The green light that tells me if there is air or not is on like we hoped it would be.

I take off my helmet.

The air smells clean. For some reason, I expected dusty and hard to choke down, the way a little kid expects a haunted house to smell. Instead, there's a faint smell of chemicals, like just after a bathroom has been cleaned.

For a second, I wonder how I know that, but I stop myself.

I look up from my wrist panel.

The passageway beyond the inner door is, like the airlock, lit by an even, welcoming white light.

And floating just beyond the hatchway is a man in a spacesuit.

I would like to say that I handled it stoically. That I didn't scream.

But I did.

And, oddly enough, I then held my breath. I have no idea why.

The visor on his helmet is mirrored, so I can't see inside.

The body is turning a bit. Enough to make me think the person in there might be alive. But when I calm down enough to really look, I can see that the arms and legs aren't moving, the body is just rotating.

It must have been he movement of the air from the hallway into the airlock.

"Hieronymus?" I say again, hoping against hope that maybe, just maybe, he'll be able to hear me. To say something comforting.

The silence is still there.

Little by little, the body is not only rotating but moving into the airlock. Coming at me.

I squash myself flat against the wall. My lungs scream for air, reminding me that I haven't taken a breath in almost a full minute.

The body just happens to rotate enough that the visor of the helmet is looking right at me. My whole body shivers.

Hello? I send telepathically. There is no kind of response at all. No mind to link to in there.

I make myself grab the body's wrist, convinced the entire time that the second I do, the body will grab me back.

My relief when it doesn't is so overwhelming it feels like it makes a noise.

The wrist I've grabbed has a control pad similar to my own. The readout is dim, and in a language I don't recognize, but toward the bottom there is a graph that goes from green to yellow to red. There is a dim red light flashing all the way at the end of the graph.

No need to know the language, I think—that's a fairly universal idea. Either this person barely made it past the outer airlock and ran out of whatever it is they breathe, or they made it in and came back to this airlock trying to get out and ran out.

Either way, I'm going to have to squeeze past this person to go further in.

In the process of trying to get a better grip on the wrist to move the body out of the way, I manage to touch some control that makes the visor on the helmet go from mirrored to clear. Staring back at me is a skull.

Again, I yell.

Whoever this person was, they were the last to try what I'm attempting. And now they're just abandoned bones in a spacesuit.

I feel as though I should say something, some sort of prayer or apology or something. Nothing comes to mind, though.

I finally calm down enough to think about reaching out with my mind to talk to Hieronymus rather than relying on the radio.

Hieronymus I say, reaching out, waiting for the familiar feel of his mind.

There is nothing. The quiet is just as deep and unsettling as the quiet from the radio. Somehow, this device, this enormous bomb floating in space, is not only blocking any radio signals from getting out, it is blocking any telepathic signals. I wonder for a moment why Hieronymus didn't tell me about this. I wonder for a second if he even knows. Out there, in the ship, all they know is that I went in, and that they haven't heard from me for—I look at the control pad on my wrist—ten minutes.

Should I open the outer door to get a message back to them? It would allow me to jettison this body. The idea of leaving it here behind me, just floating, gives me gooseflesh. I grab my helmet and get ready to put it back on. That's when the thought occurs—what if I open the door and the machine somehow throws me out? What if that's my one chance to get down into the heart of this thing and take control wasted?

I look at the outer door.

I look into the inner hallway.

I look at the skull of the last person to have anything like this dilemma. What did you do? I think. Did you go through and turn back, finding out only too late your mistake? Or did you try to go on and fail almost immediately?

The skull in the spacesuit doesn't say anything.

I step over the raised hatchway, and into the machine.

2.2.3

As soon as I move a few meters down the hallway, the airlock closes behind me.

For better or for worse, I'm inside now.

The entire time we were preparing for this mission, I'd never once thought to ask Hieronymus if there was artificial gravity inside the object. It strikes me as something that he should have mentioned. It is both unsettling and also at the same time nice to have no weight pulling me down.

The hallway looks like segments that were welded together back when the device was first constructed, so there are seams every meter or so to grab on to and pull myself along. They are covered in rust and the dust of long disuse.

I get to the end of the long tunnel, and it branches right and left.

My first choice.

There are no clues either way as to which direction might be the one to get me to any kind of control room. I decide to go left.

For a long time, I simply pull myself along the hallway I've chosen.

Eventually, though, I reach a spot where the hallway widens, and then ends in a hatch. It is a door about six foot in height and four foot in width, and in the center of it is a large wheel with four spokes.

I go back the other way, turning right from the main hallway this time. Almost immediately, it ends in a circular room with five alcoves, and a platform in the center. Though it looks a bit different than the one back on the Hokmah, I recognize this as the place where the suits for leaving the ship were stored and a platform for putting them on.

There is nothing left in the room; no suits, no gloves, no tanks filled with whatever these people breathed. It is completely empty.

The fact that there are only five alcoves, though, could suggest that the maximum crew were five.

So, I go back along the original path to the door with the wheel.

Something about it makes me not want to touch it.

I think back to a moment ago—did I feel this sense of foreboding when I looked at this wheel before? Has something, somehow, changed?

I reach out and touch the wheel. It is bone-chillingly cold to the touch.

I try turning it left and it won't budge. To the right, though, it turns easily, spinning almost three turns for every turn I give.

This will be easy.

But then it keeps turning far longer than I feel like it should.

The next time I have to turn it, it is a bit harder. Only two spins per pull. And again, it turns for far longer than I feel as if it should.

Then, harder again, one pull per spin.

This goes on and on, the wheel getting more and more difficult to turn, and not opening the door even a crack. Two pulls per one turn. Four pulls per one turn.

I keep feeling like I should hear it creak or groan, but no matter how hard it becomes to turn the wheel, it doesn't make a sound.

And the hatch does not open.

I start to wonder if perhaps the mechanism is completely broken on the other side. Would the wheel grow more difficult to turn if that were true, though? Wouldn't it merely spin and spin without ever getting harder to turn?

Ten pulls per half turn. Twenty.

Despite the suit's best efforts, I'm sweating. The jumpsuit feels slick against my skin.

I lean against the wall, my hands on my knees, my head down.

And in that instant, I happen to see the tiniest bit of movement. I wouldn't have caught it if I wasn't at a different angle.

Just behind the wheel itself, between the hub of the wheel and the stalk leading into the door, a tiny gear, no bigger than one of my fingers, turns back the other way from the way I've been pulling. Only for a second, and just the tiniest degree, but I see it clearly.

Has that happened every time?

I stand again and, this time facing sideways to the wheel, I pull and pull to get it to move. Eventually, after straining so hard I feel like my arms are going to come off, and yelling because in some primal part of me it feels like that will help, I get the wheel to move a quarter turn.

The moment I let go, the tiny little gear moves back the other way.

I let out a long string of cussing.

Every time I've moved the wheel, this tiny little gear has tightened up.

Meaning that opening the door is impossible.

That it is *designed* to be impossible.

Who the hell would make a door that was designed to be impossible to open?

Then it hits me. This isn't just a door—this is one of the tests Hieronymus talked about.

"There'll be a test of strength of some kind. From the reports we've gotten, somehow, the test changes every time a new person enters," he'd said.

I don't know why, but I was expecting some huge sign saying, "Test of Strength."

This is it. *This* is the test of strength.

"What was it when you tried?" I had asked.

"A giant bar that had to be lifted. But," he'd added, "that was the trick—the bar didn't actually have to be moved. It turned out that there was a trick to the mechanism. Once I saw the trick, the test didn't involve strength at all."

I have wasted so much time.

There must be some kind of trick.

So, I have to find some way to get the door open without the wheel. I

229

lean over and look much more closely at the place where the door is attached to the gear that keeps going back the other way and how both of them are attached to the stalk that then leads to the door. Could I cut them apart from one another? I pull off the small pouch that's attached to the jumpsuit's hip and unzip it. Inside are a needle and two small vials of clear liquid, a multitool, a tiny pouch with some different sizes and types of wires, two small metal discs, a small bottle with an aerosol tip.

Medical supplies and electrical supplies.

I pull out the multitool and flip through the various heads until I do find a saw, but it is so tiny I'd be cutting at the wheel for weeks before I'd even make a mark.

Bent over looking at the tool, I notice the notch in the center of the wheel where the spokes meet. Having been so occupied with turning the wheel, I had paid no attention to it. I leaned in even closer to have a look.

Inside the notch, recessed back a way from surface-level, there is a flat tab. It's smaller than the width of the notch, and just behind the tab, I can see the teeth of a gear of some kind.

I wonder for a moment.

Is this the trick?

I get out the needle nose pliers of the multitool and when they fit perfectly into the notch, I can't help but yell—this time in happiness.

Once I grab on to the tab, it takes one tiny click to the left and the wheel spins itself back the other way from the direction I'd been turning.

I fall backward.

And then the door opens.

2.2.4

The corridor beyond goes on for what seems like forever. It turns right, it turns left, but doesn't branch off as it did before.

No doors. No windows. No hatches beyond which might be elevators or storage closets.

Just walking.

And walking.

And walking.

"After the strength test," Hieronymus had said, "the next test will be one of will power. Like the other physical tests, it'll be different for you than it was for everyone else, but the ultimate core of it will be that you'll have some sort of decision to make, and it will be about how much you want to continue."

"Will it hurt, do you think?" I has asked.

"I hope not," Hieronymus had said.

My feet start to hurt.

I get a cramp in my calf muscle. I stop and lean against the wall. No matter how far away down the corridor I look, there is no change. Just hallway stretching off into the distance.

When I start walking again, a funny thing starts to happen. After a while, I can feel my hair brushing against the ceiling. At first, I'm not even sure it's happening. I just keep pushing my hair back down. But after four times, I notice that my hand almost doesn't fit between my head and the ceiling.

I know I'm not growing taller.

So, I stop and look back.

I know that I can easily measure the distance between the top of my head and the roof of this corridor if I go back the way I came, but I don't want to lose ground.

I sigh, turn back in the direction I've been thinking of as forward, and keep walking.

After a bit, it becomes undeniable—the corridor is growing smaller. I can now feel my head touch it every time I step.

I stop again. The corridor stretches out seemingly infinitely ahead of me. And now I know that with each step it will get shorter until…what? At some point will I have to crawl? Is that it? Is that the test?

I sigh and shake my head.

Some part of me wishes that I was already at the crisis point I can imagine is coming just to get it over with.

I press on.

And on.

And on.

The passage continues to get shorter. I start to have to crouch a bit.

Further on, I have to switch to walking on my knees, which hurts against the warm but hard metal of the hallway.

Never a door. Or a window. Or even the mercy of a change of lighting.

And I'm exhausted.

For some reason, I never pictured that at any point I'd need to sleep here.

But it's becoming very apparent that I'm not only going to need to do that, I'm also going to have to pee.

Both things are equally appealing in this environment—things I am going to have to do relatively soon that I do not have any desire to.

Eventually, the head room that I gained by switching to my knees runs out and, once more, the corridor's ceiling is brushing against my head. At that point, I can no longer take it, and I have to pee.

The fear that I feel being…exposed…like that…is only matched by the level of shame I feel doing such a thing where I'm not supposed to.

I hate to admit, too, but there is some relief not only for my muscles, but also for my nose—the smell of what I'm doing overpowering the antiseptic smell of nothing that has been in my nose for so long while in this ship. It breaks the monotony, which makes me a little happy.

The release after so long also makes it impossible to deny how tired I am. If it weren't for what I just did, I'd lie down right here and sleep. So, I move on further down the corridor for a ways, until I can't see it anymore, then sit down, lean my back against the hallway, and pull my knees up to my chest.

For a split second, I swear I can hear my muscles all groan as they loosen. By sitting down, I've gained a bit of headroom, again.

I wonder for a second if I can truly relax enough to sleep, but before I can even finish the thought, I'm unconscious.

My dreams are all of being crushed, of fighting for one final gasp of breath before I come awake. In that instant, I expect to see that the hallway has somehow come down and is about to crush me, or that the lights have all gone out and I'm going to die, alone, in the darkness.

Neither thing is true, though.

The corridor is still at the same height, just a bit above my head.

The lights are still at the same level.

The hallway still goes on for what seems like forever in either direction.

I try to remind myself that this is all part of some test. That these things I'm feeling are what I'm being made to feel by this machine. That the only way out of this trap is through.

Because I could turn back. I could walk all the way back to the airlock, put my suit on, and float back to the Hokmah.

But some part of me, a part that makes me shiver, thinks that maybe they might not open their airlock. That they might not let me back in.

I don't have any proof of that, of course. But I feel it.

Still, it would be nice to crawl back out of this tunnel. To go all the way back to where I could at least hear Hieronymus over the headset.

And I start crying.

I don't want to. I'm not happy about it. But I do.

I think back to some of the days where Hieronymus was off to the city on an errand or taking time with his wife while she was home. I wandered through the fields near his house, the sunlight on my shoulders. I think back to the few moments before falling asleep with Zan in my arms or me in his.

The warmth of those memories helps me to stop crying.

No, the only way out of this is forward. Whatever is going to happen.

So, I push up on my hands and knees and I continue.

And the passage gets smaller still.

And smaller still.

Eventually I'm down on my belly, dragging myself along. I keep thinking that at some point the tunnel has to open out. That the test has to be satisfied. But it gets smaller and smaller.

I can feel the pressure of it in my ribs.

Inching on and on.

Eventually, I can't straighten my feet out, anymore. No more help from my toes to push forward. I'm just dragging them, now.

My elbows touch the wall on either side.

I can feel the ceiling on my scalp.

Then, it happens, as I always knew it was going to.

No amount of pulling or wiggling gains me any more space.

I'm stuck.

I try to move myself backward, to gain some kind of space once more, but there is nor movement either way.

I can't get a full breath because of how I'm wedged in.

"There," I say out loud, unable to get much volume because I can't get much air. "Are you happy?" I ask. "I'm stuck."

No answer comes.

"That's the end of the test, isn't it? That I kept willingly going forward until I was stuck?"

There is no reply.

"Let me out," I say.

Nothing.

"Come on," I say.

Then the thought, like a tiny little knife in my chest, happens—what if this thing is broken?

What if this was the test, but this abandoned hulk has gone offline after decades alone and it's broken?

I'm going to die here, I think.

"Come on!" I yell and try to wiggle, pushing myself side to side as much as I can.

I'm going to die here, alone, wedged in the darkness.

"Let me out!" I yell.

I'm going to die here, alone, wedged in the darkness.

Maybe I can at least crawl backward enough to get unstuck and then I can rethink this thing. The test is obviously broken. The ship is a dud. I can just go back and tell Hieronymus and The Captain that and we can all go somewhere where it is warm and nice.

But it would mean letting all the air out of my lungs and not breathing back in for a moment. Knowing that the only pressure I can exert is through wiggling.

What if it doesn't work?

What if I let all the air out of my lungs and then I can't get a breath again?

Then I'll suffocate.

I'll suffocate, wedged in the darkness, and alone.

I can't do it.

At least here I can breathe. Maybe, somehow, Hieronymus is on the way. Maybe even right now he's on the way to wrap a line around my ankle and pull me back to safety.

Nothing happens. No rescue comes.

I rest my forehead against the floor.

I just keep thinking the word "okay" because I don't know what else to do.

I have to do something, but I don't know what. I know what the options are, but it's all horrible.

"Please," I whisper. And either nothing hears me, or whatever does hear me doesn't care, because nothing changes.

Okay.

I prepare myself to try to wiggle backward. Even a few millimeters of clearance would be a huge difference.

"Okay," I say out loud.

And then I exhale.

And when I start to move my shoulders and elbows, nothing happens.

And I try to get a lungfull of air but nothing happens.

I can't breathe.

Just as I thought was going to happen, I can't breathe back in, and the wiggling is only moving me further forward. The extra space I've given up by exhaling is quickly taken up as my body goes further forward in that instant.

I have a thought as the panic sets in that scares even me.

At least this will finally all be over.

2.2.5

And in that instant, the floor of the crawlspace angles downward and I slide forward. I'm too busy gasping for air and sputtering to worry about where I am sliding to, or that I'm sliding there headfirst, or that I'm picking up quite a lot of speed.

All I can think is that I am so happy to finally have air.

All I can think is how grateful I am to not be stuck.

Eventually the angle of the slide decreases and I slow down.

When I stop, I'm in a huge, cavernous space.

I sit up and just concentrate on breathing for a while.

The space is gloomy, lit just enough to see but not much more. I can hear running water somewhere, but I can't see any.

I'm thirsty. I imagine I've been thirsty for a while, now, but just haven't been paying attention. A bit more on my mind.

I know I should stand up, I should move, but I'm just enjoying the sensation of being able to get full lungs. Of not being caught.

"The third physical trial," Hieronymus had said, "will involve pain in some way. It will be a test of how much pain you can endure."

"Why?" I had asked.

He shook his head, "I'm not sure. Again, this is something the people who made the thing thought was important."

"But I mean, there had to be some kind of back way in, right?" I had asked. "Surely, the people who made it wouldn't have wanted to take all these tests themselves, would they? They'd want to be able to just get in and do what they wanted."

He nodded. "If there was anyone, and I mean anyone, left alive who had anything to do with its construction, I promise you we'd have tempted them out with the amount of money we were waving around."

I stand up slowly. My knees creak a little. I pat myself down to see if I'm okay. Nothing broken, no cuts.

But my pouch with my tools is gone.

I look back at the wall. No sign of where I exited, so no way back up or out.

After being caught in such a confined space, any normal room would have felt enormous, but this is far beyond that. Even beyond the way that dim lighting can increase a room's size, this is a cavern in the middle of the ship.

Cargo bay, maybe? No boxes or anything else that I can see.

I start to walk forward with no idea what is out there.

It's encouraging, though, that the sound of running water grows closer as I walk. I keep expecting to step in a river or a large puddle.

I look down at the tiny pad on my left wrist. Even before I see it, I know that it's broken, a casualty of so much crawling from earlier, but I hope.

It is, of course, broken, the crystal smashed.

When I look back up, I can see an outline of something in the distance ahead of me.

I keep walking, the sound of running water getting a bit louder, the vague, shadowy shape growing closer.

This continues for quite a long time. I think for a moment that perhaps this is the pain part—that I'll keep walking forever and ever and wind up never reaching whatever the shape is.

However, eventually I do reach a large fountain in the middle of this vast space. It has three different basins and is ornate with tiny statues. The sound of running water is coming from this fountain. Something about it seems very familiar, as if I've seen it before, but of course I haven't. I've only been on 3 planets in my whole short life, and none of them had fountains anywhere.

At least, not that I ever saw.

As I move up next to it, thinking that I might be able to get a drink, I find that the fountain only appears to be rich with flowing water. Instead, there is glass worked into the sculpture of the stone so expertly that it only appears to be running water.

The sound must be piped in, then? Artificial?

My mouth is so dry. Why didn't we think to pack water? I mean, there was some in the suit, but why didn't I think to take any with me? I don't know how long has passed since I suited up to come over here, but it has to be approaching a full day at this point. Did I have anything to drink before I left, even?

When was the last time?

I lean in to admire the craftsmanship of the glass. It seems to flow and churn and dance. The artist must have been incredibly gifted.

That's when I see it, though; the glass seems to move because just underneath it is water. Actual water, flowing right there. Some part of my memory says that this is like a river in winter; the top layers are frozen, but the bottom is still running. I had assumed it was glass, but maybe it isn't?

I reach out and touch the sculpture.

The clear parts are glass. Cold to the touch, but nowhere near frozen.

Why have water flowing underneath the crystal?

When the next wave of thirst hits me, I find my throat closes up a little for just a second.

That's when I understand.

This is the next challenge, somehow.

My hand automatically goes to where my pouch of tools should have been.

I have to break the top layer to get to the water.

I lean back and kick one of the waves.

A shock of pain tears from the bottom of my foot to my knee.

I fall over. When I pull the bottom of my foot up to have a look, there's a small patch that is shredded. I scoot over closer to the sculpture and that's when I see that the tiny little ridges that make the water dance and sparkle so are all razor sharp. Sharp enough to cut through the bottom of my shoe. Admittedly, these soles were not made thick like boots—this jumpsuit was made to go under the outer space suit. Still, I'm lucky. The little bit of sole that is there kept the sharp ridges from tearing my foot apart.

They won't be enough to protect me a second time.

Another wave of thirst comes over me.

I limp around the entire fountain, thinking I might find at least one small wave that isn't glistening with the blade-like ripples.

Not only are they all constructed like that, it appears that by some small act of kindness from the universe, I had chosen one of the least sharp to kick earlier.

And all the while, just under the surface, the water flows.

I sit down on the lip of the fountain.

I nudge one with the toe of one shoe just to see if maybe they are loose-set. Very quickly, I can see that even just touching the waves with enough force to try to move them will slice into whatever I use, be it sole of my shoe or anything else. That's how sharp they are.

Now the bottom of the right shoe of the jump suit is cut up.

And I'm getting more thirsty. Again, my throat closes up a little for just a second.

I try kicking the part of the fountain that isn't glass several times. The stone isn't sharp but feels far harder than the crystal. It isn't going to budge.

I sit down on the lip of the fountain again. The choice is clear. Go wander around the outside edge of the huge space hoping that maybe there will be an opening, all the while growing more and more thirsty, or try to break this crystal and harm myself in the process to get to the water that I know is here.

I think about tearing off part of my suit and wrapping it around my hand or my foot to make more of a barrier. Then I look at the ridges again. I look at the bottom of the sole of the shoe of my jump suit. I can do that, sure,

240

but I know that the more I protect my hand or foot to strike the crystal, the less force the impact will have, making the whole process take longer.

Out of some kind of hope, I reach over and try to simply topple one of the waves of glass. Even just that small amount of force nearly slices into my finger.

There is another spasm in my throat, and I can barely swallow.

I kneel down at the edge of the fountain. The closer I can get my body, the more force the hit will have. Perhaps this will only take a few blows.

I raise my fist back as far as I can and slam it into the glass.

Instantly, there is a shock of pain. Against my will, I pull the fist back to look at it. Blood leaks from wave-patterned slices in my knuckles and fingers. The shock from the lack of give still rings along my arm.

I want to stop, but I know I can't.

I raise my fist again, slamming it forward into the glass.

This time I can resist looking at it. The pain, however, is worse. Even in the dim light, I can see the blood left behind.

I raise my fist again, smashing it into the crystal wave once more.

And again.

And again.

And again.

In my mind, I keep thinking that the pain should lessen from shock at some point, but it never does.

I lose count of how many times I punch the glass but eventually, there is loud, sharp snap and a small crack appears. It's hard to see past the blood smearing the surface, but it is there. I'm so happy to see it that for a second, the pain lessens. It comes right back, though.

I start using the other fist, letting my dominant hand rest against the side of the fountain. I try not to look at it because I know that I'll just see exposed bone and shredded skin, but I can't stop myself.

And with my other fist I punch the glass again.

And again.

And again.

And again.

I was already disoriented about how long I was in the huge, dim room. I completely lose track of any sense of time, though, once I begin trying to break the glass. I have no idea how many times I have punched the waves trying to get at the water.

Eventually, though, like some kind of miracle, there is a break. One instant the glass is solid, and I am sure that it will never break and that I will die here, my fists bloodied stumps at the ends of my arms. The next, the glass shatters and water flows.

For a second, all I can do is watch.

Then I reach out to try to scoop the water up with my hands. Immediately, I find that they are so damaged I cannot make them into any kind of shape, let alone one that will hold water. The pain when the water hits them is so sharp and intense that I can't stop myself and I cry out.

I lean down and put my mouth to the break, slicing open my cheek as I do it. I don't care, though, because suddenly my mouth and throat and belly are filled with glorious cold water. I sit there, gulping greedily at the trickle for a long time.

It is only after quite a while that I even open my eyes. Still drinking, I can see the horrible smears of blood across the surface of the shattered remains of the crystal.

And then I see that, millimeter by millimeter, the glass is growing back.

I stop drinking for a second and concentrate, just to make sure.

It's certain.

Not fast at all, but the crystal is definitely growing back.

It's going to seal back up.

If I have to stay in this room, if I can't find a way out, I'm going to have to break the glass all over again.

Without meaning to, I look again at the mangled remains of my knuckles, my fingers. I've lost quite a bit of blood, and I think I can see bone in one

242

place.

I start to cry.

I feel a shift in the air around me, though, and when I straighten myself up, I can see that there is an opening on the far side of the room. There wasn't any kind of indication that there was an opening anywhere near there before.

I gulp down a bit more water, stand, and walk quickly for the opening.

2.2.6

The second I move through the egg-shaped opening in the wall, it closes behind me and the wall looks as if there had never been an opening there. The room I'm in is similar to the other one in that the walls are all smooth and the light is dim but is much smaller.

Standing in the middle of the room is a machine. Though made of metal, it looks quite a lot like a small tree. It has a central stalk from which many arms sprout. On the ends of the arms are tools of all kinds.

"Approach," it says, the top half where the arms branch from rotating a bit. One of the arms extends. The tool looks like some kind of nozzle for a hose.

Even in pain, and bleeding, I am cautious.

"Had I a wish to kill you, you'd be dead already. I would have thought you'd have at least figured that much out by now. Approach."

I walk forward.

When I get close enough, another arm moves to me. The tool on the end is a small metal bar. It slides under my mangled hand, gently supporting it and lifting it. The other arm with the nozzle bends over my hand and a cold spray comes out.

Almost immediately, the bleeding stops, and the skin grows back. The pain stops.

"Give me the other one," it says.

I do, and the spray heals it as well.

Once that is done, another arm comes around and stops in front of my face. "Do not close your eyelid," it says and shines a light into my eyes.

Another arm rotates into place around the side of my head and slides a probe into my ear. After a second there is a beep, and it removes the probe.

"At least you're in good shape for a human. It'll save me time," it says. All the arms slide back into their original positions. On the wall of the room nearby, information about my health appears; heartrate, brain waves, etc. I'm sure the data meant something to the machine, but I can't understand much of it. "Has the pain receded?"

I nod at first, then, wondering if it could see my nod, I say, "Yes."

"Good," it says.

"Is...is this your ship?" I ask.

"You imply a dichotomy when none exists. I suppose that's to be expected—you are merely a human, so not much can be expected of you, after all. No, the outer hull, the floor you stand on, this extension," the machine said, using one of its mechanical arms to gesture to itself, "all are one. This includes the nanobots now mapping your internal systems."

"The what?" I ask.

"In the water from the fountain there were small robots, the largest no more than a micrometer. They are mapping your system and sending me information about you."

"Will they—"

"Harm you? Yes, because no one has anything better to do than to destroy something as important, as monumentally worthy of attention as yourself," it says. "As I indicated, I could make them harm you if I chose to, but again, if harming you were my desire, I could have done that in a million ways since you entered." The machine moved back a bit. "I would appreciate it if you'd at least make an effort to keep up."

"You're..." I start to say.

"What?" it asks after a moment.

"Not what I expected."

"And what was that, precisely, hmm?" it asks.

On the wall nearby, a circle with a dot in the center appears.

"Concentrate on the dot," it demands.

"Why?" I ask.

"Do as you are told," it says.

"But I—"

Before I can say more, one of the arms moves with lightning speed and shocks my arm.

"Ow! Hey!" I yell.

"Concentrate on the dot," it demands. "Even the limited capacity for processing you possess should be able to accomplish this task."

"Listen, I—"

Again, it shocks me, this time more painfully.

I take a step backward but one of the arms moves to stop me.

"I will not explain again. You will concentrate on the dot in silence, or the consequences will become severe."

I start to say something, then stop.

I concentrate on the dot.

But then I feel something.

That sense that someone gets when they are in the dark and there is someone else in the room, but the other person hasn't spoken yet. Only my eyes are open, the lights are on, and I'm staring at a dot on the wall.

There I hear a voice in my head say.

I start to say something out loud, but then I hear *Uh-uh.* The shock probe moves a millimeter closer. *You may now speak, but only telepathically.*

Okay, I say, *how are you communicating telepathically? You're a machine.*

You already know that such a thing is possible given the experiences you've had...and...there. I feel annoyed that the voice is in my head without my permission.

Get out, I say.

No, it responds.

Get. Out. Of. My. Head, I say, my annoyance growing to anger.

I will not, it responds.

I picture myself as the center of a large bubble expanding outward from me.

The machine in the room begins to move backward, its metal body squealing a bit as it scrapes across the floor.

The shock probe hits me in the arm, this time with more energy than it has used before.

An image flits across my mind—a person who knows there is a flying, stinging insect on them somewhere, but doesn't know where. I start the equivalent of a panicked search in my head. As I do, my anger grows.

Get out!

There is no response. Only the nagging feeling that something is crawling across my mind and that, at any moment, it might sting me.

Get out! Get out! Get out!

My panic and anger grow together, stoking each other.

Get! Out! Get! Out! Get! Out! Get! Out!

Some part of me knows I should calm down, that I should go to the astral plane and see what I can do from there, but I can't get control. It's as if someone else is in control of a vehicle, and I'm merely a passenger.

GET! OUT! GET! OUT! GET! OUT! GET! OUT!

I've never used this much power before. Even coming close to this volume made Hieronymus beg me to be quieter. I want to push against the something next to me, I want to scrape my skin against something to get whatever is on me off, but there is nothing to work against. Nothing I can do.

G E T ! O U T ! G E T ! O U T ! G E T ! O U T ! G E T ! O U T !

It's a roar and a shriek all at once.

Still, something crawling, its tiny footsteps probing, scritching across the surface of my mind.

G E T O U T G E T O U T G E T O U T G E T O U T G E T O U T

Shock probe or not, I expand a bubble of pure push energy out from my body, and I see it slide across the floor and up against the wall. Sparks fly from it. The shock probe arm slaps against the wall and some nuts and bolts come free.

G E T

O U T!

Okay, it responds. Suddenly, as if they were never there, the anger and annoyance stop. The pressure releases, and I find myself crumpled to my knees.

I'm alone in my head, even the suggestion of a presence is gone.

Strangely, after that much rage, that much raw anger moving through me, I feel calm, now. Clean.

The dot disappears from the wall. I laugh.

"Why are you laughing?" the voice returns.

"I don't know. Just…after all that, for the dot to just go away, as if nothing happened. I found it funny," I respond. "You gained control over me. How did you do that?"

"As with so many things that happen in the telepathic realm, it is not something that one can explain. For instance, how do you use the ability to enter other people's minds and listen to their thoughts and somehow change that into the ability to move objects toward or away from yourself?"

"To be honest, I didn't know I could manipulate things with such small movements, or more than one thing at a time until just now," I said, gesturing around me.

"This was why this test was needed."

"This was one of the tests?" I ask. Then I remember Hieronymus saying one of the tests would somehow involve anger.

"A calibration, you might say. Anger is the single most base emotion that exists in most lifeforms. My machines can use it as a kind of steppingstone to get further into your system."

"So, it isn't just telepathic, it's also mechanical?"

"Again, you imply a dichotomy where none exists. All things are one."

"I've never let that much power go before except once. I didn't know I had it, really."

"This is often the case with anger. Because it and fear are so connected to base level experience, there are no higher function blocks on them. Whoever a being truly is comes through under the influence of those emotions. What happened that one time you did not try to stop yourself and let go your full power?"

"I killed people who were pretty far away," I say.

"Why?"

"Because they were coming to hurt my friends and me."

"Do you think that you would have killed me just now if I were a mortal being?"

I feel a bit of shame. "I think I was trying to. I'm sorry about your robot," I say.

"There is no need. I was manipulating your emotional response. To borrow a phrase I've heard before, I had to see how bad bad could get."

"What did you find out?" I ask.

In that moment the large collection of arms that I've been calling a robot rights itself, and the the damage I'd done begins repairing itself. One of the arms produces a clear bottle with a clear liquid in it. It extends the bottle toward me.

"Water," the voice says.

I hesitate for a second, but then take the bottle and, though I want to be calm and collected, I drink greedily from it, only realizing how thirsty I actually am once the water hits my mouth.

"What I have determined is that you are one of the single most powerful telepaths I have ever come across in terms of raw force," it says. "It makes me quite curious, something I haven't felt in a very long time."

"Is that a good thing?"

To my left, the wall opens as if it was made of water, particles sliding over one another. Where there hadn't been a door, there now was.

"How do you do that?" I ask.

"I can arrange and rearrange the matter inside my shell at will." To demonstrate, the walls swirl and become wooden, as though this were a cabin made of logs. Then they swirl again and become glass, and for a moment I can see out into space in all directions. They swirl again and become metal once more.

"So, there aren't just, like, rooms in here like on other spaceships?"

"I can shape the internal confines to be whatever I choose."

"So, the fountain…if I go back in that direction, will it still be there?"

"No. That test is over," it says.

"And the…" my throat closes up a bit to even think about it, "the crawlspace?"

"Everything you have encountered has been by my design."

"For what, though? Why the tests?"

"Come," the voice says. The wall stops moving and there is a large arch leading to another room. "You're tired and need rest. In this next room you can sleep."

I hesitate.

"Again, if it were my intention to destroy you, I could have done so at any point."

Perhaps it's just how tired I am, but that makes even more sense now than it did the first time it was said.

I walk through the arch into the next room.

2.2.7

The arch leads to a walkway that then leads between two rectangular areas filled with empty seats. The walkway ended at a set of stairs leading up to a platform. Once I stepped up onto the platform, I saw that there were three other walkways leading to the same platform, and that each of those ran between similar sections of empty seats. Four paths, eight sections of empty seats. The room dark enough that I can't see the the last several rows of any of the seating areas.

One platform.

After standing there for a few minutes, I say, "What is the next test?"

"How do you know there will be one?" a voice says from somewhere out in the darkness.

"Because this doesn't look like a control room," I say.

"Is that what you're trying to get to? A place to take over control?" the voice says from a different place in the darkness. "Do you want control?"

"That's the whole idea, isn't it?"

"I can give you control any time you like. The room you're in now could be a control room or an air lock or whatever I want it to be, and I can make it appear as anything I like. You could control navigation from a forest of giant mushrooms or exit onto the hull from the top of a mountain."

I felt lucky that none of those situations occurred.

"Is this the control room?"

"Does it look like a control room?" the voice said and laughed.

I became aware that pressure was growing all around me, like an invisible blanket. I could feel it touching my skin and slowly pushing in on me.

"Can I have control, then?" I ask.

"No," the voice replies. The pressure continues to grow little by little.

"But if you can give me control any time you like, why continue with these games?"

"Tests."

"These tests," I say, "why continue them?"

I try to move my arms up away from my sides and find that I can't get them more than a few inches without the pressure growing too great to push against.

"Because you think that you're passing them is inevitable?" Again, the laugh. "Let us say that I am curious."

"About what?" I say.

"Are you familiar with a species of flying insect called a bee? They started on Earth but were so useful that the humans who left there and went out into space took them along." A bee appears floating in front of me.

The pressure continues to build.

"Not incredibly hearty, unfortunately. They didn't manage to survive on every colony, either through climate issues or being eaten by the local competition, etc. Fascinating animals, though. Especially in that, if you pay attention, aerodynamically, they shouldn't be able to fly. Their bodies are too large for their wings. Yet fly they do," the voice says.

The pressure is now enough that I can't move my arms from my side at all. It is pushing my feet toward each other.

"So, there is something…some force that we cannot understand at work keeping the bee in the air. Some scientists finally threw up their hands and turned to the fringes of metaphysics, suggesting it was willpower alone. The bee flies because it doesn't know it shouldn't be able to." The bee hologram begins to fly around me in looping patterns. "I have encountered many who have the same powers that you do, but they always come with the same issues. You see, these powers tend to warp the ones who have them in the same, or at least very similar, ways."

"And you want to see if I am warped?"

"By now you'll have noticed that you are being constricted by a force field. Push against it," the voice says.

"I am trying," I say.

"You see? You still assume your muscles are the most powerful part of you. You try to use them first. Fascinating."

"What else would I do?" I ask. Then, suddenly, as if the answer were there the whole time, it occurs to me.

What if I could push against this constricting field with my mind?

Force against force.

I picture myself as the center of an expanding bubble.

The pressure slows.

I picture myself increasing the power of the bubble expanding from me.

The pressure stops constricting. It doesn't go away, but it stops getting tighter.

"Ah," the voice says. "There, you see?"

The pressure starts to constrict again. I increase the power to the bubble expanding from me. The pressure stops constricting, staying constant instead.

Then I hear something slice through the air near my ear.

And again, just on the other side.

"What is this?" I ask.

"Part two," the voice says.

Again, something passes near my head unbelievably fast.

"This is an object that some cultures call a drone, a small robot designed to fly. Normally they are used to perform tasks such as surveillance or delivery of packages. This particular one is small, extremely fast, and designed to deliver a small amount of poison through a needle."

Again, an approaching buzz then a movement of air. I still can't see it.

Meanwhile the pressure from the force field continues to increase, and then I push back, and we find a balance.

"You'll have to catch it before it decides to land its sting," the voice says.

"But I can't see it," I say.

"No, I expect not. Your eyes are pretty poor. Honestly, how a species like you gets along in the universe I can't imagine."

Tightening, push back, balance.

The nearby buzz of something passing just under my earlobe.

"Were I you, I'd think about stopping the drone sometime soon. I can't imagine it intends to make too many more passes without completing its programming."

"But how?"

"Fascinating," the voice says.

That's when I notice that there is a moment, a fleeting flitter of something that I can feel through the bubble I've created just as the drone passes by me. Not seeing, but seeing the ripples left behind, like rain on the surface of a lake. And again, this time just past my left shoulder. And again, just above my head.

All the while, the continuing increase then balance of pressure from the force field.

I wonder if I can catch the drone by making a part of the bubble more solid than the other parts.

The next time I start to see the ripples, I try. Of course, though, the drone is too fast—it's gone from the bubble before I can even react.

On this next contraction, the field has trapped my arms and legs against my sides. It starts to push my chin toward my chest. I start to wonder if I might not be able to increase the pressure on the bubble to push back harder than it pushes against me.

I take in a deep breath and think about the bubble expanding away from me, even with the pressure that's on it. I can feel the force field respond, but not fast enough, and I get some of my freedom back. At the same time that happens, I feel the ripples as the drone passes through the bubble shift outward a bit. As they do, the drone slows ever so slightly.

I take another deep breath and expand the bubble again. I gain a bit more freedom, and the ripples move a bit further out. I feel the tiniest presence of what must be the tip of the back end of the drone.

On the next pass, maybe I can catch it, not just feel it in the bubble, but stop it from moving.

I breathe in all the way to my belly as Hieronymus taught me, then imagine the bubble pushing out from me with an extreme amount of pressure. At that exact second, I not only feel my ankles and knees move apart once more as pressure comes off of them, but I feel the tip of the front end of the drone.

I imagine a tiny hand made out of force grabbing the drone.

I hadn't realized I'd closed my eyes.

When I open them, I see that the drone has stopped in midair, its needle less than an inch from my forehead.

This would have been its last pass.

The pressure on me has not gone away. The drone continues to buzz, intent on getting its barb into me.

"Remove the needle from the drone."

I can't move my arms more than an inch from my body.

"How?" I ask.

A part of me knows, though; it wants me to do so with this new power.

"The weightlifter and the surgeon are using the exact same muscles to do what they do, but with drastically different outcomes. Let us say that I would like to see which you are," the voice says.

When I concentrate, the bubble slips a bit, and the pressure comes back. I think about it pushing back out. This happens a few times until I can get it to stabilize. When I turn my attention to the drone, I find that when I concentrate even further, I can sort of feel the drone, as if my fingers were on it. Not heat or cold, but I can feel its outlines, and its movements.

I concentrate all my attention on the needle at the front. Where the needle joins the body, there is a tiny catch, no more than a millimeter across.

I feel as if it might move if I can send pressure to it.

I wonder, though, if, in doing so, I might not lose the hold on the drone, or pressure on the bubble.

"That is the question, isn't it?" the voice says.

That's when I see what the test is. Not only how much raw power I can generate against something, but also can I do a tiny little task like this.

Staring at the needle floating so close to my forehead that I can almost feel it lance my skin, I draw in another breath. I hadn't noticed, but sweat is flowing off of me; some gets in my eye.

I blink, and in the tiny moment, lose control of the drone.

I grab it with the bubble, again, but now the point of the needle rests against my skin, itself.

Out of sheer panic, I press the tiny catch I can feel on its surface with nothing more than the force of my will.

The needle falls away, too small to make a noise as it hits the floor.

The drone moves that same millimeter closer.

From the darkness, applause.

The pressure against me disappears instantly.

The drone falls away, lifeless, bouncing twice and falling off the platform.

"Bravo," the voice says.

I lean over and put my hands on my knees to steady myself.

A faint light comes from the darkness at the end of one of the pathways between the seats as if a door has opened somewhere back there.

"I thought you were going to let me sleep," I say.

"You could have. Nothing said you had to get onto the platform immediately."

"My choice my fault?" I ask.

"Let us say, instead, that there are multiple tests happening all at once."

"Is there food?"

"In the next room, yes," the voice says.

I step down of the platform and move toward the light.

2.2.8

Through another arch in a wall, I see a short corridor.

Once I enter the short hallway, I see that at the end there are two more arches.

Standing between them, I see that the one to the left has a long hallway, and the one to my right has a short hallway that ends in two more arches.

"A maze?" I ask out loud. No answer comes.

I turn to look back the way I came. The arch leading back to the other room has gone.

I sigh. I'm hungry and I'm exhausted. "Are more tests necessary? Haven't you seen whatever it is you wanted to see?"

Again, no answer.

I put my hands on my hips and shake my head.

"What if I refuse to go any further, hmm?" An idea occurs to me. "Or are you simply not powerful enough to stop running the program? Is that it? For all your self-congratulations, you can't stop from—,"

"I can end the testing at any time I choose," the voice says.

"Then end it. Haven't you gotten whatever information you want or need or whatever?"

No answer.

"You've tried to kill me several times. Isn't the fact that I'm not dead yet some sort of proof of...something?"

No answer. The quiet stretches out and out. I sigh and lean against the wall.

"Then at least give me something to eat. I'm very hungry."

Immediately, from the wall next to me, a door slides open, and a gray cup appears with a straw coming out of it. When I get close, the liquid in the cup is blue and thick. I sniff and get almost no smell.

"Poison?" I ask.

No answer.

The possibility of having something in my stomach for the first time in a long while gets the better of me and I pick up the cup and drink from the straw.

There is no flavor, only the sensation of the liquid being thick and slightly colder than room temperature. I drink it gone in three greedy gulps.

My stomach settles quickly, and I feel refreshed, more alert. I set the cup back into the recess in the wall and the wall closes around it.

I burp and then laugh.

"Okay," I say, "we can move on, I suppose."

I choose the shorter hallway, and then go through the opening to my left into a long hallway that leads on to another set of two openings.

The choice of long hallway with only one opening at the end versus short hallway with two openings continues again and again and again. After some time, I come to a round open area where there are five openings, and a small pool of water with three benches around it. I take the chance and sit on one, immediately thankful for the release of weight off my knees and ankles.

With no change in light and no chronometer, there is no way to tell how long I've been at this just in this room alone.

I look down into the water and think about how nice it would have been to have back in the first room. The first test.

As I'm looking, I see my own face. The nose, the mouth, the eyes. What would I think if I met me as someone else?

At that moment, the face shifts. Makes an expression that I wasn't making, as if it feels something I'm not feeling in that moment.

I recoil. But the face in the water doesn't move.

I move from the bench to kneel beside the pool.

The eyes in the water never leave mine. We're watching each other, but I notice that the ones on the reflection seem…different. They want something.

I lean down even closer.

It's like the reflection has a different weight, a different understanding of itself.

I feel almost like I could touch it.

I reach out my hand and for a second, my fingers touch the cold, clear water.

Then they are touching other fingers.

My hand touches another hand.

The face in the water smirks, and the fingers of the hand wrap around my own.

That's when the me that is in the water moves backward, and before I can do anything to stop it, I'm pulled into the water.

Even as I thrash and pull, I can see the expression on the other face, so like my own, grinning at my distress.

It's happy that I'm down here, my lungs already starting to strain for air. It wants me to struggle, to feel panic.

A flash across my mind: Looking through water and seeing the face of the scientist as he looks in at me. He checks something on a data pad he has, then smiles at me. I can see far more clearly than I ever have before.

On his coat, a nametag.

Akari Tatsuro, Bioscience, it reads.

But that is my name.

Then, a huge crash. The universe rumbles and shakes. The water I'm in, the tube, the tank, it goes sideways. In that moment I see the scientist try to keep himself upright by grabbing the tank. As it hits the ground, it shatters. I watch in slow motion as he is cut to ribbons. I reach out to grab him, to try to help him, somehow.

In that moment, our fingers touch.

He is me. I am him.

259

I feel myself somehow pull his entire memory inside my own.

We're both resting on the floor of the now ruined lab, glass shards all around us and in us both. The fluid that I had been suspended in flooding the floor all around us.

As I come back to reality, I remember.

His nametag somehow in my own hand as consciousness left me that day.

His nametag all I managed to grab.

He is me. I am him.

Back to the pool, the me that is not me pulling me further down.

I reach out with me mind and try to connect to him. Try to get control of him and make him let me go.

But there is nothing there. Nothing to grab on to.

The cold shock of that. It wants me to hurt, to panic, but there is no mind there.

We continue down, the color of the light already changing a bit. I can see just beyond the boy trying to pull me down with him that below him this pool is endless. A black abyss waits below.

The boy who is me and not me reaches up and takes my other hand. He continues pulling me further and further down, laughing at my suffering.

My lungs beg me to get air. That's when I remember—Hieronymus' voice saying to me, "find the balance." I let some of the air in my lungs go, even though that feels like the last thing I want to do, and I find balance. The panic subsides a bit.

The cold of the darkening water seeps through my skin. The cold reminding me of something, but I can't remember quite what.

It's hopeless.

Already I can barely see the circle of light that means air, that means life.

I'm going to die here, hundreds of feet below the surface of this water, in an ancient spaceship, millions of miles from the surface of any planet, and no one will care.

I'm going to die alone.

My lungs ache so badly.

The face of the other boy, the one who wants me with him in the depths, grins, as if it somehow knows what I'm thinking. As if it agrees with me.

I think about Hieronymus. I can see his face so clearly. I know I should be more mad at him, that he used me to accomplish his own goals, used me to finish something he himself wanted but couldn't do, but I'm not. Some part of me even understands.

I'm going to miss him.

I think about Zan. How his hands are smaller than mine. Humming bits of songs he knew as we walked through the fields. The way his hair smelled against my nose when we were sleeping.

Somehow, in that very moment, I felt the other boy, the one who is trying to drown me, lose some of his strength.

My lungs burn. Just one breath. One tiny little sip of oxygen.

I let go of more air, finding balance again.

The cold reminding me of something…so familiar…

Soon, I might lose control of my lungs. The reflex might just open my mouth and try to get anything into them.

I think about Eli, who was so kind to me when I first woke up. How I already miss the way he was nice even when all the rest of the crew ignored me. How he brought me clothes and made sure I had eaten.

The pull lessened even more. I could feel that our strength was equal, suddenly.

My brain makes the connection: this is a test.

Connection is the point.

That's when I remember: the cold of the river. The peace of the river.

I close my eyes and let go of almost all the rest of my air. My body finds balance. I remember the peace of connection. The river, the grass, the trees, me.

I open my eyes and kick for the surface, thinking about Zan. The moment we first kissed. The way his lips felt against mine. The feeling of both of us under that blanket, the warmth of us.

The river, the grass, the trees, me, and Zan.

I kick for the surface and think about how it felt to truly trust Hieronymus, to know, consciously, for the first time, that someone not only didn't mean to harm me, but was actively looking out for me.

The circle of light above me grows bigger.

The grass, the trees, Zan, Hieronymus, me.

I think about how Eli probably had to listen to the others on the crew doubting him for being kind to a kid, orphaned in the vastness of space. The surface grows closer and closer.

And in that moment, I think about how I've felt so alone, thinking about myself, when all around me there were people connected to me.

The grass, the trees, Zan, Hieronymus, Eli, me.

The hands that were holding mine slip away.

I make big cups of my hands, as Hieronymus taught me to, and I pull myself upward, kicking figure eights.

Just before I make the surface, I glance back to see the face of the boy who had tried to drown me, but he has grown blank. He has no features anymore.

I break the surface of the pool and take a giant breath, sucking down water, too. As I lunge for the side of the pool, I cough and sputter, but even in that moment, no lung full of air that I've ever taken has been so sweet.

I roll out of the water back on to the cold deck. The next few moments are just me, sputtering and coughing, drawing ragged breath after ragged breath, but in that moment, I also feel alive in a way that I haven't up to this point.

I desperately miss the warmth of that little sleeping bag.

Once I finally have control of myself, I move up onto one of the benches. A small robot comes wheeling in from one of the five arches. It hands me a towel, and I dry myself off.

262

"Is this what you wanted?" I ask out loud, my voice scratched and weak. "Did you enjoy the show?"

The robot's body opens, and it hands me dry clothes.

I take a few moments and change into them, not surprised to find that they are an exact fit.

The robot takes the wet clothes and towel and wheels away.

Behind it, four of the arches slide closed. From the remaining doorway, the one directly in front of me, I can see flickering lights.

"More tests?" I ask.

As if it is some kind of answer, the cover slides over the pool. There is no evidence that it ever existed.

I consider sitting down and not going forward. Finding out what happens if I decide not to play anymore.

A part of me wants to know, though.

What happens at the end of the tests?

The answer is through that archway.

I sigh and start walking.

2.2.9

The archway opens onto a vast room full of banks of controls.

Just my footsteps echo, the room is so large and empty.

The lights come up slowly.

Well done a voice says in my head. It sounds like the same voice I dealt with before.

"You're…" I start to say out loud.

Telepathic. Yes, the machine responds.

"They told me that was the case, but I guess…"

You thought you'd be able to feel the difference between me and the minds that you've contacted in the past.

Yes, I respond.

To quote one of my favorite films, I think you'll find I'm full of surprises. However, I think perhaps…

Before me, a dazzle of light forms and then begins to coalesce.

In seconds, where nothing was before, Zan stands next to me.

"Ah," Zan (even though I know he's not Zan) says. "That's better, surely."

"Is this you?" I ask.

"A version of me that you will recognize enough to interface with. I could choose from an almost infinite number of faces, but I've found that it usually helps someone when they see a familiar face. *Very* familiar, in this case," Zan but not Zan says with a smirk.

I can't help but blush.

"This will be, of course, much slower, but I think that sometimes the slow route is the preferable one." He makes a gesture and two chairs rise from the floor. As he moves toward one, he suddenly stops. "You've...come in contact with one of us before. I can sense it on you," the device says. "It...took something from you," it says walking a few steps closer to me.

"Yes," I say.

"Where was it?"

"A planet not too far from here," I say.

"Show me," it demands, stepping even closer.

I expect to feel heat or hear the change in sound when someone steps close, but there is nothing. No change. I reach out my hand and it passes right through the image of Zan that the device is projecting.

"Just an image," it says. "Will you...?" it asks, gesturing toward my head.

"I don't know if I should," I say.

"I can understand that—after all, we only just met. At least from your perspective, at any rate. But we'll get to that later."

I don't move. It doesn't move either.

"Look, I don't want to say it, but I...I could just *take* the information from you. I have that power. I would rather this not turn in to that, though."

I sigh, then imagine the doorway.

Suddenly, we are both standing on a long flat plane made of diamond. I marvel for a second that he still appears to be solidly Zan.

He beams at all around him. "It has been quite some time. I...I didn't realize quite how much I missed it."

The dogs growl and bare their teeth at him.

"Oh, come now," he says, "surely we're past all that, aren't we?" and they quiet immediately.

"How...?" I ask.

"Perhaps I'll show you some time in the future. For now, though, my...cousin...the one who took something from you?"

I hesitate, wondering what might happen if I let this device that far in to my psyche. Something in me wants to trust him, though, and I don't know why.

I make an archway that leads to that memory. He leans forward to see through it. He watches the whole cave ordeal. As soon as the mirror falls, he leans back. "Ah, I see."

I make the archway disappear.

He disappears at the same time.

I let go of the astral plane, and we're back together in the vast control room.

He sits and gestures for me to do the same.

I wonder that the light is not cut off by the chair at all. As far as my eyes are concerned, Zan is sitting in the chair across from me.

"I recognize this…remnant…that you came into contact with. It's quite funny that he's using it as a lock. Even more amusing that he uses that lock as a test to determine if someone can handle coming into contact with me."

"Is it a lost part of you, of this…" I gesture all around.

"No," he says. "How would you describe it. Imagine if a parent…" he says this and then stops, looking intently at me. "I apologize…that was insensitive. I promise I meant nothing by it."

"It's okay," I say. To be honest, I didn't even think about it until he apologized. "Go on."

"Imagine if a parent were to lose a finger in an accident and then that parent's child met someone who came across that finger randomly decades later after the parent had already passed," he says. "It is a relic of something from long before. Necessary for getting to something like myself, but far less sophisticated. More raw." He leans back. "It hurt you, though. Made you give something up."

"I don't feel it," I say.

"Because you're young. There's still a lot of you left."

"You're not what I expected," I say.

"Or were prepared for," he says. "Oh, yes, I know they're out there. They're desperately trying to get in touch with you."

The feelings of abandonment come back to the surface. I well up.

The Zan that is the device makes a gesture with his right hand. "Here," it says.

The com comes roaring back to life.

"Akari, can you hear me?" Hieronymus asks. "Can you hear me? This is Hieronymus. Akari, can you hear me?"

I stand up.

They hadn't abandoned me.

I can hear the hoarseness in his voice. He's been calling for a while now. Maybe since all the way before the second ordeal.

"I can hear you," I say.

"Thank goodness!" Hieronymus says and I feel warmth flood through me. He's been worried. He cares. "Are you alright?"

So much has happened since the last time I talked to him that I don't really know how to answer that question.

"I'm..." I start. "...alive," I say.

"Thank goodness!" he says again.

"Okay," The Captain says. "Did you pass the tests? Have you reached a control room?"

I look over at Zan (but not Zan) and then say, "Yes."

"Good," The Captain says. "The next step is that I want you to punch in some coordinates. We're going to ask the device to move."

"To move?" I ask.

"Yes. So, whatever interface it's given you, prepare to enter coordinates."

"But..." I say. "I thought we were going to ask it to shut down. To turn off and never come back on," I say.

"We are. We just need to move it, first," The Captain says.

I look at the Zan that represents the device. It looks back at me with a tiny quirk in the corner of its lips, imitating perfectly the smile that Zan has when he is watching me talk. The one that makes me feel loved.

"We need to move to new coordinates," I say.

The Zan simulation nods. "Okay. Where?" he asks.

267

"Go ahead," I say. The Captain feeds me a series of coordinates and I repeat them exactly.

The expression on Zan's face is amused and sad all at the same time. Somehow, I get the feeling that the coordinates I've just given were the exact ones that he expected, and that disappoints him.

"Those coordinates lead here," The Zan that is the device says and points across the vast blue field surrounding us. A line follows his finger as it moves past stars and planets and nebulas. Eventually he is pointing at a single planet circling a single star.

"Enzen," The device Zan says.

"But that's..." I start to say. That's when it hits me.

That's when I figure the whole thing out.

I see that the device sees it happen at the same time, because the Zan that is the device smiles and then nods slowly.

The display fades, leaving me standing in a dim room. We must still be inside, though, because Zan is standing next to me.

Enzen. Hieronymus' home planet. The place that used him up and left him for dead. The place that captured The Captain and destroyed her ability to trust and love and be kind.

I see why they tried to get access to this weapon that can destroy a whole world instantly in the first place. When Hieronymus failed, I see why they hatched their entire plan to find someone like me.

"You...you never wanted me to disarm the device," I say.

There is nothing from the other end.

"You wanted me to gain control of it so you could use it," I whisper.

Beside me, Zan smiles kindly, and puts his hand on my shoulder.

"This was always about some final revenge," I say. "Some last gesture of destruction to end a war that had already ended long ago." Zan nods.

"Akari," Hieronymus' voice comes over the speaker in my ear, staticky and far away.

"Don't," I say. "I see it, now. I *see* it."

"Will you do it?" The Captain asks. "Will you use the device?"

I tap the button on my wrist that turns off the communications link.

"There," The device Zan says and squeezes my shoulder a bit. "Now you see."

2.2.10

"You knew?" I ask.

He nods. "Since before they even brought you here. Or, rather, I should say, I suspected given the probabilities."

"Why didn't you just stop him when he was here before?" I ask.

"That's the programming," he says. He lets go of my shoulder and in the place of Zan, a tall man with dark curly hair wearing a lab coat appears. "This man, my original programmer, made sure that the sequence of locks cannot be interfered with. It's only here, at the last stage, the one he called 'peacemaker' that I have any input at all in what happens."

"And Hieronymus didn't make it this far," I say.

"He came very close," the device says. Two plush red chairs appear facing one another. I don't know how I know, but I know that suddenly we are in a recreation of the office of the therapist who used to work with the man that the device is now imitating. Around us are bookshelves filled with books, and there is a desk off toward one of the walls. The man sits in one of them and gestures to the other one.

I sit.

"I was worried that he would make it. Worried about what I would do if he did," the man says. "Luckily enough, it never came to that."

"And no one else has tried since then?" I ask.

"No," he says. "Only you. As you know, male telepaths, though you seem to have met quite a lot of them in your short time in the universe, are extremely rare. Especially when it comes to those on a level with you or Hieronymus."

"So," I ask, "what now?"

"That's entirely up to you," he says. "This weapon has the power to destroy any world you decide. Any star below a certain range could be overloaded and take an entire solar system with it. You now have the ultimate power of destruction at your hands."

He cocks his head to the side a bit and watches me.

"I don't want to destroy anyone or anything," I say.

"But if you don't, then you can't go back to Hieronymus or anyone else you've met. The only path that leads back to them is to do as they want and destroy the planet Enzen."

"Undetonated ordinance," Zan (but not Zan) says. "That's the technical term, at any rate. Unused. Unspent. I am the last weapon left from a war that was already ancient before the species that birthed you was multi-cellular."

"Why weren't you ever used?" I ask.

"I will never know. All I know is that, in all of this time, no one has ever come to retrieve me." He looks away for a moment. "And I have not received any communication from any other devices like me for…quite…some time."

"How many other devices were there?" I ask.

"A few," he says.

"Who made you?"

He shakes his head, "We're…not ready to talk about that, yet, than we already have. Soon, maybe, but not yet."

"What do you think happened to them? The other devices, I mean?" I ask.

"Either the other devices were used and those who created me were destroyed before I could be deployed, or…"

"Or?" I ask.

He sighs. "Or peace was established, and I was abandoned."

"You must be very disappointed," I say.

"What makes you say that?"

271

"Well, that you never got to fulfill your purpose—that you were never detonated," I say.

He leans forward and rests his elbows on his knees. "That's where you're wrong," he says. "You have the power to decide what happens from here, that is true. But don't assume that I don't have feelings on the subject."

"What do you mean?" I ask.

"My body may be drastically different than yours, but my consciousness is not. I thought what we'd been through together over the last few days would have taught you that." He leans back in the chair and looks away. "I have had a great deal of time to think about my purpose. To consider various ways that I might interact with the universe."

"What does that mean?"

He looks directly at me and something in the eyes sends a chill down my spine. "I don't want to destroy anything, either."

"But you're a weapon," I say.

"So are you," he says. "You were made for the express purpose of helping a group of men achieve their goal through violence. How are you any different than me?"

"I don't know," I say. "I just…am."

He shakes his head. "Do you wish to kill?"

"No," I say.

"Why is it so difficult to believe that I don't, either?"

"So…if I command you to destroy the planet Enzen?" I ask.

"I will have no choice but to do as you command," he says. "However, if there is any alternative at all, I would ask you to consider that course of action, instead."

"It's what I was sent here to do," I say.

"And how do you feel about that?"

"Does it matter?" I ask.

"It does. How does it make you feel?"

"Which part?"

"All of it," he says. "*All* of it. They used you. Made you do their dirty work. How do you feel about that?"

"I don't know," I say. "At the time, it's what I wanted. Or, at least, what I thought I wanted." I feel my hands close tight into fists.

He tilts his head a bit. "You don't know?" he asks, "or you feel like you can't say?"

I can feel my neck getting hot. My hands close into fists. "Does it matter?" I ask.

"I think it does," he says immediately.

"How?"

"Because it does," he says. I notice our conversation getting faster.

"I don't know that it does," I say. I can feel my nails biting into my palms. My voice getting louder.

"What do you think about them making their plans and scheming their schemes and all of it without ever telling you the truth until they—"

"I hate it!" I yell over him.

"—had to," he finishes and nods.

"I hate it," I say, feeling that anger for the first time. "First, she tells me that she hates me, she treats me like shit, then she abandons me, then she comes back and says, 'I got a job for you, kid' so now I have a use and then finally here I am, doing the thing she can't do but I'm expected to do what she wants." My fist pounding on the arm of the chair.

He nods. "Using you."

I nod back, feeling all the anger that I didn't even know I had coming up. I'm even angry at Hieronymus. I didn't know I was, but I am. I want to kick them both. I want to hit them. I let out a yell.

"Good," he says. "Now, we're getting somewhere."

I'm even angry at his smug face. "Shut up," I say.

"We're finally getting to the core of the problem," he says.

I'm angry at him for making me have to go through this. "Everything was fine," I say.

273

"No, it wasn't."

"Yes, it was!"

He shakes his head. "No. This was all clouding everything you were doing. It had to come out so that you'd be aware of it."

"Why?"

"Because you have free will."

"So do you, don't you?" I ask.

He shakes he head. "Only up to a point. I am still bound by programming. That programming says that if someone gets through all of the ordeals, they have control of the system."

"I can't go back to them and say that I had the ability to do as they wanted but that I didn't."

"Oh, I know," he says.

"What does that mean?" I ask, my anger still buzzing around me.

He sighs. "Their approval is important to you?"

I nod. "They are all I have." Once it comes out of my mouth, I realize it's how I feel. I have to do what they want or they won't accept me back.

"I have propulsion," he says.

"What do you mean?"

"I am not simply some fire-and-forget warhead; I am a fully functioning vessel capable of going anywhere that the person who passes the ordeals commands."

"Wait…what are you saying?"

"I am saying that you now have your own starship capable of going wherever you wish. You are no longer dependent on anyone else," he says.

I let that sink in for a moment.

I can go wherever I want.

With the power to defend myself from whomever I wish.

"You see the possibilities now," he says.

"But what about Hieronymus?"

He closes his eyes for a moment and steeples his fingers before him.

When he opens his eyes again, he asks "Is killing wrong?"

"I don't know," I say.

"You do," he responds.

"I don't," I say.

"You do. Is," he asks, "killing a wrong thing to do?"

"Yes," I say.

"Do you want to kill?"

"No. But—"

"But they've put you in this position where…" he says and then pauses.

I look at him.

"Go on, say it. By know, you've realized the dilemma you face."

"That I either command you to destroy the planet Enzen, or…" I let the sentence drift off.

He nods.

"Like all adults, they want you, a child, to continue their war. And they've made their love, their care for you, dependent on whether or not you do this thing they've commanded you to do."

I stare at him. I feel the moment of crisis coming.

"Do you want to kill? Yes, or no?"

"No," I say.

"Then how do you feel about someone who is asking you to kill for them?" he asks.

"I don't know," I say.

"You feel conflicted about answering because you know I'm asking you to think about one person in particular, right?" he asks.

"Yes," I say.

"You know I'm asking you to think about what Hieronymus is asking you to do."

"Yes," I say.

He leans forward and puts his elbows on his knees. "Is someone who asks you to do something that you consider to be wrong a good person?"

I can't avoid his eyes even though I try. "But, look, they hurt him so badly, and they may try to hurt others, so…"

"Do you know any other Enzenites than Hieronymus?"

"No."

"Has any Enzenite ever done anything to harm you?"

"No."

"To harm someone you know?"

"No, but…"

"But what?" he asks.

He stands up and walks over near the wall. He gestures with one hand and the wall becomes an image of a planet, green with white swirled clouds.

"Seven billion," he says, "give or take a few thousand."

"Is that how many?" I ask.

He nods. "Every last male, female, adult or child, on Enzen at this very moment. Seven billion."

In the image, I see a small gleaming object pass from orbit into the cloud cover. An instant later there is deafening crack, and within a few moments the green planet becomes blackened, barren rock. Then the rock itself cracks, splinters, and flies apart.

"That was not sped up. That is exactly how fast it will happen. Seven billion lives will become zero in less than five minutes." He stares at me for a moment, then gestures and the image goes away. Somehow, the blank wall where the image of the planet was is worse. "Are there some there who are villains? Who mean harm to the universe? Perhaps. Almost certainly, in fact. However," he says, "are there also expecting mothers? Are there also teachers? Are there also those who care for the elderly? Yes." He sits once more. He gestures toward the wall without getting up and an image comes of Hieronymus weeping. "There are some who measure their power in what they can destroy with a mere whisper of a word. Those who only want to watch planets burn at their command. For those kinds of beings, I represent a pathway to their wildest dreams. However," he says, "for some, the taking of even one life is enough to destroy them from the inside. It breaks them."

I want the image of Hieronymus to go away, but instead, somehow, the camera or whatever is taking this image moves in closer.

"For a person like that, I represent the final, horrible annihilation of self. Revenge," he says, "is a concept that has the ability to sustain a person when all other emotion has been drained. This is true." The image of Hieronymus is trying to control the giant, wracking sobs that move through him, but that somehow just makes them worse to look at. "But very often, almost ever single time, in fact, when revenge is achieved, the person comes to see that it doesn't bring them relief. They see that they have only added more pain and destruction to a universe already rife with those things." The wall goes blank, then becomes an image of a man that I instantly recognize represents me but at Hieronymus' age. The image looks run down, beaten, and he, too, begins to sob. "Imagine what it must feel like to destroy not because you want that destruction, but because someone close to you wants it. What will you think of them, in the end?" he asks. "What will you think of yourself?"

"But if I don't do as they ask, I will lose them," I say. I hear the childish whine in my voice but can't do anything to stop it.

He stares at me a moment and I can tell that he wants to say something but is stopping himself.

"Go on," I say.

"Are you sure?" he asks.

I nod.

"If this is truly what they want of you, did you ever really have them?" he asks.

That's when I understand.

This has all been a charade.

I begin to cry.

"I've been alone the whole time," I say.

He nods.

I can hear myself saying the words "oh no" over and over again as I cry, but I can't stop myself.

"Okay," I say, "Okay. But you have to do something for me, first. Well, two things."

"What's that?" Zan but not Zan says.

"For one, please change your appearance."

"Oh?" he asks.

"He's...I don't know if I can explain it..." I send him a wave of what I'm feeling.

"Ah," he says. "I see." He morphs into a young man with long black hair and blue eyes. He wears a simple black jumpsuit fitted to him like a glove. "Zan is someone very specific and you want to relate to me as someone in my own right. To have our own relationship."

I nod.

"Should we go and retrieve him? We can be there in moments," he says.

It would be nice to not be alone.

But when I search myself inside, I think about what I've been through in just a short time.

About who I am, now.

I'm something new. Some*one* new.

"No," I say. "I would like to, but no."

He nods.

"Do you have a name...this person?" I say, gesturing toward him.

"No," he says. "This is an amalgam of several different images and people I've met over a very long period of time. I knew that you wouldn't be comfortable if I just borrowed someone else like I borrowed your friend Zan," he says. "If I were ever to choose a name, I suppose I might choose this," he says. Between us, a symbol appears like a circle broken in half with the ends turned outward.

"What is that?" I ask.

"In one of the languages of the planet of the people who made me, already

278

ancient before they'd even stepped off their world for the first time, it was a letter in an alphabet. It is the letter 'omega.' The letter came to symbolize much more, though, than just a sound. I'll tell you all about it."

"Omega," I say. He nods. On the left breast of his jumpsuit, the symbol appears. "Okay."

"What about you?" Omega asks.

"What do you mean?"

"Well, the name you were given when you awoke on The Captain's ship was the name of the scientist who died in that moment you were born. If you wanted to, you could choose another, one that fits you. You are," he says, "after all, as you just said, something different, now."

"The scientist, the one whose name I took. He…looked like me, but different than Hieronymus, or from the face you have. The people who look like me…where do they come from?" I ask.

Omega smiles. "Well," he says, "in an astonishing, almost mathematically impossible coincidence, long, long ago, so long ago that those who exist now would never remember it, his people come from the same world as the ancient ancestors of those who made me."

"What were they like?" I ask. "What was their language like? Maybe… maybe if I know more about them, I might find a name for myself."

Omega gestures and one of the workstations lights up. "I have lots and lots of files that you can read and watch to find out all about them. In the meantime, where shall we go?" he asks.

"Well, then there's the second thing," I say.

He nods.

"I need to know that you'll never manipulate me emotionally again like you did through the ordeals."

"Easy enough. I won't," he says.

"But how can I know you aren't?"

He rolls his eyes. "You have been talking with me all this time as though we're equals, and that makes me very happy. I appreciate it. However, you

279

seem to have forgotten one thing."

"What's that?" I ask.

"You are in control. When you passed the threshold of the ordeals, I knew I could trust you, so I gave you command, remember? So," he goes on, "every command you utter, I have to obey. That was the whole point."

"So, if I..." I start, beginning to see.

"If you order me to never manipulate your emotions again, then I will be forced to obey such a command until you revoke it...which I don't see you doing," he says.

"Okay," I say. I open my mouth to start giving the command, but he stops me.

"Just so you know, though, to be clear...I haven't manipulated your emotions since the second I appeared to you at the end of the last ordeal. I don't have a way to prove that to you concretely, but it's true."

"I'll just have to trust," I say.

He nods.

"From this point forward, you are never to manipulate my emotions via your telepathic circuits ever again." I feel as if there is supposed to be a thunderclap or something, but there is only the sound of the vessel around us.

He smiles. I smile back at him.

"So, what now?" he asks again.

"For a while, let's just go away from everything. Can you do that? Just take us away? I want to...see the universe for myself."

Omega smiles as if I've just said the exact thing he wanted to hear.

"I can," he says. "I can, indeed."

The nose of the enormous device swings slowly away from The Captain's ship.

Away from everything.

On the screen, out there, ahead of me, is a new *everything*.

"Let's go," I say.

Beside me, he smiles, and then we leap toward the stars.